"Soldiers and memor... can and can't recall, what you wish could forget, what you wish you had back. Nik Korpon takes you there and back, in writing as fine as I've seen and with a story you'll remember."

Stephen Graham Jones, author of Mongrels

"Nik Korpon's *The Rebellion's Last Traitor* is a mesmerizing mix of post-apocalyptic SF, war/adventure, criminals dealing in memories, and black-as-hell noir. It's full of attitude and atmosphere, and I couldn't put it down."

Paul Tremblay, author of A Head Full of Ghosts

"*The Rebellion's Last Traitor* is a delicious dark delight of sci-fi noir, with an atmosphere that virtually drips from every page and an ingenious story that will hook you from the very start."

Adam Christopher, author of Made to Kill

"*The Rebellion's Last Traitor* is an explosive tale of betrayal and revenge in which allegiances prove as dangerous and unreliable as the memories the citizens of Eitan City buy and sell. Korpon crosses genre lines with ease, and imbues this post-apocalyptic tale with the rhythm and immediacy of crime fiction."

Chris Holm, Anthony Award-winning author of Red Right Hand

NIK KORPON

THE REBELLION'S LAST TRAITOR

ANGRY
ROBOT

ANGRY ROBOT
An imprint of Watkins Media Ltd

20 Fletcher Gate,
Nottingham,
NG1 2FZ
UK

angryrobotbooks.com
twitter.com/angryrobotbooks
The boys from County Hell

An Angry Robot paperback original 2017

Cover by Steve Stone
Set in Meridien and Q Type Square by Epub Services

Distributed in the United States by Penguin Random House, Inc., New York.

ISBN 978 0 85766 656 7
Ebook ISBN 978 0 85766 657 4

Printed in the United States of America

9 8 7 6 5 4 3 2 1

This book is dedicated to the memories of
Patricia and Charles Bangert,
Ken Korpon, and Jeff Laughton.
May Nahoeg hold you close.

"Down near the river where our brothers bled,
I knelt on the bank and my father said,
'This is our land, all that you can touch,
and we'll water our crops with Tathadann blood.'"

TRADITIONAL WESTHELL COUNTY BALLAD

1.
HENRAEK

Dust motes float in the manufactured light that sluices through my target's hallway. Muted explosions from outside this tenement, bombs maybe. Most residents walk down the middle of the floor and, over time, work some of the nails loose, so I creep along the edge to remain undetected. When I get to the door with *12B* scribbled across it, I press my ear to the door and make sure it's quiet.

Inside the target's apartment, I take small, soft steps. A fan with stretched-leather blades pushes hot air around the room. The old man's clothing is scattered, most of it cut near to rags and stained with soot. Turned on end in the middle of the room is a spool that once housed the industrial wire used to power the water-drilling rigs that sprang up in the hills around Eitan City after the Resource Wars. A plate and a few pieces of silverware sit on top of the spool. The wilting dandelion perched in a can – the same thing my wife used to do – is so sad I can feel my heartbeat slow. He snores on a mattress in the far corner, the thin sheet covering him pocked with holes.

The two slivers of coal clack together in my pocket, and I'm sure this will be an easy job.

Tacked to the wall beside him is a newspaper clipping with a poorly focused photo. A quick glance is enough for me to recognize the article. It details the bombing of a Tathadann party community center during a failed rebel raid. The photo that accompanies the article is a picture of me, carrying a wounded rebel fighter away from the building. I read the article a hundred times the day it came out. I've seen it a thousand times more in my sleep.

The man snorts himself half-awake, mutters, rolls over and resumes snoring. His elbow nudges a green-and-white striped coffee mug. I inhale and blink a few times.

Hung beneath the newspaper clipping are a faded funeral card and a photograph of a log cabin, two men and a younger boy standing on either side of the cabin's doorway. They all smile the way fathers and sons do. Illegible writing crawls along the border, likely recording who's in the picture, when and where.

I look from the photograph to the funeral card and a phantom blade lodges in my gut when I realize that the boy on the card was one of my soldiers.

Riab was his name and he caught a gae bulg, one of our barbed spears, in the face during the failed raid I led. His blood splashed on my lips. The old man asleep beside me – his grandfather – is a shriveled, sadder version of Riab.

I pull the slip of paper from my pocket and scan the list of addresses until I find this one, check it, check it again.

This is deliberate, Walleus's sick idea of a prank, because this family has obviously suffered so much already without subjecting them to more. I wonder if he snickered as he read through the list before giving it to me, whispering under his breath, oh, man, Henraek is going to be pissed. Or maybe he cringed, sucking air hard through his teeth. For all I know, he didn't even look at it. In all the years I've known Walleus, the only thing I can get a steady bead on is the space his loyalty had just occupied.

But really, his reaction yesterday afternoon when receiving the list from Lady Morrigan doesn't matter, because I have no say in whose memories I harvest and my failure to do so will mean it's my back against the firing squad wall – again – not his. So I take a long breath, then resign myself to the job.

Kneeling, I lay out my kit on the disused produce crate that serves as a night table beside the bed. Two cloth squares and one pipette of iodine. A needle, two empty vials, a round bandage. And the two slivers of coal.

His hair is thin; the temple is easy to find. A drop of iodine hangs on the tip of the needle before I slide it in. I stretch his skin with my index and middle fingers, and with a little probing I navigate past the firmer portions of the temporal lobe until I find the soft section of his hippocampus and begin to bleed his memory cortex.

His eyelids flutter like a flurry of ashen moths are trying to beat their way out. Fingers claw and twitch. Slowly, the vial attached to the end of the needle fills with milky liquid. I shift him onto his side to help it flow faster so I can sooner leave him be.

As memory drains from his skull, I stare outside the single window in his apartment, Eitan City throbbing faint crimson. A red sky at night is a sailor's delight – but if the red is the flames of the Amergin neighborhood, a twisted collection of shanty buildings set ablaze ten years ago that continues to burn, and we haven't seen direct sun in thirty – then what do sailors know? This heat is tactile; instead of rain, we get condensation, languid smog that chokes the air. Each day we're convinced it's the day that smog will break, the day real light will cut through and actual water will fall from the sky. Each night, we go to bed thinking tomorrow, tomorrow will be the day.

I thought that way for years. It was one of the things that attracted my wife Aífe. She'd said that, even after all the fallout of the decades-long Resource Wars and the Tathadann-sanctioned death squads of the Struggle, I still hoped for sunlight, even though I hadn't seen it since I was a child. It was the perfect complement to her feisty cynicism, another way that our contrasts brought us closer, made the passion burn brighter and hotter than an exploding star. But now, I can't remember the last time I closed my eyes wishing for the sun. Oh, that's right, I can. And ever since I've been closing them wishing for nothing.

The old man's twitching becomes violent and it takes both of my knees to hold him still. I press my thumb against his carotid artery until he falls limp. I switch out vials, setting the one meant for Walleus on the floor beneath the bed and inserting another I'll sell on my own.

The vial fills – picnics and birthdays, the way young Riab liked his sandwiches cut seeping from his temple. Drip by drip.

Something reminiscent of bells rings out in the street, but it might only be shots from home-modified weapons. In the distance is the old county airport, which was converted into a food-augmentation factory after the Resource Wars and the ensuing chaos cured everyone's yearning for travel. The fighting started in the west, between competing resource companies – sort of like the old oil companies, but they'd harvested any profitable commodity, and they each had their own army for protection. They scrapped and clawed for any bit of land they could develop and exploit. Then conflicts gradually spread east with no heed for oceans or language, eventually crossing the channel and razing the fields of Westhell County. My father told me that the mountains gave him and the other fighters inside their watchtowers a better sightline, and with their rifles they were able to keep the hordes away from Eitan City, the largest city in Westhell. But by then it didn't matter, because the massive amount of chemical weapons the companies used to fight one another and harvest resources had already tainted the atmosphere and stopped the rain. Each new company that swept through promised the sun would melt the snow in the mountains and that would help us collect the water for our crops, but the people had already believed in too many lies and refused to accept any more. It was tragic, he'd said, that the people then believed the lies of the Morrigan brothers as they were building the Tathadann party, which capitalized on our fears and seething distrust of outsiders.

In the central park, I can see the dull glimmer of Regent Pond, a fetid repository for the run-off from Macha and the other center-city neighborhoods. Next to it is the pagoda where Walleus and I stood years ago, where my wife would proudly watch as we whipped the straggling few listeners into a fervor back during the early congregations that turned into our Struggle against the Tathadann. Even now, the irony in their name – which means something akin to unity in our slang – makes me smile like my teeth are made of glass.

A voice startles me.

"Who the hell are you?"

I spin around, almost pulling the needle from the old man's skull. A silhouette stands in the doorway, clutching a sack in his arm.

"Get away from him." He has the kind of voice that accompanies a face painted with scars. There's no wavering in it but the timbre is higher than his bulk would suggest. He takes a step forward. "Get that out of him. Now."

"Calm down." I realize how obnoxious that sounds. I know a man will kill for family without a second blink. Hand behind my back, I keep the vial level and the memories draining. It feels almost full. "There are no problems here."

The bag falls to the floor, spilling a survivalist cornucopia: two misshapen oranges, a chunk of bread, half a bottle filled with muddy brown liquor and a sprinkling of jagged metal shards. He takes two quick steps forward, a thick scar where his left cheek used to be, and I see the genes in this family are strong: this man is no one if he is not Riab's father, the other man in the cabin photo. I nudge the old man's head back so the needle won't snap, let my jaw go slack as the father's fist kisses my mouth. The man might have a glove full of iron rivets. It has been years since I felt something like that.

I stagger along the wall to keep the scuffle away from the bed. I rub the white dots from my eyes, and look up as he pulls something from his waistband. A flare gun, likely retrofitted.

The trigger clicks and I flinch.

Nothing.

He smacks the handle and I duck. Then he fires and a hundred tiny metal teeth chew the wall behind me.

When he charges, I step to the side, sweep his leg and use his own mass to send his shoulder through the wall. The gun skitters across the floor.

Before I can inhale, I find myself with a knee on his throat, ready to crush his windpipe.

His face is the picture of repentance. Eyes beg for mercy.

Nostalgia sloshes around me: a man's life, violence in the air. My face must project indecision bordering on abject horror because the father swings at me, scraping some hidden weapon across my eyes.

I roll away but he's on me before I can sit up, his hands wrapped around my neck. His finger placement is wrong, though, and I'm able to swallow, to catch my breath, to say, "Be calm," before clapping my palms against his ears. He rears back and I pounce on him, cinching the crook of my elbow beneath his chin.

With one twitch, I could sever his spinal column. With one hard squeeze, I could pop his eyeballs from their sockets. With one well-executed yank using the right pressure point, I could remove his skull. But I swore to never take a life again. I took too many during the Struggle, ruined too many others.

Five seconds and he's swimming in his unconscious mind. He's not on Walleus's list, so I fold a sheet under his head then lower him to the floor beside his father's bed, his spine intact and my hands clean. I remove the needle from the old man's skull, swab the area with iodine and bandage it, then slip Walleus's vial into the protective padded case and put mine in the belt beneath my shirt and leather jacket, and gather my kit.

After removing every trace of my being here, I pull the slivers of coal from my pocket and stand between the two men, debating which one to anoint. The old man did nothing to deserve this but I understand the weight the father carries, how the soul of a son can be marred by his father's sins. I lay the coal on the old man's eyes, whisper be well into his ear then slink away. The two lie as quiet as an abandoned catacomb, full of cobwebs and dead skin.

Out on the street, a barker calls for patrons in the gilded doorway of a bar. Gold paint flakes away as if the building has eczema, revealing part of a pictograph etched into the wall, a symbol from one of the animistic religions in Amergin. I keep my hands near my stomach, shielding the vials from pickpockets and lumbering, drunken Brigus, the nomadic people who claimed the neighborhood as their own. In all reality, they could have had it, because no one else wanted it.

Repurposed air conditioning units sit in most of the windows, sucking moisture from the oppressive air to give these people something to drink. In Findchoem, my neighborhood, we can usually count on running water most of the week, even if it's varying shades of rust. But over here the Tathadann isn't concerned with placating the inhabitants, so water of any color isn't a given.

Children climb piles of discarded furniture and hunks of collapsed buildings in the alley, dirt and ash streaked across their faces. One stands at the top, holding a broken table leg in place of a scepter, shouting that she is Queen of the Struggle as the others scramble toward her, wielding makeshift versions of gae bulgs, hoping to steal her spot. My stomach clenches at her declaration. In the streetlamp's pulsing, their faces oscillate between playmates and ghouls.

Amid the wreckage of the Resource Wars, two brothers called Macuil and Daghda Morrigan came to the city from their mountain home several counties away. They mobilized bands of fighters, diverted the water from our crops to the city center, learned how to create food from chemicals, and drilled deep into the mossy boulders that covered the mountain, searching for wells, all with the vision of creating a city where, carefully allocated, the remaining resources could serve their optimal population. Which meant if you weren't optimal – like the Brigus, the Amergin, the other people who'd sought refuge in Eitan after being driven from the rural homes by resource companies – you were funneled into neighborhoods like this, stacked atop one another like cords of wood, waiting to be burned for fuel. Eventually things began to burn, but it wasn't the people.

Someone grabs my shoulder.

My fist curls as I turn, then relaxes when I see it's only Fergus. Once a fierce fighter, he's now gaunt-cheeked and sunken-eyed. He looks at me but his gaze is focused somewhere beyond, trying to remember what he was about to do. When you become accustomed to having memory fed to you, your brain has trouble creating its own. He's definitely not the worst lagon I've seen, nor the most tragic.

"Been looking for you," he says.

"You said that already."

He cocks his head, searching the air for his words, and I feel a little bad for messing with him.

"It's fine, Fergus. What do you need?" I keep my hands over my belt, guarding the vials. Regardless of whether or not they're a good source of supplemental income, a lagon is still a lagon and he will rob me as quick as buy a vial.

He scans the sidewalk, wary, as if those kids would care what he's doing. As if half of Eitan City isn't doing it too.

"You got something?" he says.

"Like?"

He shrugs, says, "Not picky. Someone old, but nothing creepy. No babies or bombs or nothing."

Fergus is one of the sensible ones, whatever counts for sensible these days.

"How many?"

He holds a clutch of folded bills.

"Sure." I turn away from him, using my back to block his line of sight, and pull out the vials on top. I hold them out, then snatch them away when I realize they're from Riab's grandfather. "Actually, this might be too much for you."

I don't know why Riab's family landed on my list, but I don't want to give away their pasts before I have the chance to find out.

After I take his money, I hand him two vials procured earlier in the day from a woman in Fomora, a neighborhood in the north of the city where the older – and forgotten – population tends to migrate.

He hurries away in the slow but frenetic way lagons do, probably to one of the abandoned basements converted into a lagonael den where he can view memory.

The Tathadann's goal had been to unify the people. But as their grip on the city tightened, anger burned inside every citizen who felt like a commodity, until the people finally did unify, and unified against the Tathadann. I was a teenager when my father was killed for speaking out against the party. It was filed as an accidental death, being in the wrong place at the wrong time, but even at that age I knew better. A few years later, Walleus and I took up his mantle and started preaching against them. Our speeches attracted attention, then followers, then devotees. Then, when all of those who were dispossessed gathered as one, we became a movement. A rebellion. A mass of people with one goal: take down the Tathadann and reclaim the city as ours.

And we tried. And we fought. For ten years.

Walleus had seen the writing on the wall, that the Struggle was doomed, and defected to the Tathadann. I was captured while holed up at what I thought was a safe bar not long after the Struggle finally collapsed – everything we had built after the Wars falling beneath their feet, the smoke from scores of fires obscuring the sun that was supposed to save us, leaving the city in perpetual twilight. But Walleus bargained with his new leaders to secure my future as a memory thief for the Tathadann, instead of a target for the firing squad. He told me it was a coveted position, one that would afford me some security, and I could thank him later.

Sometimes I think the job is his form of retaliation, that he hasn't forgiven me for slapping him in front of our men when he announced his decision to leave the rebellion and join the Tathadann, and stealing memories from the people we tried to save is the only suitable punishment for me embarrassing him.

Other times I think he was taking pity on me because my wife and son were crushed in the riot that I incited.

I stand across the street from Johnstone's and survey the faces, looking for any Tathadann scouts. When I'm convinced there are none, I hurry across, head down, then push open the heavy wooden door to Johnstone's, already tasting the bourbon. I know it won't wash away the image of life draining from someone's face – it never does – but that's never stopped me from trying. A lone man sits on a stool at the bar, a scar tracing the curve of his face from above his mouth up into the hairline by his ear. Even from across the bar I can peg him as a longtime lagon without seeing that dead-eyed stare.

Emeríann leans down to eye level behind the bar, bottle in hand, drops of clear alcohol slipping into a cracked tumbler. She's prettier than any woman I could've hoped for under our circumstances, her hair dirty yellow like my memory of the sun. When I said that, trying to compliment her, she waved her slender hands in wispy circles, so I stopped saying it after the second time.

She lays her hand on the bar top when she's done with the alcohol. The man sets three bills in her hand and she curls her fingers for more. Another four bills and she stuffs them in her pocket, pulls out a lighter. She takes a swig of the liquor, presses two fingers between her lips, then lights her fingers and spits out the alcohol, the burst of flame setting the man's drink on fire. He spins the glass in slow circles, enraptured by the flames as they scorch the liquid, small specks sifting downward. Emeríann swishes water around her mouth and cleans her fingers and chin with a towel.

"Let me guess," I say. "He's chasing either arson or explosion?" I sit, three stools away from the man.

"Campfire, actually," she says.

"Really?"

"You don't always have to assume the worst." She sets a tumbler before me, holds a bottle of bourbon in one hand and homebrewed liquor in the other. I nod at the bourbon. "Feeling sensitive today?" she says.

"I don't want to piss fire later."

"It's OK, love. I'm only having fun at your expense."

I spin the glass in my hand, liquor coating the side then slipping down in elongated spikes. Though everyone on this side of the city knows liquor is made with the same contaminated water that's in our homes, the sting of alcohol is pungent enough to cover it up, strong enough to help us forget. If you want actual water, you need deeper pockets and different credentials.

The man waves his hand over the dying flames, trying to nurse them back to their full height.

"To be fair," she says, gesturing toward the man, "I think the campfire popped and one of the people burned to death."

I nod.

The Tathadann took complete control after our failed rebellion, revising the historical dead. There was no longer a Struggle against the party, no Resource Wars. There was only the Tathadann. To ensure that, they outlawed memory of anything that came before them. And around that ban, like weeds growing from a sidewalk crack, a black market emerged.

Straight lagonael can become frustrating. By nature, there's a barrier between you and the experience, and when you can no longer mentally put yourself in the memory it can be worse than not watching at all. Most longtime lagons will resort to vaporizing Paradise to make the memory immersive, to create smell and taste – sometimes even touch if you vaporize enough. But where years of lagonael will only make your brain lazy, Paradise completely dissolves memory. The more a lagon fills his skull with artificial memories and Paradise, the less personal ones he retains, until he can't remember who he is, where he is, and sometimes how to speak.

The man sighs as the flames snuff out, tips his head back and pours the alcohol in his mouth, letting it sit there, absorb, reconstitute into something approximating grey matter to tide him over until he can score again. I'd try to sell him something, but Emeríann doesn't quite approve of it, especially not in her bar. When he returns to the present, he looks my way and a smile spreads across his face like oil on water.

"Hey." He extends his hand. "I want to shake – thank you for everything – then, back then, during all that fighting."

I give him a stately nod and shake his hand. Emeríann scratches her nose to disguise a snicker.

"It's a shame what you have – you working like – a tragedy, I say." He bows his head for a moment. Then he focuses and he looks at me from the top of his eyes. "Say, you – you have anything, do you?"

"What the hell do you know about tragedy?" I clear my throat and move away from him, swallow my drink, squint away the liquor burn and images of Riab's grandfather. "Damn junkies."

"They're an important part of the community," Emeríann says. She manages not to smile when she says it. I raise an eyebrow and she holds up the cash.

"They keep us employed, anyway."

I wet my lips and hope the nod is implicit.

"Well, hell, King Sunshine," she coos, with a girlish twang. "'How was your day, Emeríann?' 'Oh, it was OK, Henraek, but it's better now that I get to see you.' 'Oh, you're so sweet.' 'Well, ain't that the goddamned truth.'" She moves her head when she changes parts, carrying both sides of the conversation for us.

I slide her my glass.

"Lovely to see you too." She snatches the glass from the bar but I grab her hand before she can move away, kiss her knuckles, her elbow, her jaw and lips. She gives me a patronizing smile and says I'm cute but still have to pay for my drinks.

I reposition myself, the stool rocking beneath me. I test the one beside me, and the one beside that, but none sits evenly.

"You should combine all these stools and get one that works," I say.

"Or I could set them all on fire as payback for the problems they've given me."

"You could do that, yes." I stretch over the bar for a bottle to top off my drink – which elicits a smack from Emeríann – and almost knock over the smooth, carved rock that sits on a shelf. It's an abstract version of a woman, three inches high, except with a snout and two tusks where the face should be. I nod to it. "You trying to catch spirits?"

"Don't start," she says, picking up the statuette and wiping away the dust beneath.

It's from the grandmother of Forgall, the other bartender. His family was hill-people, a couple counties over, and this is Nimah, their family god, one of the old ones. She's an avatar of Esin, who rules over Nahoeg, and in this avatar Nimah is the goddess of safety. She had a son or lover who was a boar, or something. I can't remember. The Tathadann outlawed any open worship of Esin when they came to power – especially the cultish subsets Nimah attracts – and I wasn't much for religion in the first place. I don't know if Forgall actually believes the totem will protect the bar or if he thinks it will send out some signal audible only to Daghda Morrigan, in whatever world he exists, the natural or the ethereal.

I sip at the remainder of my drink, and, as if conjured, the door opens, sending a ripple through the thick air. I clock a massive reflection in the glasses, then glance behind me and see Forgall, carrying rolls of paper.

Emeríann says, "You're back early," then looks down at his hands and gives him a headshake so slight I would have missed it were I not two feet from her.

"Had to meet a contact. It went quicker than I thought."

I spin on my stool to face him. His hands are stained purple and brown from what I now recognize are schematics. Red, yellow, and white wires hang from his jacket pocket.

"Congratulations on your promotion," I say to him.

"What?" he says.

"Henraek," Emeríann says, "knock it off."

"You're a secretary now, right? I thought that's why you were carrying all those prints," I say to Forgall. "Because if you told me you could actually read them, I might die of shock and–" I look around the bar, "–it's too nice a day for that."

"Every day's been the same for years," he says. "Or do they only allow you to read the revisionist weather reports?"

He starts past me but I hold my arm out.

"No one allows me to do anything," I say. "You need to understand that."

"Hey," she says. "Come on."

Forgall lowers his head, smiles as if something on the floor is incredibly amusing, then shifts the papers and takes a deep breath.

"You were not my lieutenant back then," he says. He looks up and his jaw could have been chipped from a piece of granite, with rivers of burned skin and buckshot pockmarks. "And you sure as hell have no authority over me now."

The lagon slides his stool up, his belly cascading over the edge of the bar. "Miss, can I – one for the road – and the ditch, please."

"You," Forgall says to him. "Get the hell out of here." He sets his jaw, exhales hard, his nostrils flaring. "This is your fault," Forgall says to me, motioning to the junkie. "What's happening to everyone."

"She doesn't seem to mind," I say. "They tip well."

"First you made us believe. Then you deserted

us. Now you're taking the city apart one person at a time."

"You are one to talk." The glass is heavy in my hand. It would be nothing to drive it into his eye socket, twist and cup and pull the whole thing out. I look over to Emeríann, possibly to gauge her response, to mentally implore her to look the other way for a moment, but she's staring at the schematics in Forgall's hand. She flicks her eyes to the side and he deftly pushes the wires for rigging pulse-explosives down into his pocket.

"Emeríann," I say, "what are you planning?"

"Nothing," she says. "I don't want arguments in here."

"I don't know if he would understand it, Emer."

"Don't call her that," I say. "You're not familiar enough to call her Emer."

"Both of you shut up," she says.

"Forgall, if I can take down the Tathadann comm systems with a handful of men—"

"It was a power substation," Forgall says, "not the comm systems."

"The substation powered the comm systems, correct? So, yes, we took out the comm systems." I wait for him to argue but he only seethes. "What I'm saying here is, I'm pretty sure I can figure out the bottlerockets you have planned."

He gives that smile again and even though I'm sure he could snap me in half, the only reason I don't smash a bottle against his teeth is because Emeríann would have to clean it up.

"You might be able to hurt me, but it'd be hard to do any actual damage without your four-hundred-pound pet rat here to help," he says. "You're a team, right? One can't work without the other."

I jump to my feet, my face inches from his, and despite all the battle wounds the prick still manages to remain handsome. Pride has a strange way of preserving a man's looks, even with all that wicked blood coursing through him.

"Enough," Emeríann yells, but from the tone of her voice I can tell she won't get involved. She will be rightly pissed at home tonight, however.

Forgall and I shift on our feet, the reptilian parts of our brains feeding our self-image as men of violence, of conviction.

She growls, "I said, enough."

"What are you planning, Emeríann?"

A soft fwap, her wipe rag landing on the bar top.

"Emeríann, don't," Forgall says, a forcefulness in his voice that almost brings me to hit him.

"Dammit, Henraek." She glances at Forgall, then back to me, and sighs hard. "We're going to blow up the water supply."

2.
WALLEUS

I'm standing at the front door of the Gallery, next to the seven-piece hologram band playing some crap from hundreds of years ago that's supposed to make people feel safe and nostalgic but to me sounds like the musical equivalent of a psychic fugue. I have to be near two hundred paces away from Lady Morrigan, way in the back, with fifty people milling between us. And I can still see her raven-feather hat from way over here. Looks like some ancient monster devoured a nest of birds then threw them up on top of her head. All she has to do is add a handful of dirt-stained pearls and she can call it a day.

I lower Cobb from my arm down to the floor.

"How about you make something for a little bit while Daddy takes care of some business?" I shuffle him into one of the leather booths meant for Gallery patrons and flip on the screen in the table then select the sculpting module. "You remember how this one goes, right?" He clicks twice. The program loads, projecting a dozen shapes and forms that Cobb can mold into something. They have better modules with more options, but they tend to overwhelm him.

Before I can deal with Lady Morrigan and get on about my day, the door swings open and two soldiers enter, their Tathadann fatigues splattered with dirt and blood, dragging a man between them. His clothes are all torn to hell.

"Hey, I'm trying to run a business here," I say to the soldiers. "Don't bother my customers."

One gives half a laugh, and the other a hearty, "Yes, sir."

The beaten man appears to have been shot with some sedative, probably to avoid an outburst that might shake the patrons' faith in the Tathadann's control. Judging by the slashes of blood ringing the man's mouth, I doubt he'd give much fuss anyway.

They pass the booth where Belousz and a few others from my crew sit gambling, then give Lady Morrigan a quick salute. She appraises the man then nods. The soldiers exit the main gallery through a cloaked door in the back.

Gonna be a bad day for that guy.

Stilian, who coordinates the separation and cataloging of harvested memories under the supervision of Doctor Mebeth, is set up in another booth, recording it all in our ledgers then organizing the vials in groups: food, nature, family, sex. Things that used to be inalienable rights. The fact that a

Tathadann man sells a Tathadann-banned product in a Tathadann-controlled building for money that will go to back to the Tathadann cracks me up. In a city as dysfunctional as Eitan, it's refreshing to know the government is consistently corrupt.

"Imagine my surprise," Lady Morrigan says as I approach, "when I came to check your progress on the new cells and found you were out at the park eating ice cream cones with your son."

"I had a soda. Cobb wanted something salty." I nod toward the back, where the man is likely begging for his life. "A good leader compels his men to perform without him."

"Without and in spite of don't mean the same thing," she says.

"And we were walking through the park on our way here, not sitting and eating and staring at the pigeons." I stick a toothpick between my teeth, feel the point scrape against my gum. "Seems you need to get me some new ears out there if that's what you heard."

"Oh?"

I shrug. "Dairy upsets my stomach."

"For such a dull brain, you've got an incredibly sharp tongue." She presses a feather back into place, her fingers cold and slender like claws.

"That's part of my charm, Lady Morrigan."

Greig, one of my intel gatherers who also happens to be a real shitbird, lays his chips on the table, forfeiting to the rest of the crew, and leaves the game.

He moseys into our periphery like a hyena to a carcass, looking for an opportunity to insert himself into our conversation.

"Then why don't you draw on that charm to infiltrate the forming cells as I've asked, instead of relying on your friend Henraek?"

"Is my face different yet?" I say.

"What?"

"I figure there must be some kind of connection between my features changing and you asking me the same question over and over." I wait for her to answer and a howl erupts from the back room.

"Is this one of your interrogation tactics?" she says. "Attempt to be witty until the subject can no longer bear it and gives you the information so you'll stop?"

"What I'm saying is, there's no way they'd let me get anywhere near. Ever. I am persona non grata. Carve my ass with a piece of glass, hear? You understand what I'm saying?"

Her dress makes sharp rustling sounds when she shifts positions, the capped shoulders digging into her purple-tinted skin. I'll give it to her: dead husband or no, she's determined to stay true to the vision of the party, regardless of how ridiculous she looks.

They say her first husband, Daghda Morrigan, didn't share his brother's penchant for aristocratic excess, which Macuil had picked up to overcompensate for their hill-people roots. Ridiculous clothing. Pointlessly elaborate food. Refusing to incorporate any of our advances into their home, the same way those old kings inbred until their gene pool was as contaminated as Regent Pond. Story goes, after he and Macuil formed the Tathadann and saved Eitan from the chaos of the Resource Wars, it quickly became obvious to the Lady that Macuil – not her husband, Daghda – was the more flamboyant and easily manipulated one, so the Lady turned one brother against the other and had Daghda shanghaied out in the hinterlands with orders to shoot him on sight should he return, then married Macuil. That pretty much set up the Tathadann's MO and they've been screwing people ever since.

Rumor has it Daghda has become something of a roving mercenary over the years, returning occasionally to the hills to try to spark unrest against his brother and ex-wife in between facilitating coups in foreign lands and killing rival heads-of-state for whoever sees to paying him the most, though I don't know how anyone would understand him with that thick-ass hill accent. But some people say he was murdered across the straits way south of Westhell. Others say he never even existed, that he's a story the Tathadann created to keep citizens in line. If you ask me, the most convincing account I've heard has him dead ten years ago. Chewed a cyanide pill after being captured during a failed uprising in one of the far eastern countries with too many z's and strange accent marks in their words.

"What I understand, Walleus, is that they are out there creating sympathy for another uprising by threatening to disrupt the anniversary celebration, and it is your job," she says, poking me in the chest, "to stop these things before they come to fruition."

"Which I have, Lady Morrigan, for the last six years."

"They will not destroy Macuil's statue, nor tarnish his legacy. Am I clear?"

Oh, the irony. It was Lady Morrigan – wanting Eitan to see her and Macuil as their saviors – who declared memory illegal to erase any trace of Daghda. But making memory illegal only put a premium price on it. The Promhael – the cabal of Tathadann generals who took over a few years back when they saw Lady Morrigan's calculating edge was dulling and appointed her something like an honorary figurehead – saw money to be made, so they allowed the memory trade to flourish, replacing half of the history she's tried to erase. Now no one really knows for sure if Daghda is even real because no citizen can talk openly about him for fear of being stripped were they to be heard invoking his name. But talk about him they do, in whispers and lagonael dens, an altered history mixed with hearsay such that he's become a projection of political stances: a savior to some rebels, a conqueror to others; an example of Tathadann efficiency and justice to its members, a cuckold to its dissenters. In the battle between Lady Morrigan's nasty god-complex and the Tathadann's greed, god didn't stand a chance.

I suppress my gag reflex, and she motions for Greig to come.

"Greig has been quite proactive on the matter." She turns to Greig. "Tell him."

He steps forward and says, "Johnstone's is a rebel bar, Walleus. That's where they're planning everything."

"That's Protectorate Blaí to you," I say. He nods, deferring. "And when did you speak with Lady Morrigan?"

His lips curl into the slightest grin possible without it seeming like gloating. Greig's father fought at the end of the Resource Wars and went on to become a general in the Tathadann. He could've used his influence to get Greig a high-ranking position, but instead wanted his son to earn like he had. So now Greig carries all the entitlement and accent of privilege while still harboring the conniving, backstabbing tendencies of someone continually trying to prove himself. Yeah, he's a goddamn joy to have around.

"Do you read your reports, Walleus?" she says.

"Of course. And there were no substantiated claims in any reports I've gotten from him." I turn to Greig. "You never said anything like that to me. If you're sandbagging your gathering, we need to have a sit down."

"No," she says, snapping her fingers at me. I swallow the urge to break them like stale breadsticks. "Explain, Greig."

He puffs up a bit. "I've seen people in there wearing green and white clothing. Some scarves too."

"So there's a draft and they're cold," I say.

"When has anyone in the last fifty years been cold?" he says.

"Doesn't mean it's a rebel bar."

"Nor does it mean it's not," Lady Morrigan says. She speaks without looking at me, her eyes focused squarely on him.

Greig clears his throat, assuming an authoritative tone, that posh goddamned accent making me want to tie his tongue in a knot. "As I mentioned, ma'am, they're using it as a front. There's a room in the back where they store maps, blueprints of our facilities. One of the bartenders there, Forgall Tobeigh, looks to be the main architect. He was known as the Lumberjack, because of his size–"

"It was because he cut a dozen men in half with an axe," I say. "And no one called him that. At least not to his face."

Greig peers at me, swallows, then continues. "The woman there, Emeríann Daele, hasn't shown any signs of involvement, but her late husband was killed during the Struggle."

"We were watching Tobeigh before the last bombs went during the Struggle. There are too many people gathering on him to try anything," I say. "And everyone had someone close killed during the Struggle. I mean, Daele's an artist. How violent could she be?"

"You've seen her profile," Greig says.

"I have, so I know her statistics, locations frequented, occupation, and known associates, but that doesn't mean I know anything about her."

"It all matters," Greig says.

I flick my hand, batting away his theories. It's bad enough she has to hide living with Henraek – and that she has to put up with Henraek – she doesn't need Greig bothering her as well. "I thought you knew better than to believe everything you heard. Were you the one who told Lady Morrigan I like ice cream too?"

Greig considers me for a minute, debating whether or not to pursue this point in front of her. If he can prove Johnstone's is the hub of this plan, he'll embarrass me and bolster his position in the Tathadann. And all in front of the other men, no less. But there ain't no way he can prove it. Not with the way I've heard Emeríann and Forgall run that place. They should run it right, because Henraek was the one who taught her.

And I taught Henraek.

His point made, Greig gives a respectful nod to Lady Morrigan then turns on his heel and leaves before I can confront him.

"He's quite the young prospect," she says. "Perhaps his talents are being underutilized in his current role."

"I doubt it. If he were any good he would know about my stomach condition. I'll re-evaluate his gathering but I wouldn't expect anything." I scratch my chin. "And if you don't mind, ma'am, I have to go over some reports before meeting someone, so I'll be on them."

"I do mind." She clucks her tongue once. "Let's ask the man in the back what he knows about Johnstone's, shall we?"

"I guess the files can wait, then," I say. I turn to check on Cobb, who has curled up on a bench, and when I turn back, my stomach brushes against Lady Morrigan.

She looks down like a rat cozied up to her ankle. I follow her into the back room.

The man is lashed to two crossed pieces of wood by leather restraints. Long streams of blood run down his arms, the bare space where his fingernails had been still pulsing wet. His head hangs, eyes closed and lips slightly moving, his barely rising chest pocked with spear-sized holes. He's older than he looked at first, even through all the blood, but I still don't recognize the face. The soldiers who brought him in sit in padded chairs on either side of him, taking a breather. Their blood-crusted probes rest against the man's legs. At the sight of Lady Morrigan, they both stand at attention.

"He's an undercover rebel, ma'am," one of them says. "We picked him up in Macha. He was loitering – arranging a pickup, we believe."

"Are you going to ask or should I?" Lady Morrigan says to me, nodding at the bleeding man.

"Ladies first," I say.

"What has he said about Johnstone's?" she asks one of the soldiers.

"He hasn't said much of anything, ma'am. We

did find this transponder in his pocket." The soldier holds it out for me, staring like he expects a medal of commendation.

I shuffle the metal oval around in my palm, looking over the pitted surface, and cold threads spread through me. The tusks are broken off down to nubs, but I'd know Nimah anywhere. Hill-people juju. Some of the rebels used to carry them during the Struggle, calling out to Daghda. I always thought it was worthless, both the calling out and him saving us. No one in Eitan carries them anymore.

"Good work, men," I say to them.

"He won't tell us anything, ma'am." The soldier looks over at his partner for backup.

"No, ma'am," his partner says. "We've been on him for two solid hours and he won't say anything. He keeps singing."

"Singing?" I say.

"Yes, sir," the first soldier says.

I drop the totem on one of the steel tables and step close to the bleeding man, set my ear beside his lips. His words are only breath but I know what he's saying by the rhythm. Down near the river where our brothers bled. My fingers tingle. Last time I heard that song, Henraek and I were leading a group of two hundred men in choruses as we marched through the streets. The old rebel song doesn't give me anxiety, though; it's his accent that makes me sweat. Thick. Muddled. This man is actually from the hills, and that's probably worse than being a Nimah-worshipping rebel.

"Why did you come down here?" I whisper to him. "What are you doing?" It might be the shadows playing over his bloody face, but I swear to god he smirks.

"We can't tell what it is, ma'am. Might be some sort of code," the soldier says.

"He's praying," I say to them. "He's making his peace."

"How do you know?" one of them says. "Do you speak Amergi?"

"Does this pasty bastard look Amergin to you?" Sometimes I'm amazed this party has ruled for so long with soldiers like him on the ground. "You're not going to get anything from him," I say to her. "He's not even here anymore."

Lady Morrigan lets out a long sigh, then flutters her hand at the man. "Strip him." The soldiers exchange a glance, then peek at me, as if I have any say. "Don't look at him," she says. "I told you to strip him. The rebels must understand who they are fighting."

One of them clears his throat. "Lady Morrigan—"

His compatriot cuts him off. "It's taken care of, ma'am." He crosses the room to a closet and pulls out a cart. Sitting on it is what could pass for a small generator, clear tubes snaking from the base and leading to a stochae, an oblong glass container that doctors used to hold small amounts of medicine.

After the hill-man is hooked up to the machine, one of the soldiers will flip a switch and the man will be stripped of his consciousness, which will be held in the glass tube on a shelf in the basement of the Gallery to fester in the darkness next to his countrymen for the next however many years. Or centuries.

During the Struggle, we told our men that there were worse things than death, partly to motivate them to fight bravely, and partly because it sounded cool. Then Doctor Mebeth invented stripping.

"Post his body where they will see him," she says. "And make sure you hose down the floor before you leave. The tiles will stain."

I open the door for her, and as we're leaving the room, the man erupts in one last howl that raises my hair.

"What will you do about Johnstone's?" she says to me as we pass through the main Gallery.

"It's all under control." I shape my face into a comforting smile, see her to the front door. "You go home and relax. It's been a long day and I've got someone coming in."

She gives me a smile that could be mistaken for a paper cut, then adjusts her hat and steps into the street, leaving without another word.

I go back to the booth where Cobb sleeps. His sculpture pulses over the table, something that could be either a pile of debris from a bombed-out building or an abstract person. I shut the screen off, then lean down and run my hand over his head, his patchy hair so fine it's almost invisible.

One of the soldiers calls my name and hurries through the patrons, his hand cupped by his side.

Belousz gives me a crooked look from his booth then returns to gambling.

Cobb stirs and blinks his eyes open, woken by the soldier's yelling. Now he's going to be cranky as hell because he didn't get a decent nap.

"Sir, you left this in the back room." He hands me the totem.

I give him a nod, gritting my teeth. "Thank you, son. Thank you for your commitment and service to Eitan City." I look him up and down. "Now go clean yourself up. You look like a used tampon."

He thanks me and hastens back to the room. I wait until he's gone before I throw the totem in a garbage can.

3.
HENRAEK

The Gallery lies in undulating shadow, the prized flower in Eitan City's crown of thorns, nestled among cafés with metal bars striating the windows and water repositories guarded by teenagers wielding nail-speckled boards. Even with badge readers at the front doors, the Tathadann wants to make sure that what is theirs remains theirs. Thick nets of Spanish moss hang from the streetlamps' ornate wrought-iron armatures, a constant symbol of Tathadann decadence at the expense of the people.

I swipe my badge and enter the Gallery, the cold air hitting my face like a fist. This is one of the few buildings left with air conditioning, but the system is so old it needs every advantage possible, such as the marble floors. They're wonderful for keeping the space cool but create a constant murmur that rolls through the room. Considering some of the conversation topics, that might be a positive.

Patrons line up before the paintings hung on the walls, pointing and whispering to one another, or squinting and tilting their heads. Some of them sway in time to the hologram band, the same music Emeríann plays at home, though ours is from a pirated network feed because our kind can't afford holograms. One woman asks if a painting is hung the right way. Fifteen years ago I would have laughed and called her a philistine, but I have a similar reaction now when Emeríann shows me her sculptures.

Primary colors dominate the art, scenes from a time before the Wars: the reflection of a cloudless summer sky shimmering on glassy water; the emerald knolls, ripe with the musk of fresh rain; the face of a child smeared with candy. Whoever painted these must be either biblically old to remember times like these, or have access to dangerous amounts of Paradise. Once I asked Walleus if he knew the artists. He clapped my shoulder and smiled then walked away. I'm not sure he could identify a painting from a photograph.

My father used to tell me stories about scenes like these from when he was a kid, lush green forests beyond the hills he'd explore and slow-moving brooks brimming with fish that he and his brothers would catch. I'd spend nights with my wife Aífe recounting those stories, both of us lying on the living room floor of our house, imagining that the ceiling was some distant, better, brighter sky, a reason to fight harder against the Tathadann and reclaim the city as ours. But sometimes I wonder if these paintings are what the land actually looked like years ago, or if it's merely Tathadann-sanctioned reality. Another way for Morrigan and the Promhael to rewrite history, position themselves as our saviors and gods.

When patrons stroll through the Gallery, the paintings create a longing for an unknown, idealized past. Patrons need to experience green grass and clean air, to hear birds chirping and watch a child dig into a sandy beach. As they slink farther toward the back of the Gallery, the ache grows until they're nearly scratching at their throats and begging for help, for communion, for air. Walleus soothes them, answers their prayers, gives them air: he sells them memory.

And I harvest the memories for him.

My heels thump on the floor as I weave through the crowd, oblong polishing droids scuttling between people's feet. Guttural laughs undulate from the back of the Gallery like vultures thrown down a well. Walleus's lackeys occupy a booth, all of them dressed in brown Tathadann fatigues. I lobbied Walleus to let me out of wearing the uniform, saying that I'd better be able to slip amongst the people, but in all honesty the soldiers look like walking pieces of actual shit and I've suffered enough indignity.

They push gambling chips back and forth, grunting and arguing and sniping at one another. Someone pushes it too far and a shiv comes out, then tentatively lowers. Their conversation disintegrates into whispered laughs as I approach. I set the case on the table and try to stare a hole through Belousz. One of his eyes is shocking blue and the other is grown over with skin, slightly sunken like a tarp lying across a gaping hole.

"You look lost, son," he says, not even bothering to smile. "Need some help?"

"Only if you show me on your trip to Hell."

"Ah," he nods. "I'm sure you're well on your way."

During our raid on the Tathadann outpost he commanded, Belousz stepped on a hastily buried scatter bomb and sent jagged metal bits into his face. I considered it a fair trade, considering he was in the middle of beheading Josihe, my second-in-command and the husband of Aífe's best friend. Since then I try to view every interaction with Belousz as a testament to my self-discipline, that swearing to no longer take lives really does mean something, because there are few things I'd rather do than put him in a cage and set him on fire.

"If you two're going to fight, then fight. If you're going to screw, get on with it. Otherwise, shut up," Walleus says, coming up beside me. "You've got something red on you, Henraek." I wipe my hand across my face. A slash of blood in my palm, from Riab's father cutting me. I'm surprised Emeríann didn't notice or bother to tell me.

He uses a handkerchief to blot away sweat on his massive forehead, even though it's cold enough I expect to see my breath in a burst of fog.

Walleus nudges one of the lackeys – he's new to the organization and under Greig's wing, which means I haven't made any concerted effort to learn his name yet – and flicks his wrist, telling the kid to move over. With a great exhalation, Walleus lowers himself to the leather bench. I imagine the wood groaning beneath him.

He leans back and knits his fingers together behind his bald head. With his white linen suit, thin gold chain and chunky rings, I would expect to see him selling luxury vehicles used on vacations a hundred years ago, in one of the southern lands across the channel, not sitting inside a Tathadann-run art gallery that doles out the very memory they stand against, lest the people remember how they used to live and want it back. With everything that has died since the Struggle began, it's nice to see at least capitalism can survive. "Any problems?" he says.

"Nothing I couldn't handle," I say.

"'Nothing I couldn't handle' doesn't sound promising," Walleus says. "You need a helper next time?"

This elicits snickers from the cronies. Belousz simply stares at me.

I nod at the chips in the middle of the table. "They seem pretty integral to this operation here." I measure my words, not putting too many teeth in them but enough to keep his lackeys from getting the impression that I can be insulted by anyone.

Walleus hefts himself up, points to an empty booth, says, "Sit."

I take my time getting there, though it is only

twenty feet away. When I look inside, I find Cobb drawing meandering shapes on the table screen. He yawns, his lopsided mouth opening only halfway. My skin prickles on seeing him but I sit nonetheless, albeit on the opposite side of the table.

Once Walleus lowers himself into some privacy, he says, "Things would be a lot more pleasant for you if you quit that little pissing match. There ain't that much difference between the two of you, anyway."

"Aside from cutting off Josihe's head."

"He was a worthless soldier from the start. And if he'd been paying attention, Belousz wouldn't have gotten a jump on him. You only gave Josihe the nod because your wives were friends." He hooks his thumb over his shoulder. "We might've broke a lot more necks if we had Belousz on our side back then."

"But back then, you would've rather broken your own neck than say something like that."

He purses his lips, arches his eyebrows. "Well, I learned to move on."

"Is that what this is called?"

Leaning forward, he sets his jaw, ready to unleash a torrent. Then he switches gears so quickly it's almost disorienting. Such is Walleus. "Did you find the jewelry?"

"What jewelry?"

"The hangman's widow in Fomora?"

"I'll be all right," I say, shaking my head.

"It's not charity if you're working for it," he says. "It's a tip."

"I'm all right."

"Fine. Starve. See if I care. I'm only trying to help the family."

I give him a blank stare. "My family is dead."

"I'm well aware of that, Henraek." He closes his eyes and lets go a long, exasperated sigh. "I meant Emeríann."

He shakes his head and smooths the silken strands of Cobb's hair. His boy sits beside him like a trembling peregrine falcon, staring at his drawings, his fingers pressed so hard against the screen that I half expect it to crack. Still, I swear I can still feel his gaze burning on my flesh. He rubs his gnarled, stunted body against Walleus's suit. His scaled skin, a product of his blood disease, scratches on the linen fabric.

I've been toiling as a memory thief for more than six years, draining citizens of their pasts and coming in here to trade them, and still my skin feels too small for my body whenever I am near Cobb. There's no reason a grown man should be so unsettled by a twelve year-old.

"That was low," I say. "You didn't tell me I was going to Riab's address."

He flinches slightly, as if this surprises him. "I didn't know," he says. "I get paid to hand them out, not read them."

"You also didn't tell me there'd be someone else home," I say. "It almost cost me."

"Surveillance isn't my wheelhouse–"

"I'm painfully aware of that, Walleus." I'm tempted

to say something more, something about watching dead families that I know will cut him, in return for all the slights he's given me to maintain his position of authority, but shut my mouth because there's no point in arguing.

"Look," he says. "I give you names, you give me brains. Your list is your word, hear? That's all I need to worry about." He purses his lips then exhales. "If you're not up for this anymore, let me know. I'm sure I can scare up a hole for you. Might even have the old one still waiting."

"Vials are in the case. Everything else is under control." I lean closer to him, changing tack before he tries to bait me into another argument. "Do you remember that power substation we did? Out in the fields?"

"I don't know. Maybe."

"I know you remember it. You were still with us then, weren't you?" I keep my voice low. "You never leaked anything, right?"

He closes his eyes for a long beat then opens them abruptly. "We are sitting in the middle of a prized Tathadann building."

"Tell me I'm right."

"What's it matter what I say? You always think you're right anyway." He shakes his head. "Let me get your list for tomorrow." Walleus clears his throat and calls for one of the lackeys, another new one it seems from the way he hustles over, still eager to please. He hands a piece of paper to Walleus, who lets it hang out before me. I snatch it and he smiles.

Four addresses down and I stop.

"What is this?"

"What?" he says.

"I was there today. Why do you want his dad too?"

"Word from on high." He shrugs, not even needing to ask the address to know what I'm talking about. "Look at it positively. They trust you above all the others."

"Why are they interested in Riab's family?"

His mouth a knife line, Walleus says, "Because they are, and we work for them."

A rapid click silences the table. Walleus turns to see the lackey staring at Cobb so hard it almost makes me uncomfortable. Cobb nestles closer to Walleus.

"Is there a problem?" Walleus says.

The lackey doesn't answer.

Walleus clears his throat to get the man's attention, only to swing his hand like a blade at the man's neck. The sound of cartilage shredding his breath is like a dying breeze over a broken glass bottle. His body collapses into a writhing pile beside the table, his legs kicking and hands slapping at his crushed windpipe. His face turns so red it's purple. Walleus soothes Cobb with one hand while calling for one of the plebes to get this man some medical attention.

"You're still here?" he says.

"Whatever. I'm going home. See you tomorrow morning."

He nods at Cobb. "We're making special pancakes

tomorrow. Let's push it back half an hour."

"I don't care," I shrug and step over the man, legs barely tapping the floor. "It doesn't matter."

Blackened lines climb along the stairwell to my apartment like the EKG of a cinder heart, the residue of a fire that spread from the building on the left. The exposed light bulbs in the hallway sing in the frequency of hornets, the one before our apartment flickering long-short-long-short. A sprinkling of crushed glass lies along the baseboard, either an old memory vial or glass dropped by the lagon woman across the hall who constantly forgets where she lives. Half the time I come home, I expect to see her in my living room, looking for her cat.

Earthen spices hit me as soon as I open the door with my key. A pan sizzles in the kitchen, Emeríann singing quietly as she cooks. I call out to her then kick off my boots by the couch, my bare feet leaving tracks across the recently swept floor. The gnarled wood remains dull, the color of stagnant coffee.

Emeríann stands before the stove, swaying to the rhythm of the song. I set my hands on her hips and she startles and spins, wooden spoon reared back and ready to gouge my eyes.

"Goddammit," she says, lowering the spoon. "I almost killed you."

"You're halfway a criminal already, apparently. I said hi when I came in."

"Oh, I couldn't hear." She kisses my cheek then

returns to stirring the root vegetables and strips of brown meat. "Dinner's ready in ten if you need to change."

I kiss the back of her neck then go into the adjoining living room and open a window, swinging the iron bars aside.

To the west is the pale glow along the lid of the world's eye, the mountain range cutting a dark, jagged line against the red sky and the silhouette of rigs puncturing the land. Past the mountains are the charred fields of Westhell County, where Walleus and I come from. And past that, well, people from here rarely go that far, and none of them venture here. Beyond the hills, there are likely only roving bands of scavengers with bloodlines long mingled. Or there could be nothing at all anymore, which might be the worst.

When the wind is strong enough to blow away some of the haze, I can sit on the ledge with a glass of Emeríann's bourbon and watch the flames in Amergin samba up to the sky. Today, though, the air is dead, thick with sulfur and ash.

The dull thrumming of Eitan City is as hypnotizing as Emeríann's singing. At our rallies during the Struggle, she would always break into song and work the crowd into a frenzy. Aífe and I would dance a two-step while Emeríann sang, her late husband Riab nearly iridescent with pride while watching from the crowd.

I lean out the window and extend my arm, whistle,

and wait for Silas to land.

My dead son, Donael, named his last two cats
Silas. I thought it appropriate, despite the city slowly
burning itself to death, to continue the tradition.

Silas's fellow pigeons strut along the ledge, pecking
at the bowl of rock salt I leave out for them. If anything
could have survived the Struggle, I would have put
my money on cockroaches. The pigeons adapted by
molting their feathers into something like leather
and augmenting their diet. They were the dark horse
of the evolutionary arms race and I cannot help but
admire their ingenuity.

Silas lands on my forearm, his feet warmed
from standing on concrete. His coos grotesquely
affectionate, he presses his head against my palm,
forcing me to pet him. I turn around to sit at the table
and catch a death-stare from Emeríann. If she weren't
holding a plate of food in her hand, she would surely
press both fists into her cocked hips and exhale hard.
I stop in place, consider her, then look at Silas.

"Sorry, pal." I set him back on the ledge where he
pecks at the rock salt with the rest of his flock, then
pull out Emeríann's chair.

"He's sweet, I know," she says, setting the plate in
front of me then sitting and draping a piece of burlap
over her lap. "But he's also a filthy flying rat."

"But a filthy flying rat with personality," I say.

"Of course."

Two dozen found-art sculptures hang on the walls
of the apartment. Emeríann's mother had been an

artist – a classic artist – back before the Struggle, and Emeríann definitely inherited that creativity. But since everything went to hell, paints have been hard to come by, so Emeríann has had to quell her creative demons by making art out of the debris she collects from the streets. I don't pretend to understand what her projects mean, but she likes making something beautiful out of all the pain and suffering out there, and I like her liking something.

"So," I say, "blow anything up yet?"

She stabs vegetables with her fork. I bite into the meat. Squirrel, I believe, though the marinades she concocts do wonders to take the game out of it.

"I'm sorry," I say, changing tack. "How was the rest of your day?"

She gives an affected smile, but it feels more relieved than pained.

"No one vomited on me, so that was nice." She cuts her food into equal-sized bits, shifts the fork to her right hand and chews with tiny bites.

"The apartment is clean," I say.

She smiles and winks, smoothing back her hair with her palm, as if saying she worked a shift then cleaned the apartment and still her hair looks perfect. Which it does. It always does.

"So you can speak freely if you like." I motion around at the room with my knife. "Without regard to me or them."

"If we talk, we'll fight, and I don't want to fight. Besides," she raises her eyebrows as if nudging me with her elbow, "you're the pacifist, anyway."

"That's ideological, and could–"

"Henraek," she says, her voice controlled but with an undertone of warning. She takes a breath and gives me a strained smile. "Your dinner's going to get cold."

I concede and take a bite, flicking my tongue at a hard bit of gristle stuck between my back teeth. "Where did you find steak?" I say.

She stops chewing and cocks her head, a smile blooming over her lips. "How do you stand yourself?"

If only I could answer that.

I resist the urge to interrogate her about the impending bombing for the sake of civility, and we finish the rest of the meal in pleasant fashion. She sets the dishes in the sink and I tell her to leave them, that I'll wipe them off later, as the water here usually makes them dirtier. I pat the space on the couch next to me, invite her to sit.

"I love you, Henraek, but I want to set your couch on fire."

"It's got character," I say.

"You can't use the same justification for a couch and a flying rodent."

I guide her down beside me, set her feet onto my lap and rub my thumbs into the arch. Her eyes drift closed.

But as I massage, I see the image of Riab's grandfather on the back of my skull, his father's name written beneath it. I examine it from a hundred angles, trying to find some way to approach Emeríann about her former in-laws and the Tathadann's sudden interest in them. Even though her face is the picture of relaxation and it would be a cardinal sin to disturb her, I can't shake the memory of Walleus wincing and wonder if it's all connected.

"So." I clear my throat, though I don't have much to follow with.

She sighs. "Really?"

"Is everything OK with Forgall?"

Her eyebrows rise slightly. "How so?"

"All of your plans, and whatnot. Everything's secure?"

"Things are quiet and in motion, if that's what you mean." She takes a deep breath, blinking away the promise of sleep.

"But no one's talking? Forgall hasn't told anyone?"

"He's told his people but I highly doubt anyone else." She breathes half a laugh. "He was pissed I told you."

"Why? He think I'll try to take it over?" I feel the blossom of pride in my chest. "Or that I'd do it better than him?"

"No." She blinks a few times. "Doesn't trust anyone who comes near Iagonael. His brother was one."

"Then it's a good thing I'm not," I say. "When are you going to do it?"

"Next week."

"During the statue dedication? That's dangerous."

A small smile crosses her lips.

"Hell, Emeríann. It's the twenty-fifth anniversary of the Tathadann founding. Do you have any idea how many soldiers they'll have guarding the area?"

"Do you have any idea how many cameras they'll have filming it?" she says. "When they see the boar-face hologram on the statue, then hear the big boom?" She shakes her head, grinning at the image.

I nod, stretch out the cramps forming in my fingers. She's got a point. "That's only ten days away. Has he looked at all the logistics? Do you have all the supplies? Capacitors, charges, shielding wire? What about trigger points, escape routes?"

Pulling her feet from my lap, she pushes herself to sitting. She leans in and peers at me. "Are you worried about me?"

"If I didn't think you could handle yourself in a stressful situation, I never would have suggested we live together."

"I don't know what happened with you and Forgall back then," she says, "but it's none of my business."

"It's not back then. It's all the time. His family has Morrigan blood, but no one spits on him in the street and calls him a traitor. And then he has the gall to suggest that Walleus–"

"Love," she says, grabbing my hand. "It doesn't matter. Who gives a damn what some assholes say? He knows what he's doing, and I need to do this. I'm sick of being their victim, all of us living the way they tell us to. They've ruined thousands of lives here and they're going to keep doing it even after Morrigan dies.

This is my home now, the place I want to raise a family. And I'm not going to let them rule over my family's lives. And before you ask – no, I'm not pregnant." She punctuates it with a brief wry smile. "I spend all day getting people drunk and helping them forget about life for a while. Sometimes I make pretty things to put on our walls. But these fireworks? They're my opportunity to do something real, something my kids will be proud of. I need them. We, all of Eitan, need them. Now is the time for them."

"No, I know, but it's…" I scratch my stubble and try to collect my thoughts, push away others I'm not willing to acknowledge. "You could've asked me. I would've helped you."

She gestures toward the belt of vials sitting on the table in front of the couch. "I didn't ask you because I care about you."

"I know, but–"

"Come by tomorrow when you can. I'll show you what we've got so you can sleep peacefully." She stretches her hands over her head, leaning back until her hipbones pop from beneath her shirt. Arms spread like a swan, she leans down and touches her toes, letting out a deep satisfied breath. "Are you coming to bed?"

I nod. "Got a few things to go over first."

"Surveillance again?" she says, knowing it's not, but it's our unspoken agreement not to discuss it.

"I'll be in soon," I say.

"I have things I should be doing too, you know, but

I'd rather spend time with you."

"I know. I won't be long."

She chews on her bottom lip, stares at me with those eyes for a moment, then lets out a short breath. "How many times is that this week?"

"It's fine, love. That..." I swallow, restart. "The Paradise was only a couple times, and that was a long time ago. I'm fine." It was five years and eleven months ago. I lost several weeks in lagonael dens and on friends' couches, vaporizing and watching the only memory I had of Aífe and Donael, trying to bring them back into existence through hallucinations and tears.

"You understand this is exactly why Forgall doesn't trust you, right?"

"Don't confuse doing a job with being one of them," I tell her. "You should know better."

She sets her fists against her hips, bristling at my condescension. "Then come to bed."

"I will."

A hard moment stretches between us before she exhales, her hair drifting aside. "Well, I don't know if I can wait up for you. Tomorrow's going to be busy."

"I understand."

And I do, but my dead family is waiting.

4.
WALLEUS

"Can't believe you left the house without your umbrella, Mister Walleus," the man in the gatehouse says to me. "Might've gotten your new haircut all wet."

"Good thing I can clean it with my hand, then." I pat my bald head. "Work smart, not hard. It's in my genes."

We've had the same exchange every time I come home for the last five years and still he smiles like it's the funniest joke ever told. Life in Eitan must be a lot easier with blissful stupidity like his.

The scanner and my car exchange their information, then the gate yawns open.

"Hopefully tomorrow will be a dry one," he says, waving at Cobb as the car drives itself forward.

It navigates through Donnculan, each court's name honoring a different Tathadann dignitary: judges, generals, politicians, police. If I'd been in charge of planning and development, I would have named everything after their whores, because no statesman can get anything done without the promise of some pussy once he's finished.

Cherry blossoms line the main drive. Two small droids hover at the tips, pruning away the errant growth so that the branches will arch like a canopy over the sidewalks. Thick bushes with some kind of red flower keep the street out of everyone's yards. A mother chases after her son who is going too fast on his bike, the training wheels rocking him back and forth. He takes a corner without any brakes and flips over, the handlebars pinning him to the concrete. She yanks it off him and he rights himself, wiping his tears and a bloody cut on his sleeve then taking off again.

This is the second section of the neighborhood I've lived in, the one with connected houses. When I first joined the Tathadann, they gave the boys and me a detached home two miles inside the gates – fully furnished and with a closet full of white suits so finely tailored to my body the old man had to move my balls aside to get the right measurement – sort of incentivizing my switch, or at least not making me feel like such an asshole about it, and looking sharp while I did it. Every third house had a fountain sitting in its front yard – which likely meant there were at least two more at the back, if not a pool as well. In here, there's no landmarks in the landscaping or architecture, and all the houses are white. That suggested solidarity, they said. Our house was so far back that, if I hadn't been issued a Tathadann car – one of the newer ones that drove themselves by radar triangulation – I would have had to track the mileage to remember where I lived.

As fast as my position within the party grew, from managing the water dispersal to wrangling intelligence and commoditizing memory, the size of my house shrank and moved closer to the community's perimeter. Those suits got cheaper and came less often, too. At first, it pissed me off, but after a few drinks it occurred to me that I'd moved past the need for constant surveillance and they would finally leave me be.

At Mayhe Court, we swing left then drive to the end of the street, kids chasing each other around the asphalt circle.

Yeah, I live in a goddamned cul-de-sac now.

Cobb scampers up the sidewalk to the brick steps and hits the front door with so much momentum he tumbles backward. He stares blankly at the house like it attacked him. I step up to the sensor, say, "Open up." The voice sensor is as bad as the biometric reader and I have to clear my throat and try twice more before it opens.

Inside, I call out hello but it echoes through the house, so I scrounge up some food for us. I throw containers of leftover roasted pork, potatoes au gratin, and poached asparagus in the top part of the dual-oven and tell it to warm up. "But not too hot this time," I say. "You burned my mouth yesterday."

I call out to Cobb, "Do you still want some chicken?" When there's no answer, I assume he's hungry and turn on the indoor grill in the center of the kitchen island of burners, put on a couple pieces of chicken and tell it to grill them medium.

While the food cooks, I go into the living room and draw the shades then press my hand exactly four feet above the seam in the carpet. The laser inside the wall analyzes my DNA, then there's a pneumatic hiss beside the bookshelf.

The sudden interest in Riab's family is a little unnerving, but I don't really know who's writing the orders, and Riab's family seems a little small to concern Morrigan. What has me curious is Henraek mentioning the power substation, something I haven't thought about in years. I'd say it has to be urgent for him to bring it up inside the Gallery, but this is also Henraek, the man who shot three holes in the door to our old apartment because the tumbler inside the knob kept catching. For a man who constantly bitches about his dealings with others' pasts, he damn sure loves wallowing in his own.

I push on the wall and open up the panic room.

More than three dozen green and white scarves hang on the walls, some striped, some printed with mantras, some with notable dates or player names. Against the far side is a bookshelf crammed full of photo albums holding clipped articles that damned the raids, old pamphlets, blueprints of buildings and schematics of bombs. More albums rise like towers around the foot of the shelf. I installed the room myself after I'd been here a couple years. Even cloaked the reader by altering some old plans from a bomb-maker called Nael, rejigged to read only DNA related to mine, in case of emergency or an official stopping by for a surprise inspection. Seemed safer than hiding all of this under my old foul weather gear in the back of the closet.

I pop open the lid of the surplus bullet box, sift through the vials until I find the right one, then step out of the panic room, close the door, and seal it. I stick the vial into the projector unit that I jury-rigged up to the TV so it'd project from within the wall, creating a three-dimensional hologram – state-of-the-art twenty years ago when they built these houses, another vestigial benefit of Tathadann life – then let it boot up while I check on the food, forking the chicken onto a plate for Cobb.

"Your dinner's going to get cold," I yell down the hallway, then dump my food onto a plate, plop on the couch and hit play.

The power substation comes into focus, down in the distance. Giant green tubes extend from all sides of the building, housing the conductors that provide electricity to all the Tathadann offices, bars, and shops on the southeast side. No electricity, no communication capabilities. No communication, no way they could raise the soldiers when we went in to gut their headquarters.

A razor-wire fence runs the perimeter of the

grounds. Twenty feet of bare dirt stretches between the fence and the tall reeds covering the floor of the valley. It's all supposed to make it impossible to approach the plant unnoticed.

Unless you're going at night, dressed in all brown.

And you have a schedule of the guards' rotation and a fistful of bullets.

I'd told Henraek for weeks that this was a stupid idea. It would never work and he was leading us into the killing fields. He told me I would owe him two drinks for every side of the building that went. He was throwing up all the next day.

While Henraek led the team to the station in the distance, I stayed on the high ground, tucked in between patches of reeds with a .50 caliber rifle mounted on a tripod at my feet. One of our plebes had a sister who had attracted the attention of the clerk working in a Tathadann weapons office. She kept him busy for five minutes – apparently she was as good as the plebe had boasted, though no one wanted to ask how he knew – and we relieved them of some heavy artillery. One of our soldiers, Fergus, brought out the new pulse cannons the Tathadann had developed, but I said to keep it old school. I sat up there half wanting something to go wrong so I could use the gun to mow down a line of the plant's guards.

On the bottom left, the team creeps through the reeds, and from the zigzag pattern they take – a tactic Henraek would later be obscenely proud of – it only looks like a breeze through the barley. So far, there is nothing new, nothing different I notice from the hundred other times I've watched it, which doesn't mean that I'm missing something as much as Henraek's got a new bug up his ass, different from the usual one. When the point man reaches the dirt at the edge of the reeds, the floor behind me creaks.

I jump up, fork in hand and ready to stab.

He's standing there with a large bowl in his hands.

"Goddamn," I say, turning off the memory. "Donael, you scared the hell out of me."

"I said hi when you guys came home. Didn't you hear me?"

"No," I say. "Obviously I didn't."

He looks at my dinner splattered on the carpet but doesn't comment on it, then holds out the bowl of popcorn. "Want some?"

I shake my head. "Have you seen Cobb?"

"I thought he was tired so I asked him if he wanted to go to bed but he wants to read books." He hops over the couch and sits in my spot.

"Where is he?"

He shrugs. "Reading?"

"Can you go get him? So we can have a family night? You know, for once?"

"Can we watch a movie instead?" he says. "Memories are creepy. I don't want to end up like those freaks who can't talk."

I kneel on the carpet and scrape the food back onto the plate, picking through the threads of the shag to get the big chunks of asparagus and potato because the cleaning droid they gave us is old and will clog. "Do you want his dinner at least?"

He holds up the bowl like that should be an answer in itself.

"You can't eat popcorn for dinner. That's not very healthy."

"There's milk on it too. Well, butter."

"I'll bring you something real."

I dump the food down the disposal and I leave the dishes in the dishwasher. There's not much left in the fridge, so I take two mostly clean plates from the counter and drop some chicken on them.

I hand one to Donael then sit next to him on the couch.

"I think the popcorn would've been healthier," he says, not looking at me but focused on the TV screen he didn't even want to watch.

"What are we watching tonight?"

He shrugs and shoves popcorn and two bites of chicken in his mouth. "Something funny." A chunk of chewed meat falls from his lips and lands in the shag. I lift my feet and call out for the cleaning droid.

After I upload a movie from the network I sit back next to him and listen to his crunching, consider my makeshift meal, drop it on the coffee table. He sets the bowl between us and rests his feet atop mine on the ottoman. I tell the system to play.

5.
HENRAEK

As I lean out the window, Silas perched and preening himself on the ledge, I watch Amergin flicker until the noise in the bedroom quiets and I'm sure Emeríann is asleep. "Stay quiet, bud," I say to Silas as I wave him in.

Hanging above the couch is Emeríann's least favorite piece, the jaw of a dog attached to a bird skull with copper wire, beaded feathers wrapped around interlocking twigs and shards of metal. She'd wanted to take it down, saying it was trying too hard, but I told her to leave it, that I actually understood this one, which seemed to satisfy her.

In truth, it reminds me of Aífe and Donael in some oblique way. Possibly the dog jaw, for the way Donael would run around the living room chomping his teeth as he tried to bite us. I'd pull my arm inside my sleeve and roll around on the floor in ham-fisted agony, begging to get the lower half of my arm from inside the dog's belly. Possibly the bird feathers and beads, for the way Aífe would sound like an exotic bird when I'd do an impression of Lady Morrigan dominating her husband Macuil and she'd laugh so hard she couldn't breathe. Possibly, or probably, I like it for the way it tries too hard and yet still doesn't work.

Quietly, I push back the couch then pry up a floorboard. Sitting beneath the floor is Aífe's green and white striped scarf and a pistol with a barrel so clean it looks wet. Wrapped inside the scarf is a glass vial, the metal rings tarnished with rust. I set the memory viewer on a wooden crate before the couch and flip on the power to warm up, turning the volume knob all the way down. One of the men in my platoon was also a mechanic, and converted an old video recorder into a viewer using some solder and two magnetic rods. There are much nicer – and smaller – ones out today, but I've used this one so many times I've begun to associate it with the people it displays, as if my wife and child would be different people on an unblemished projection. Silas flaps to the arm of the couch and perches there.

I wrap the scarf once around my neck, place it against my mouth and nose, close my eyes and inhale. Hold it, hold it. Exhale and inhale again. Though it smells mostly of dust and thick air, a few tendrils of jasmine perfume still cling to the threads and if I focus hard enough, I can bring them out. Or maybe I will them into being. She'd worn the perfume on our first date, when I got us tickets to see the Hoep's play, and I bought her a bottle of the same perfume on our first anniversary. After another quick inhale, I fold the scarf into thirds, then halves, then set it back beneath the boards. I know she won't leave the bedroom, but the random chance that Emeríann might find me with Aífe's scarf wrapped around my neck tight as a noose would warrant too much mollification, and she has dealt with enough already.

I don't have enough energy tonight to survey the memories from Riab's grandfather so I set the vial next to the scarf and go to the kitchen to pour myself a glass of bootlegged bourbon.

I sip it and inhale quickly through my nose, the burn nearly taking my breath away, then crouch next to the viewer and insert the vial. The electrodes crackle and light up. The lines of a football pitch materialize in the steam, the warbling crowd noise cutting through the hiss. I take a belt of liquor, suppress a cough, then lie on the couch. Silas wobbles his way to my lap. His coos reverberate in my chest and he might vibrate me to bits. I press play.

The stands heave with fans singing partisan songs. Players scatter across the field. Donael cheers when the blue player takes the ball near our goal and slips in a sneaky one early in the first half. I see myself telling him that those are our Hoeps out there, the green and white team, that it's the people's team and the blue guys are supported by the Tathadann party, but his favorite color is blue so he doesn't care. Sitting next to me, Aífe tucks back a piece of her chestnut hair, her fingers long and slender. Piano player fingers, I'd call them, though she didn't have a musical bone in her body. Her neck is pale and smooth and, even though I spent hours nibbling on them, I always forget how elfin her ears are. The striped scarf draped over her shoulders flutters in the breeze.

Since our first date had been at a Hoep's match, we made it a tradition to come every year and sit in the same seats, bringing Donael in a baby carrier when he was young, then getting him his very own top – to match ours – as he grew. The fact that she wore perfume – the jasmine one – to a football match, combined with the way she put down her whiskey without cringing, was part of the reason I fell in love with her in the first place.

The field of vision goes back to the match. This memory came from my friend Séta, one of my sergeants who would come out with us. Later, after everything went to hell, it took me an agonizing week to track him down.

Our team equalizes late in the second half with a goal through a series of clumsy one-touch passes that were saved only by the skill of Concho Louth, widely considered to be our Hoeps' all-time best player, but Aífe's breasts bounce as she celebrates the goal and Séta instead follows them with his eyes. Unimpressed by the on-field antics, Donael shovels fried potatoes into his mouth like he's a giant monster and the wedges are helpless villagers. He pulls on my sleeve, chunks of potato hanging from his mouth. Aífe tells him that he's gross, which only encourages him. He wedges two more in his nostrils and turns toward Séta for approval. Behind him, Aífe leans close to me and asks me to tell him not to encourage Donael. I can still remember the pomegranate scent of her shampoo, mixed with the beer, sweat, and the sharp smell of freshly cut grass. Séta watches us for an uncomfortable amount of time.

On the other side of the stadium, a finger of smoke twists between the blue jerseys in the stands. It's military-grade plastique set by Tathadann loyalists with the intention of framing the rebels, though we didn't know it at the time.

The game remains tied until the eighty-fifth minute when one of the opposing players breaks through our defense and notches the go-ahead goal. Our side groans. The Tathadann supporters erupt in song. Donael is so happy he grabs Séta's coffee and throws it on a kid wearing a striped jersey then calls him a Hun. The memory fades out.

But three minutes later, Concho Louth scored the most famous goal in Hoeps' history, collecting a cross with his chest and unleashing a deadly right foot into the corner of the net. Thirty seconds after that, during the celebration, Aífe flinched, as if she could sense it. Then the plastique exploded.

The following morning they reported on the explosion, blaming us. It wasn't even the obvious bias that pissed me off, but the fact that they used my name when I had nothing to do with it.

Two days later, I led the raid on the power substation. The Tathadann countered by driving an explosive-filled truck through the front door of the Parkhead, the bar where Walleus and I had earlier devised plans for the uprising.

That kicked off a riot, the one that would eventually collapse like a dying star on Aífe and Donael.

They said she'd been trampled in the street, shielding our son. The only way they knew he was dead was his grey skin. To this day, I can't even remember where I was when they told me. The shock of hearing they'd been killed wiped everything clean, and all that remains are jumbled glimpses of scenes. An old woman falling to the ground as I sprinted through the streets. Pressing my face against the pavement where they had been found, trying to recover any stray molecules of them. Punching a Tathadann soldier in the mouth as he tried to stop me from climbing over a Tathadann barricade that was in my way. A broken bottle glittering in the gutter where the riot had been, the way it seemed to wink at me. Walleus's face as he held me back from killing the medic who said the bodies had already been transported for burning. The way my throat ached from howling all night long and puking up liquor during the day. I couldn't even say goodbye to them, take her slender fingers in mine or muss his hair one last time, apologize for not being able to protect them.

I take the vial from the viewer and cup it in my

palm for a minute, giving my dead family a good night hug as I do every time, then wrap it up in Aífe's scarf. I set the viewer beside it and replace the board, slide the couch leg back over it.

I undress in the kitchen so my rustling won't wake Emeríann, then slip into the bedroom and under the sheets. She drapes her leg over mine and nestles her face in my neck, our bodies becoming one. Her skin is warm and soft on mine.

"Did we win?" Her voice is thick with sleep.

I stare at the ceiling, listening to her breathing and feeling her skin, until the room lightens once more.

6.
WALLEUS

Cobb's feet jump around like a fish's tail and one of his jagged toenails catches my forearm, leaving a nice little slash in its wake. His leg wiggles the shorts off and back to the floor.

"I said, give me your goddamn foot." I manage not to scream which is nearly a miracle, though he probably wouldn't be able to hear it if I did because Donael is standing beside us and he will not shut the hell up.

"And everyone's going to be there, and Craesa's mom said it's fine and she doesn't care and they cleaned the pool."

Cobb smiles and clicks. His legs fall back into their marching pattern, matching the cadence of Donael's pleas. His joints move like a robot in one of the old movies Liella, his mother, used to watch. Half the time I'm not sure if it's his mouth or knees doing the clicking.

"Her mom doesn't care because she can't remember anything without vaporizing it," I say. I grab Cobb's foot and it slips from my hand. "She'll be facedown and drooling before it's lunchtime anyway. Someone's going to drown."

"Not if we know how to swim."

"I said no, OK?" In the next room, the phone rings. "Can you get that for me?"

He gives me a blank stare. I snatch Cobb's left ankle when it comes near and shove it into the leg of his shorts. The phone keeps ringing. I ask Donael again. Cobb yanks his leg back, kicking out his right foot and clipping my chin. I throw the shorts across the room. "Dress your own self. Or don't. Do whatever you want. I don't care." I retreat to the kitchen, snatching the phone on my way with Donael following and yammering the whole time.

"Dammit, son, give me a minute." I put my mouth to the phone. "What?"

"It's me," Belousz says.

"I'm busy."

"I'm calling for Morrigan."

I pinch the bridge of my nose. "What would her highness like now?"

"She's, uh, inquiring to make sure that boy – what's his name?"

"You have to be more specific."

"Boss, you know exactly who I'm talking about."

"Riab?" I say. Donael pulls at my arm and I wave my hand at him to leave me alone.

"Yeah. That his dad and granddad are coming in."

"Dad's on Henraek's list. Should be in today," I say. "Granddad came in yesterday."

"You sure about that?"

"Yeah, why?"

"Because Stilian said it wasn't there."

"Goddammit." Donael yanks again and I retreat to the walk-in cupboard and close it. Donael calls my name but I stick my finger in my ear.

Belousz breathes into the phone.

"What?"

"Nothing," Belousz says. "But – Greig's gotten it into his head that Riab's ex and the muscle she works with might be planning something big and bright. My guess is that's why those two are on the list, sort of a precaution."

I thump my head against a shelf, jars of sauce and oil clinking against one another. "I told her there's nothing to it. He's trying to get a leg up on me."

"I told her the same," he says. "But you know how she is. Given Henraek's," he fumbles for words, "connection with that side, I thought you might want to keep an eye on him."

"Does she know about them?" I say. "Wait, how do you know about them?"

"It's my job, boss." I can hear his smile through the phone. "But I'm a lot better than Greig, so they're fine for now. Long as Henraek's OK."

"He doesn't wear the uniform but he knows what team he's on."

"I get that. But he's also been known to take down a building on a whim and a whole lot of our capabilities with it. Then with him not delivering his full list..." He lets me fill in the blanks.

"He dances a lot but knows where the line is," I say, as much to myself as to him. "I'll look into it to make sure."

"Wanted to keep you appraised of the happenings, let you put your face on before you come in, you know?"

Donael says Hello?, drawing every letter out to obnoxious proportions.

"I appreciate the call." I glance toward the door, remind myself, You love him. It's a good thing he's here and safe with you. And selling him to the brigus for a couple bottles of hooch would be a bad idea. Even if it sounds tempting at the moment. "Hey, have you heard anything new on Daghda?"

He pauses a moment. "Isn't he dead?"

"You can't kill a myth."

"Occasional things. He took over a state in the west. He drowned in the sea up north. He's actually Lady Morrigan, with a wig. Nothing I thought was credible, or even real." I can hear him swallow. "Why do you ask?"

"Nothing," I say, shaking my head, though he can't see it. "How's your mother doing?"

"She is. She always is." He gives what I think is a laugh, though he could have something caught in his throat. "Hey, boss?"

"Yeah."

"Be careful. They're gathering."

I say, "On who?" but he's already hung up. I stand and let things settle, the dead air humming in the darkness.

I take a deep breath and open the door, startling Donael, who sits cross-legged beside the cupboard. He jumps up and continues as if we'd never stopped.

"And if I don't become comfortable in the water then I might accidentally fall in and drown because I panic and don't know what to do."

"You already know how to swim. I took you to lessons last year."

"But that pool was inside. This one is outside. It's different." Donael knits his fingers together like he's pleading. "So if I can't go then I might die."

"Oh, come off it, Donael." I slug back the rest of my coffee and think about pouring a little something extra in there. "I told you no, so listen to what I'm saying."

He stomps his foot into the ground. "Goddammit."

"Watch your mouth, boy. You don't talk that way in this house."

"You're not my dad. You can't tell me anything," he says. "My parents are dead."

I clench my jaw and breathe out hard through my nose, trying to remain calm. "And that means I'm all you have left."

He storms off to his room, slamming the door for my benefit. Cobb stares at me from the doorway.

"What?" I say to him. "Now I'm the bad guy?"

He gives no response, instead parading barelegged from the living room into the kitchen then down to his room, his arms pumping over his head and clicks coming in rapid fire. I pour the dregs of coffee into my mug. Grounds float on the surface. I take two belts straight from the bottle and pour a little in my mug before stepping outside to get some air for a minute.

Cobb's mother died pre-labor from the same blood disease that made him the way he is. Touched by the holy hand, according to the Brigu woman who'd lived down the hall when he was born.

She tried to abort him by using a broken bottle to cut him out. The doctors had to tear the cuts further open so they could pull Cobb out before he suffocated. They'd been surprised she even made it to term and said Cobb was a very lucky little boy.

I had no kind of response.

Medical know-how has advanced a lot in the last twelve years, but that doesn't mean dick for Cobb. Nothing's going to speed up his clock now that the time's been set.

His clicking echoes down the hallway as he makes his way back to the kitchen. I drink half my cup even though it's gone cold, squint away the burn of bourbon. When Cobb comes into the kitchen, he's fully dressed in long sleeves. Donael skulks behind him.

"I told him he'd be too hot in that but he didn't want to hear it," Donael says. He looks at the toy in his hand when he speaks, though he's not doing anything with it. "I thought you could use the help."

I crouch down to be eye level with him, my knees popping like a snapped stick. I feel like we should have some moment here. Like I should offer some koan or a sprinkling of sage advice he'll remember and tell his kid when this situation arises with them.

But I've got nothing, so instead I say, "I'm sorry too, kid. I'm only looking out for you."

He mutters thanks then makes off to the living room and uploads a movie. I gather a few things to occupy Cobb at the Gallery later today and throw them in his bag, then run my hand through Donael's hair, touching the flat spot on the back of his head.

"Tell Craesa she can come over here," I say. "It's her mother I don't want you round, not her."

He says OK and leans back against my hand, his passive-aggressive version of a hug.

"Remember, Cobb needs to be at Miss Neicy's by nine, so don't play around, OK?" I say. He nods. "Be good in school. Don't get arrested." I kiss them goodbye and step outside the front door.

Now. What the hell is going on?

7.
HENRAEK

I pay for my coffee and find a table in the far corner. I drop three coins into the music player to give our conversation a little cover and select a torch singer that Emeríann likes but I don't know very well. The six-inch hologram flickers into shape, a dark woman wearing an elaborate evening dress with a gardenia pinned to her hair.

Three tables over, a man strikes his lighter while another holds a vial of Paradise above the flame. They put their faces into the stream of smoke, inhale hard, then snatch their pocket-viewer and hurry into one of the bathrooms to lagonael. If I had been smart, I would have learned to repurpose old devices into portable viewers. Most of them are the size of a hand and only need a screen and a slot for the vial. It's not always the best viewing, but if you're resorting to stealing your sister's pocket-jukebox so you can lagonael, quality isn't much of a concern.

Walleus waits at the counter while they warm up his muffins – regular muffins, dry and with unevenly ground flour, not one of those rehydrated, designer ones like on his side of the city – then makes his way over to the table. Before he can even sit down, I start on him.

"We're in a public space now, so tell me when you turned."

"Come on, Henraek. I haven't even had a chance to enjoy this muffin. Reminds me of those ones your mom made." He smells it, revelling in the sensory associations of our youth, of my mother before she disappeared after she refused to license our property to the resource company.

"Then answer me and I'll stop asking," I say.

A slight smile creases his lips. "I thought you wanted to know about Riab's family."

"That was my next question."

"What's with the inquisition?"

"Morbid curiosity."

He bites into his muffin, closing his eyes while he chews. After three nearly pornographic chews, I repeat my question.

Eyes still closed, he swallows and says, "Is there anything you'd like to tell me first?"

"No," I say. "Should there be?"

"You tell me, Henraek." He leans forward to stare straight through me, the light in the corner reflecting off his eyes in brilliant points.

"I have nothing to hide."

He hooks a thumb over his shoulder, says, "You'll excuse me if I go shit myself from laughter?"

"I can wait."

"Maybe it's in that vial you didn't turn in yesterday? Riab's grandfather?"

I sip my coffee to conceal any expression he could read as guilt or deception, taste the hint of wood bark. I believe the girl at the counter gave me the wrong kind. "Have Stilian check it again. My orders are always correct."

The hologram sings Hush, don't explain, then sings it again, again, the player skipping as the electric current lapses, and I begin to wonder if she's advising Walleus or me.

He looks over, says, "Turn off."

"Wrong neighborhood, Walleus."

He reaches over and yanks the plug from the socket. The torch singer freezes with her head arched back and arms curled, mid-climax note, then dissolves into nothing.

"I'll have him take another look, but it'd better be there. Word around the campfire is there's something brewing at Johnstone's. I don't buy it, and as a fellow member of the Tathadann, I'm not suggesting you're involved with anything. Maybe someone else is, or two someones. And maybe that's related to the names on your list," he says, then takes a considered bite of his muffin, trying to peer inside my skull while chewing. "I can't get blindsided. It'd be bad for both of us, and anyone else who might be involved. So things need to be where they need to be, and if there's something I need to know, I need to know it."

"That statement is the ultimate summation of the superfluous presence of a bureaucracy. You have officially been there too long."

"You officially need to speak in words I can spell."

"Walleus, get yourself another coffee. There's nothing to worry about here."

He leans back, nodding with his lips sucked in, and unwraps the second muffin before breaking it in half and slipping it into his mouth. I plug the music player back in but my credit is gone and I don't have any more coins.

"Don't say I didn't ask," he says, holding up the other half of the muffin like the gesture should mean something. "But you and Emeríann might want to lay low for a while. For all our sakes."

"Why are you eating anyway?" I say. "I thought you were making special pancakes."

"I was planning to until my kid turned into an asshole."

"Yeah, well," I say, sipping at my coffee, "I wouldn't know what that's like."

His eyes flick up, narrowing when they focus on me, challenging me. Maybe my pissing and moaning has become too much for him to bear, but there is no such thing as too much when discussing a family torn from you, and as I prepare to tell him that, I realize he's actually looking behind me. I turn, and we both regard Greig and Belousz with long, dead stares.

I can hear Walleus swallow on the other side of the table and wonder if they did too. He and Belousz exchange a quick glance.

"We need him," Greig says to Walleus, indicating me.

"I'm sitting right here. You can address me."

He gives me a disgusted look, then turns back to Walleus and repeats it.

I tap my wrist, an archaic gesture that we still do for some reason. "I've got a job in ten. Sorry."

Belousz doesn't even blink his eye. "If Lady Morrigan wants you, Lady Morrigan gets you. So," he exhales, "as we said."

Pressing my fingertips against the mug, feeling the give of flesh against the cooling porcelain, I estimate how hard I could smash it against his head before it breaks, then take a deep breath and push my palms against the table to rise.

Walleus grabs my wrist to stop me.

"Is this moving on?" I say to him. "Because it looks the same to me."

He does not look at me nor the two men, but instead stares through them.

"Were you following us?" he says. The words leave his mouth but his teeth do not part. He barely glances at Greig, but from the way Greig tries to conceal his flinch this is not a tone he uses lightly. Still, Greig remains silent.

"Don't ignore me," he says.

Greig pulls back his shoulders to stick out his chest,

some new kind of confidence I haven't seen in him, then nods to Belousz for back up. "By the order of Lady Morrigan, we need Henraek."

I say, "It's fine," quickly to Walleus then stand and push my chair into Belousz's legs twice, waiting for him to move before I put it all the way under the table.

"Appreciate your company," I say to Walleus, "but you can't dodge the truth forever. Light shines on everything, no matter how hard we try to hide."

"Henraek, you have no idea," he says. "Make sure your orders are filled."

I walk out the door, waiting for Belousz and Greig to catch up.

When they come up on either side of me out on the sidewalk, I ask what the hell they want. And when they answer, "We need you to get us inside Johnstone's," my blood turns thick with anxiety. I never thought the Tathadann could move so quickly. I wonder how long this word has been going round their campfire.

"I thought that burned down," I say and continue walking, calibrating the amount of ignorance I can plead without it becoming obvious. "Even if it didn't, they'll cut me if I walk in there."

No response.

"It's a little early for me, but I'll take us to a better bar, OK?"

Greig looks toward Belousz, but receives no answer. Finally, Greig clears his throat. "I have information that—"

"We're thirsty," Belousz says. Greig shoots him an angry look.

"Don't sit down. I heard you can get a staph infection from their chairs." I pause in front of a barter store at the corner, the walls long faded from rich brown into something closer to a scab. Sinewy dried meat hangs behind wrought iron bars in the window, partially obscuring shelves of canned goods and liquor brewed in bathtubs. I scan the dirty sidewalks for Emeríann as we wait for a line of cars to pass. Someone bumps my shoulder, spits at my feet and calls me a traitor. I start after him but Belousz holds his arm out to stop me.

"Stop with all the theatrics," Belousz says. "I've got a headache and my sinuses are clogged."

I ask if he's tried ginger to help with that.

"I don't feel like dealing with your crap or listening to your chatter, is what I'm saying." He presses against his cheeks with his fingertips. "Shut your mouth before I stick my boot in it."

I breathe deep through my nose and quell the urge to end him here in the street. In this neighborhood, they might not even notice. At the right time of day, they might even join in.

In the alley behind us a man gathers a handful of old papers, some pieces of wood, the discarded insulation lying around, and throws it all in a dented trash container, then collects more.

As the last car passes, I get ready to cross until I hear the hint of a whistled refrain. Hush, don't explain. Half a block down, Emeríann winds through passersby on her way to Johnstone's. Ringlets of hair bounce and sway as she walks in time with the song.

Greig nudges me in the back, suggesting that I don't want to delay them, so I cross to the opposite side.

Belousz grabs my arm in the middle of the street. He points a crooked finger. "It's that way."

A soft-top convertible honks at us but Belousz doesn't respond. The guy yells out the window and I only stare at Belousz, willing him to break eye contact. Another honk, more yelling.

I have to relent first and glance down the road. Emeríann now has almost two blocks on us but is still two blocks from the bar. "I must've gotten turned around."

The horn blares and I take four long steps to him, reach inside the passenger window and grab him by his ascot. "Tell it to honk," I say.

"What?" His hands remain on his lap, likely out of shock. The engine idles, dials and numbers flashing on the autodrive display.

I stick my head inside the car and pull his face to mine. His skin is so pale it's tinted blue, and he is definitely in the wrong neighborhood. "Tell it to honk at me one more time."

Greig says something I can't make out, him and Belousz coming toward me.

"Do it," I say to the man. Emeríann should be a block from the bar by now. She'll soon walk inside and lock the door behind her before retreating into the back room to evaluate the latest plans with

Forgall. The bar will be empty and ordinary.

Hand shaking, the man touches his mouth with manicured nails and meekly says, "Honk."

I almost laugh, then slam his forehead into the dashboard, breaking open his brow and loosing rivulets of blood. He shrieks and presses his palms to his face to staunch the bleeding. He screams drive and the car jerks away. I pull my arm out before the window frame breaks my elbow and fall to my knees, the wheels barely missing my outstretched fingers.

Greig throws himself aside as the car passes him. Then Belousz, with his feet planted firm, cracks the guy in the side of the head with his fist. The man yelps stop and the car's brakes lock, causing it to swerve onto the sidewalk and crash through the plate glass window of the barter store. Through the shattered glass I can hear the owner yelling, though I don't know if it's directed toward us or the vehicle perched in the meat display.

Belousz yanks me up by the elbow.

"You done yet?" The tone of his voice hasn't changed and it pisses me off that even now I can't get a rise from him.

"He deserved it. He was wearing an ascot."

He shoves me forward then beckons for Greig to hurry up. Greig's fussing about the store but Belousz only grunts. I try to slow my pace but the two flank me on both sides and force me along. Taking the sidewalk at a brisk stride, passing buildings and banks and shops, all various shades of faded maroon and cracked umber indicative of the neighborhood, we're in front of Johnstone's within a minute. There's no name painted on the heavy wooden door, no hours or rules for entry, no obvious markings that would make the building a rebel bar. Here, if you don't know then you don't know.

Behind us, a crowd gathers around the barter store.

I pull the door gently, in case. It rattles in my hand. "Guess it's closed," I say.

Belousz and Greig cup their hands above their eyes as they peer in through the front window.

I hang back a couple feet, casually wandering to a position where the shadow of a streetlamp falls over the window. Above me is an advertisement for goggles the resource workers in this neighborhood used to wear, painted on the cement wall years ago and faded by the weather. Something is rotting back here, the vicious tang heavy on my tongue, and I hope it's a discarded lunch. I catch a vague outline of someone at the bar drying glasses. Even from back here it'd be hard to mistake Forgall for Emeríann, him being a good foot taller and wider, especially when he bellows something at the two onlookers.

They ignore him and spend another moment peering inside. Greig says something to Belousz that I can't understand. Belousz shakes his head, says, "He's right. They won't let him in."

"Then what good is he?" Greig says.

When they turn, I have my hands clasped before me, channeling indignant at having my time wasted as much as I can.

"Still thirsty?" I say to Belousz.

"Dying."

I clap my hands once. "Well, if you gentlemen are done chasing ghosts, I'm going to go do my job that I'm now late for. If Lady Morrigan has a problem, you'll be hearing from her."

"Where are they hiding it?" Greig says.

"Hiding what?" I say.

"There are no scarves," Belousz says to him. "You might want to adjust your report."

The muscles of Greig's jaw tense and flex. "This is a rebel bar and you damn well know it."

"Look at all the buildings. Nothing's new, nothing's painted bright, or even repainted in the last twenty years," I say. "It's a working-class neighborhood. They're just normal people getting by."

"You can call a brick a bunny rabbit," Greig says, "but it's still going to give you a concussion when someone throws it at your head."

"That's lovely." I clap my hands again for some reason. "But I don't know what to tell you."

Belousz glances over his shoulder once more, then nods toward me. "I believe him."

Greig might have given himself whiplash turning to his co-conspirator. I appraise Belousz with a long look but can't get a bead on his intention.

"I'll sit on it for while, to confirm," Belousz says to Greig. "You go on."

Greig does not look pleased.

"I'm going to leave you to it." I turn and walk away, half-expecting them to call my name or try to stop me. When I get to the corner and they've not said anything, I double-time it to Riab's father's apartment, anxious at the thought of finishing this job and destroying what's left of Emeríann's past.

The same dust, the same soot. The spool with the dandelion and silverware. The room, the city, the life is almost exactly the same as yesterday, as the day before.

The only thing different in the room is the wet, slurping breath of an old man lying in his bed. A depression has formed around the needle mark, like his skull is collapsing. His eyes are open, though it's obvious they're merely a fogged window.

The difference between a memory junkie and a memory husk is focus. A junkie stares into the distance, but has a point in staring. He can't grab what he's searching for, but he knows it's written somewhere in the ether. The husks are a complete void. They blink and twitch and occasionally seem to respond to stimuli, but there is nothing behind those movements. Their body hasn't figured out there's no longer a reason to move. It might be possible for me to take only part of their memory, but there's no way to know what you're harvesting until you watch it, and there's no easy patch for the hole in their cortex membrane. I figure that if I'm going to ruin someone's life by stealing what might be his best years, I might as well destroy him completely. Maybe, in some small way, I'm preserving the history of the country; by stealing and distributing memories I'm preventing our history from being completely remolded in the Tathadann image. And by selling those memories for booze money, I'm preserving my liver by pickling it. So, everyone wins.

Either way, this poor man has done nothing to deserve his fate, but not deserving Tathadann treatment doesn't mean you won't get it.

A creak in the next room. I hold my knife before me, tipping my head to listen. A grunt and long exhale. Without putting a full foot on the ground, I creep to the edge of the mattress and see a candle flickering in the reflection of a glass on the wire spool. The father sits in a worn chair beside it, his back to me. From the thin crinkle, it sounds like he's reading a book. Still no sign of the wife.

I try a closer look and he coughs then reaches for his glass, drinking half of it. Another cough and he'll have to come through here and this will again be more trouble than it's worth.

I pull out my kit and assemble the vial and needle. No time for the pleasantries of introductions or iodine. Sorry, Riab's father. Sometimes things don't work out the way we expect. We should both be aware of that to a lethal degree.

When he turns a page, I take two quick steps forward and slip my arm around his neck, pressing my bicep against his throat. He swings his arms back, one finger catching me below my eye, while his other hand claws at my forearm and his legs try to topple the chair backward. I can't remember if Riab ever said his father had combat training, but he has good instincts.

I readjust my grip to steady his head and stab his temple.

First shot.

He slackens in my arm, hands slapping me more out of muscle memory than attack strategy. Within a minute he's a lump of flesh in the chair. I tip his head slightly to aid in the flow. My stomach sinks when I glimpse the cover of the book lying on the ground. It's an underground book, one that's not sanctioned by the Tathadann, about how they exploited the Resource Wars to assume power. Of course. Of course.

The fluid barely passes the halfway line before I switch Walleus's vial for mine. This man, who lives at an address that has popped up on my list twice in two days, whose name made Walleus flinch, his memories are coming with me. In some way, I owe it to him to not let his memories languish along with all the others. The Tathadann's methods for choosing targets are as arbitrary and varied as their vices, but targeting Riab's family – and giving the list to me instead of another harvester – this feels like a test of my loyalty. His name will show up in my order to keep them satisfied. But his memories – some that could be used against Emeríann – they will come with me.

As the second vial nears the full line, I slip in a

third, turning his head completely horizontal. And though I know it's ridiculous, I still squeeze his skull as if it was an orange to get out every last drop.

When I'm assured I have everything I can get, I stow away my kit then heft the father up and over to the space beside the grandfather. I place two coal slivers on his eyes, then sing a short verse for him and hope his wife returns soon. And if not, it will be only two more entries on the long list of lives the Tathadann has torn apart.

8.
WALLEUS

The man's head bounces off the dashboard so hard I expect it to separate from his neck and fly out the window. But he was wearing an ascot, so he kind of deserved to have his face broken.

The car speeds away only to crash into Hurleigh's barter shop, throwing out shards of glass like party confetti. I stay against the corner of the building and watch Belousz and Greig lead Henraek down the sidewalk. Headed to Johnstone's no doubt, if Greig's here.

When they're safely three blocks down, I push off the corner and follow. I bump into a man with dirt caked in the deep furrows of his forehead. He looks up at me, says, "Goddamn traitors. Everywhere I look. To hell with you all," then shoves me aside. I start to go after him when I hear a huge whoosh and a wall of heat hits me. I duck back with my arms over my face.

Five-foot flames burst from a trash container.

A man holding two sticks stands ten feet from it, mesmerized by the fire.

"What the hell are you doing?" I yell at him.

He turns to me. The flickering makes the scar on his face twitch like it's alive. His eyes are on me but his brain is worlds away. "I have to know," he says.

What the hell is wrong with this city?

This business with Belousz and Greig is more important than some lagon lighting trash on fire, so I leave him behind and continue.

They stand in front of the bar, Henraek hanging back, likely so he's not seen as leading the Tathadann right to their door. Henraek eventually leaves and Belousz and Greig argue, Greig stomping off like a petulant child.

Belousz, he hangs back and waits. He pulls something out of his pocket and cups it in his hand, almost stroking it. I walk to him quick as I can while not making a scene or getting too out of breath. He startles when I touch his shoulder, shoves his hands in his pocket.

"You OK?" I say to him.

"I'm observing," he says, looking at the ground, pointing at the bar. "No scarves."

I squint, though there's no way I'd be able to see in anyway. At least this little field trip was in fact Greig's idea. "Is she gathering on me or gathering to move on them?"

"Does it matter?" he says.

"To me it does."

"I don't know." He says he has to go, too quick to be natural.

"Wait." I lay my hand on his arm, hunker my shoulders down to look him straight in the eye. "I need something from you."

"Name it." He still won't meet my eyes, only the space around me.

"Toman."

"Toman?" He cocks his head, finally looking at me. "What of him?"

I glance around us, checking for anyone within earshot. "You know where his store is?" He nods. "Good. He needs to go."

He leans away from me. "What did he do?"

"He let himself get greenlit. That's what he did."

Belousz takes a deep breath, looks over toward Johnstone's then quickly back my way. That big bastard stands behind the bar, staring at us. If Greig had any idea who Forgall Tobeigh actually was, he wouldn't even consider calling him the Lumberjack. I wasn't there when he took out that platoon with the axe, but one of my soldiers was positioned across the street and watched it. He said it looked like a big, bloody ballet. No wonder Henraek is jealous of him, proud warrior and loyal rebel that he is. Even overcame the taint of Macuil Morrigan that runs in his family's blood. Handsome fella, too.

"I've been keeping an ear out for Daghda," Belousz says. "There's some talk, same as usual, but I have seen a couple new hill-people show up. I don't know if it means something or if I'm seeing it because you said it."

"I'll worry about them later," I say. "Listen, this thing with Toman, it has to look like an accident. Understand?"

"OK?"

"If your fingerprints are on this," I say, "he's going to kill you."

"Who, Daghda?" He snorts out a laugh.

"No." I scratch my chin, exhale, feel a heaviness sift down through my chest. "Henraek."

9.
HENRAEK

The sky is a dome of pitted steel, even at midday. A half-dozen droids hover alongside an office building the color of old charcoal, spraying a flame-retardant solution on the walls that aren't burnt. The mist drifts down over us, the closest approximation to rain.

The pile of rubble in the alley where the young girl had crowned herself Queen of the Struggle has been usurped by a family of seven, reconstructed with the lintels of a shipping pallet, the makeshift sleeping area spilling out beneath a tarp attached to the buildings' sides with metal spikes. One girl sits before her sleeping family, bouncing half a rubber ball on the ground, playing jacks with splinters and nails. The white scarring of chemical burns radiates through the dirt on her neck and arms.

I cross the intersection of Muirin and Eisol, the proximity to Johnstone's and inches of bourbon tingling like an electric field on my skin, when I hear Emeríann's voice.

"I need a strong man," she says. She points at something large hidden beneath a swatch of old canvas. "Help me with this, will you?"

I glance around to make sure no one's following us.

"You OK?" she says.

"Fine." I peek under the canvas and see a stained dry sink, tarnished brass handles and cloudy yellow filigree accents at the corners. "You couldn't happen upon some stools that don't wobble?"

"Beggars and choosers, love," she says as we grab the ends. "Saw it on my way in this morning and covered it up so no one would take it."

"It's a step away from kindling. I don't think you have to worry about someone putting up a fight."

"Don't look at it now. Look at what it will be in a month." Her words come in spurts, between grunts of exertion. "A couple coats of lacquer, some baking soda-polish and a little paint, I'll have people coming to the bar just to look at it."

My Emeríann, the eternal optimist.

I catch a glimpse of us in the front window of Johnstone's and smile, thinking of the brick that Walleus would shit if he saw me now. "You realize we look like we're carrying a bomb, right?"

"If we were carrying a bomb, I don't think we'd be so brazen about it," she says. "And a bomb this big would level half the neighborhood."

"Maybe we were going about it wrong the whole

time and this is the way to do it." I hook my fingers around the handle and open the door for her. "Act like it's a bag of groceries and walk like it's nothing."

"How about we walk like it's something so we can eat. I'm starving." We pass the campfire lagon sitting at the bar again – I'm surprised Forgall let him back in – and set the dry sink against the side wall.

The junkie holds the same type of drink in his hand, the singed flecks perpetually drifting through the clear liquor, though he looks disappointed this time. Maybe the smell of burnt plastic and insulation that surrounds him is dulling his sense of taste.

Emeríann whips off the canvas with a dramatic flourish, admiring the new addition for a minute. "Only need the right shade of lacquer to pick up on the flecks in the bar. Polish up the handles real nice."

If I squint my eyes, the dry sink could, surprisingly, be a nice accent to the place. I never thought there would be a piece to complement the bar top Emeríann fashioned from a salvaged bowling lane – we were never sure if that was a message from the Tathadann or if they actually believed the bowling alley was housing artillery – but she has a knack for piecing together disparate items.

She plops down on the stool next to me and wraps her arm around my waist. Her fingers rest less than an inch from the memories I stole from her former father-in-law.

"Are you doing anything tomorrow?" she says. "I heard they're raiding the Gardenia tonight. Want to see if I can procure myself some stools."

"A lagonael den with stools?"

"Fancypants wanting to slum it sometimes doesn't mean they want to get their fancy pants dirty," she says. "Anyway, you want lunch? The market's got some meat that looks good."

"I'm going to pass on that."

"You're missing out."

"I'm sure I am." I pat her hand and whisper in her ear, asking to see the plans.

"Ah, right," she says.

There's a glass tink and the flick of a lighter. She whirls around and catches the lagon lighting up a vial of Paradise.

"What the hell are you doing?" she yells. "Get the hell out of here with that."

A dirty tear rolls down his scarred cheek as he contemplates his drink. "I'll never – know, will I?" he says. "I'll never know."

"No, you won't," she says. "You smell like death and you need to go."

She opens the door for him. He leaves his drink unfinished, says, "I want – understand," then walks into the street. A tuft of yellow insulation sticks to his heel.

"Goddamned junkies," she says.

She locks the front door. Then we cross the ceramic floor to the end of the bar. The tiles are a deep shade of dirt, so speckled with stains they are the perfect camouflage for spilled blood.

Emeríann removes the outlet cover above the floorboard and reaches her finger inside the socket, moves it up-down-up-right to engage the switch. What she wouldn't give to have some of the security I've seen. The lock clicks and she slides the panel into the wall.

"Where's Forgall? Won't he be pissed I'm entering his inner sanctum?" I should be able to expose any miscalculation in his plans before he gets back, but I'd like to take my time, be thorough.

"He had to meet his contact." She motions for me to follow her into the small vestibule. "He'll be back in a little while."

When she closes the door, it's full dark but for a thin blade of light coming from the back room. Her hand searches out my hip, brushing over the vial-belt on my stomach.

"Hey," she says. "Wanna make out?"

"You're ridiculous." I kiss her forehead. "Let me see these plans."

She slaps my cheek gently. "You're no fun."

We step into the back room. The light makes me squint as it blasts away the darkness. Schematics and plans with calculations crawling around the edges cover the brick walls, and there are piles of paper on two corners of the square table in the middle of the room. On the left wall are two manacles secured to the brick with four inch-wide screws, remnants of the former owners' predilections, inside of which Emeríann has hung a half-dozen found-art roses.

I run my fingers over the architect paper, feel the vertiginous swell of nostalgia as the faint dusting of blue powder presses into the whorls of my fingerprints. I taste gunpowder smoke, the powdered coffee Walleus and I would eat during a stakeout, which was the solution to what he deemed my titmouse-small bladder; I told him it was the sign of efficient kidneys.

Some are a look inside official Eitan City buildings, ones that were formerly available to the public as free information before the Tathadann seized control. Others are schools – primary and other, public and private – and stores and office buildings. On the far wall is a hand-drawn map of the tunnel system rumored by conspiracy theorists to have been dug beneath the city to smuggle food and water during the Wars, in the years leading up to the Tathadann's formation. I sent countless men in search of them, thinking it would give our outnumbered and outgunned teams a slight edge against the government forces during the Struggle, but the men either came back with nothing or they were captured and killed. Or who knows, maybe they really did find something and the tunnels led them to Nahoeg to live in eternal glory.

"Need one?" She hands me a towel and her smile is equal parts smug and tender.

"Where'd you get all these maps?" I say, leafing through the rolls. Water distribution plants. Comm stations. One that looks vaguely like Clodhna with a few extra annexes, likely the dummy plans they used to distribute as disinformation. Another with the approval stamp of a Promhael member. "These are official. You have to be someone to get into the room where they store these, much less the actual filing systems."

"Forgall has–" she clears her throat, insinuating extracurricular activities, "–made a few friends among the clerical secretaries who have become sympathetic to our cause after meeting him."

"Good friends to have," I say. "They like his big hands?"

"They're huge, if you ask him."

She leads me to the four-fold plans spread across the table. A dozen pins with green or red flags at the tip sit inside various corridors. I run my finger between them, tracing the flow of power from the breakers to machinery, following the design of the wall to determine which are load-bearing and which won't be useful. Old habits.

"I know," she says. "Pretty snazzy."

"This is east of Fomora?" I look up at her. "Near the high rises that burned down?"

"Damn, you're quick."

She starts to say something but I hold up a finger, running my hands over the plans, analyzing, feeling, absorbing. She sidles up beside me, waiting for a cue.

"Explain it to me," I say.

She points to three red flags with her left hand, three others with her right. "If we attach doubled-up atomizers on these posts, we can knock out the structural support and bring the three upper floors down on the vat level. Delay charges on these ones will bring the whole mess down on the capacitors in the basement, sending a lot of debris up at Nahoeg." More green flags with her right hand, her voice swelling with confidence, imagining the metal and chunks of concrete raining down. "Then a sequence of single pulse-charges on these to short the sensors on the way out–"

"And straight down the line they go."

She smiles. "Straight down the line."

I examine the plan for another minute, doing quick calculations in my head as I trace her lines with my finger. I'm not so sure about this. This could be a bad idea.

"Well," she says, and I didn't realize I'd said it aloud, "you know how pissed you get when you've been working all day and the whole way home you're thinking about how good a glass of water – any water, even the brown ones – would taste, then as soon as you get home you find out we're dry? How angry that makes you? Is there a better way to kickstart the revolution than by creating that feeling all over Eitan?"

"There has to be a better way to disable it," I say.

She clucks her tongue. "Not one that will make a statement like this. Especially with all those assholes gathered around that stupid statue."

Part of me is proud that I taught her to evade detection well enough that they have to resort to years-old memory as a way to gather – hoping that she kept in touch with and confided in Riab's family, probably avenging Riab, because they don't have much to look at otherwise – but I also have to wonder how Morrigan would know anything about this. Who talked?

"You can't regulate those sequences," I say. "If one skips a line they could–"

"I know, Henraek." There's the hint of an edge in her voice. "I'm not completely inept. And Forgall's done this a couple times, you know."

"Yeah, so have I. More than Forgall." Someone had to have talked, possibly one of Forgall's people, or one of his new clerical friends. Are they setting him up? "Does Forgall understand that you'll likely set fire to every house that this pulse touches? The crew inside the plant is one thing, but those others haven't done anything. Not to mention the ones who'll die from lack of water."

She shoves her fists into her hips, pissed that I'm disassembling something she's worked hard on. I'm not ruining Forgall's plan now. I'm ruining hers. "I understand that people will die. People who don't deserve it. It's an unfortunate reality but sometimes you have to break some eggs to make an omelet."

"When was the last time you saw a chicken, much less had some eggs?"

"It's a saying." She steps away from me, pulling her hair back then letting it go, her hands needing something to do.

"Well, you can call a brick a bunny rabbit, but it'll

still hurt when it hits you."

Her face tries to turn itself inside out. "What does that even mean?"

"It means," I say, flipping my hands like a flightless bird before exhaling and sitting on the edge of the table. I press my fingers into my temples. "I don't know. I don't know."

"You don't think it'll work?" Her voice softens as she approaches me.

"It'll work. It'll definitely work."

"Good. Because it has to. We're not going to get another chance to make a statement like this."

I look down at the plan again, some sharp, jealous point prodding the inside of my chest. "I guess I'm saying, what's the cost?"

"I don't know," she says. "But I know the reward."

She licks her thumb, takes my hand and rubs off two blood spots from the ascot man that I hadn't noticed. She doesn't ask what it is or where it came from. I don't know if she doesn't want to know or doesn't care.

We sit listening to the expansion and contraction of the walls, the faint shush of passing traffic, the jagged rattle of words and theories tumbling inside my mouth.

"Who knows about this?" I say.

"Me. You." She counts two on her fingers. "Forgall's cousin's half-brother, Lachlan Parnell. He helped with some of the technical stuff, getting some supplies. He's good. Smart. Used to run jewels across the border after the Struggle."

"I don't know him. What about his people? You said something about them."

"Guys he knows from the hills, guys he fought with here. It's the same as..." She scratches her cheek as she trails off.

"It's the same as when I was leading?" I swallow the words that come instinctually. They wouldn't be useful anyway. "Do you know how many other people there are?"

She shakes her head. "There are five total, including Forgall. Then everyone's got their own little crew."

I know there's no way to vet everyone else's soldiers, that you have to have faith in your fellow leaders' ability to suss out any leaks. But knowing that doesn't make me feel any better. "What about the clerks? The ones he got the maps from?"

"You really think he'd tell them what this is for?" She laughs. "What's with all the questions?"

I shake my head. "It worries me. With the ceremony coming up, and all the scouts out now–"

"Cut the mushmouth, Henraek. What did you hear?"

"Walleus," I say. "He said we should lay low."

"What else?"

"You know Walleus. The 'word around the campfire' and–"

"Exact words." She grabs my hand. "What did he say?"

All the plans hanging on the walls almost make me

woozy, as much with longing for the adrenaline and purpose of the days during the Struggle as with the desire for her not to get sucked into the violent fallout that this bombing will bring.

"He said they heard something was brewing at Johnstone's and that someone – or two someones – might be planning something. Told me to lay low."

She inhales sharply, and looks around the room. "Look, I know you want to be a part of this, but you can't be. I shouldn't have brought you back here. With your job and all, it's – we shouldn't talk about it. We need to be a little more careful."

"I know. It's fine." I pat her leg. "You're going to do great." And I wonder if I'm saying it for her benefit or mine.

Outside the back room the bar is still locked, empty.

"You want me to get you something to eat so you don't have to close again?" I manage a small smile. "I'll get some mystery meat, if you really want it."

A pat on my cheek, she says I'm sweet but we don't need to give them more chances to catch us.

When she walks behind the bar and pours herself two fingers of liquor, I notice that the boar-faced Nimah is gone. I nod at the empty space. "You sure all this will work without the hill-spirits watching over you?"

"Wishful thinking isn't the same thing as crazy talk." She gives a thin smile.

"Like hoping Daghda won't come back to conquer the city again?"

"He didn't. At least, not at first," she says. "My parents said they did a lot of good in the beginning, before Fannae got her hand inside Macuil."

"But that's not the definition of crazy, doing the same thing and expecting a different result?"

"Insanity and crazy are two different things." She throws back her liquor then pours another, effectively ending the conversation.

"Are you going to drink and sulk at home all afternoon?"

"Actually, yes." Her smile comes naturally this time.

"You promise you're only going to drink and sulk?"

"Yeah." But from her pursed lips, I can tell what she's thinking.

"I told you before, you don't have to worry. I'm fine." She stares at me until it's uncomfortable, then gives a noncommittal shrug.

When I get to the door, she calls my name. "I need you to support me on this, even if you don't like it," she says. "Even if you don't believe it."

After a beat, I nod. She gives a small smile. The corners of her eyes wrinkle and her chipped canine tooth catches on her bottom lip.

I pull the door closed behind me and start off down the sidewalk, that underlying concern about destroying innocent people not dire enough to ward off the visceral charge of planning an attack that still tingles in my fingers. I walk away from the bar, but in my head, I continue to trace the direction of the power flow.

As I turn the corner, I glance up and catch Belousz, checking both ways at the edge of an alleyway. I duck into the alcove of an abandoned storefront, watching him in the reflection on the windows. He drags his hand across his mouth then hurries away, head down and looking like he's doing everything in his power to not run.

When he is fifty feet down the sidewalk, I come out and continue to walk. Pulling even with the alley across the street, I peek down it, looking for a body or some ritual sacrifice, and instead see Forgall with a cigarette pressed between his lips, a roll of paper tucked in his armpit. Forgall buckles his belt then leaves the alley, walking toward Johnstone's with the gait of a man who has not a care in the world. There is no one else in the alley, no corpse or assailant lying in wait. There is only a shimmering puddle of oil and a pile of old papers, wavering in the breath of ghosts.

I've never once heard Forgall mention Belousz. I wonder what Walleus knows.

10.
WALLEUS

I collect Cobb from Miss Neicy outside the Gallery and bring him inside, set him up in his booth and fire up the screen before taking care of some intelligence analysis. That coffee with Henraek this morning was tasty in a nostalgic way, but it didn't have the scientifically engineered kick I've gotten used to. Damn if I'm not getting a caffeine headache without it. Or maybe it's from sifting through rumors of uprisings and nonstarters about stolen property.

A lot of times I wish I could bring Donael in with me so Cobb would have someone to play with, someone to color and sculpt with. And because, after a while, I miss being around him. But bringing him in here would risk them seeing each other. Even if I planned it right, someone would inevitably start talking and it'd get back to Henraek. I feel bad enough lying to Henraek – all right, sometimes I feel bad, and sometimes Henraek is a self-righteous, obsessive, egomaniacal, narcissistic son of a bitch who shouldn't be trusted with a pigeon, much less a child – but feelings aside, it was best for the boy, so it's the decision I made.

I weave through the throng of customers on my way to the coffee synthesizer in back.

Fresh mug of augmented coffee in hand, I make my way over to Stilian to tear him a new one, but his booth is empty.

Then Greig's voice rings out.

I squint and focus on the throb building in my skull, not ready to deal with him yet. I pull the flask from my jacket and pour some whiskey in my coffee, continuing to ignore Greig while I check on Cobb. He's trying to turn a brochure for an upcoming exhibit into a paper airplane. His clubbed fingers crush the folds with every movement. He gets frustrated quickly and crumples the paper into a ball then throws it next to the others, pulls another from the stack. I smooth it out for him, whip out my handkerchief and wrap it half a dozen times around a stylus so it will fit in his pincer grip then select the drawing module.

"Draw me a picture of a dragon eating a little rodent, OK?" I ask him.

When Greig is close enough that it's obvious I'm avoiding him, I finally raise my eyebrows.

"Are you cold?" he says.

"You have no idea." I sip from the flask, making a point to not offer him any before slipping it back into my jacket. "What do you have for me?"

"Scarves." Even with one word, he can make that goddamned rich-boy accent sound like a nail against my eardrum.

"Look, I've got a headache and don't feel like dealing with any more of your crap today, so tell me what you want or go away."

He straightens his back, repositions his hands. "I sat on Johnstone's for a while this morning with Belousz."

"Was that before or after you interrupted my breakfast?"

"I observed six people enter wearing green and white," he says, ignoring me.

"You want my place?" I step close to him, let him feel the heat coming off me. "You want to be where I am, you stop with the lies and come straight at me."

"I don't know what you're talking about."

I take a deep breath, if for nothing else than to not let him get me agitated in public. "I get that if, in your eagerness to get in good with Lady Morrigan and prove yourself to your father, you were a little overzealous in your reports – even if it's something as tiny as scarves – and want to fix them. I won't hold it against you," I say, "this time."

And the little bastard actually steps in closer. "Are you suggesting I fabricated surveillance?"

"I'm not suggesting anything, but I know where Johnstone's is and I can also stand outside a window." I move forward and press my chest to his. "You can't find anything current about Emeríann Daele to support your theory, so you beg Lady Morrigan into harvesting old memories of the poor woman's father-in-law to cook something up? You've obviously never been married because no one confides in their in-laws like that. You don't understand how people work or the emotional landscape of marriage. And then, knowing you don't know shit, you expect me to buy that Tobeigh and Daele, a woman who has no prior instances of fighting, are the face of the new rebellion? How stupid do you think I am?"

His lips and nose twitch like there's something inside his mouth trying to burst out. "I don't like what you're saying."

"I tolerate you now." I pat his cheek. "But you keep pushing with this horseshit gathering and I will end you."

11.
HENRAEK

Sometimes, I believe that telepathy is an evolutionary byproduct of his leather skin, because Silas is already pecking on the window when I step into the apartment. I swing back the iron bars and let him in, as Emeríann is not here to get upset.

I set up the memory viewer while he flutters around the room, seemingly inspecting the arrangement of things since last night. As the electrodes crackle and steam hisses, I pour the dregs of coffee into a cup.

I sit on the couch and Silas lands beside me, nuzzling his head into the back of my hand. I pull out the vials from Riab's father and insert the first.

Emeríann's face materializes in the steam. Beside her sits Riab, sipping a drink. They're all in a bar, the Parkhead it appears, back before the Tathadann blew the place half to hell. My finger hovers over the play button. This is not my life and this is not spying. I'm not concerned with Emeríann. She loved Riab and I loved Aífe. The bed we now share is incidental, but the rushing swirl of voyeurism remains.

They talk about a football match and what color to paint the kitchen. Emeríann wants avocado but Riab insists on off-white. She asks, who is the artist again? His father laughs and mutters something about being narrow and pleasing the wife, to which Riab counters by dipping her dramatically and giving her a long kiss. I feel a strange pang of jealousy that rivals the guilt of watching this. At least she's at the bar right now and there's no risk of her walking in like I'm reading her diary. I endure another five minutes of small talk that should remain private, fast forward and watch her cut sandwiches into triangles – which makes me think of Aífe preparing sandwiches for Donael while I pored over schematics at the kitchen table – then fast forward again, scanning through a few years of his life before pressing play again.

They're sitting at a kitchen table; the overhead light exacerbates Riab's exhaustion, turning his faint crow's feet into ravines leading into the dark canyons beneath his eyes. He pulls on a hand-rolled cigarette but I never remember seeing him smoke. I wonder if Emeríann knew.

"You're not seeing the full picture, athair," he says, using a different dialect than we had in Westhell. It occurs to me that I don't even know where Riab is from, where or how he and Emeríann met, or if that's even something I should know.

"That's because you ain't holding the brush, Riab.

He is, and he's painting you out of the picture." He takes a long drink from a can then crushes it and throws it aside. From the sound, it bounces off the sink and lands on the floor.

"He's got other things to plan. This thing won't go down without attacking on all fronts." Riab stands and gets a new can of beer, foam spilling over the edge when he opens it. "This is my moment to fight against what oppresses us all. This isn't for me, this is for my inion, and her inions." I never knew Emeríann wanted daughters.

"You read that in their book? They did give you a book, right?" He takes the can from Riab as he starts to drink, leaving Riab to stare at his hand. "You're my maic and there ain't no way you came up with that yourself. Been indoctrinated into you."

"You don't understand."

"You're right I don't understand. I don't like the Tathadann neither but blowing up a bunch of kids ain't going to do a thing. That ain't revolution, jack, it's murder." The sound of him slurping beer is near deafening. It's the sound of repressed anger trying to choke paternal love.

"It's a community center, athair. Not a nursery."

"I ain't talking about the building. I'm talking about you." He pushes the can to Riab and gestures around the room. "They got ears all around, maic. Trust me."

"You're scared of them."

"Because I was one of them."

"They weren't even the Tathadann when you

joined. It's different now."

"You're right, it is," he says. "Because she's been hellbent on reshaping your history. You even know how the Wars started? You know what it's like to not have water for days, even this tainted crap?" Riab starts to answer but his father cuts him off. "No, you don't. You remember what you read in their books. What they told you happened. How are you going to kill for something you don't even understand?"

"I understand what I'm doing, athair."

"Look, I don't like the sons of bitches any more than you do, OK? And I have good reason because I've seen a lot of bad stuff go down in my years, even worse than during the Wars. We had a chance once, then that woman threw him out for the other one and sent us all to hell. But I bit my tongue the whole time because those bastards put the food on the table that helped you grow up into the man you are now." He opens his own can. "So trust me that when I say they'll know you're coming, you're going to be walking into a trap."

"You're paranoid."

"Damn right I am. With good reason too, reasons you won't see cause you're young, dumb, and full of cum."

His dad creases a rolling paper and sprinkles in tobacco then tries to roll it but his hands shake too much and the paper tears. Riab reaches for the tobacco and his father shoves away his hand. This time he rolls it properly, then lights it and exhales a long cloud of smoke, the kind of cloud that signifies an immense amount of thought beneath the quiet façade.

Riab says, "It's because I love Emer, our future–"

"I love you, maic," he says, waving away Riab's canned speech that I remember giving to new recruits. "And I don't want to bury you."

He gives a slight laugh that settles into a smile. "I don't want you to either."

"Sometimes the best way to fight is to lay down your weapon." He hands the pouch and papers to Riab and leaves the table.

I hit fast forward, tipping back my cup and emptying it as his life blurs before me. When I look down, I see the image of a casket, Emeríann sitting cross-legged on the ground amid the wilted flowers and photos that surround it.

I watch Emeríann until I have to hit stop, then switch out the vials. Walleus does not deserve to have this, to allow anyone to either exploit her or learn from her misery. I have to give him one vial for the order and wonder what would happen if I drained some random brigu and used it in its place.

The image materializes, a control room with two smaller video panels on either side of a larger panel. The main panel displays a brick path with immaculate landscaping, and standing in the middle is a feminine silhouette that I would recognize even if I were blind.

My legs turn to water, palms become damp. I need a drink but could not pry myself from this seat even if I wanted to.

I hit play and watch Aífe walk down the path, running her hands over the leaves of the shrubs the same way she would touch the plants in our house -- thanking them, she'd said – but the longer I watch, the more it looks like she's actually angry, smacking them.

A faint buzzing in the scene, a voice in an earpiece. Riab's father shifts and flexes his hands over the screen to adjust the camera view. "Yes, sir. She's approaching, near the cross." More buzzing. "Yes, sir. I will as soon as she reaches you."

He mutters something I don't catch and Aífe turns right when she reaches a lush palm tree as if she has been here a hundred times. He flicks his wrist and the main panel switches to an exterior shot of a café. Three tables sit in a portico, with large ferns in ceramic planters acting as a border.

A diminutive man with a cup of coffee lounges at the middle table. When he sips, he arches the pinkie of his left hand with an aristocratic effeminacy that leads me to believe the two men flanking him at the other tables, one conspicuously reading a newspaper and the other partially blocked by the fern, are his security and likely heavily armed. The camera angle changes and, when I get a good look at him, everything crashes down around me.

This is Doctor Mebeth.

The man who delivered Donael.

The man whom Aífe used as a counselor when the Struggle turned especially dark, until I vehemently forbade her when it came out that he had been performing procedures on unconscious patients and he sought refuge under the Tathadann.

The man who invented stripping and memory harvesting by way of medical experiments on captured rebels and comatose patients when the Tathadann gave him full reign over all their research facilities and staff.

The man who now oversees my daily life.

The man on the right sets his paper on the table and his protruding mouth – like a rat's snout – is vaguely familiar but I can't quite place it. I remember seeing it in the newspaper once, I think. He places his hand to his ear and I hear the buzz by Riab's father. "Yes, sir," Riab's father says. "Discontinuing video now. I'll wait for your word to continue."

Riab's father mutters again and this time I understand it clearly. "Goddamned cocksucker," he says. "You're going to get it."

Aífe approaches the table but refuses the chair the security has pulled out, instead standing before Mebeth and yelling at him.

She crosses her arms tight over her chest, her left foot pointing at him, a posture I recognize from our early-morning arguments because I'd lost track of time and spent most of the small hours in the backs of bars with blueprints instead of in our bed with her.

Mebeth responds only by sipping his coffee and making small hand gestures.

I can feel Aífe's skin radiating with anger. His lack

of a reaction pushes her to pick up a wrought-iron chair and slam it down on the ground.

Rat-face to the right of Mebeth keeps his hand on his hip even after Aífe releases the chair, and his frightened, impotent expression triggers it: he's the one who set fire to Amergin. Morrigan wanted to burn down the poor neighborhoods and replace them with Tathadann-built housing, but before the man could get too far on her errand, the Amergi tore off his legs and beat him with them.

Aífe takes two steps forward, encroaching on Mebeth's personal space, and launches into him again. Her arms thrash through the air, her foot stomping repeatedly. She shakes her finger in the man's face. This continues for a minute, his dispassionate expression almost a feat by now.

Riab's father makes grunting noises that could pass as violent or sexual.

When she takes a deep breath, ready to attack again, Mebeth stands without warning and gives a patronizing smile before opening a plate-glass door and entering the café, the man behind the fern following. Aífe stands stunned.

The man behind the fern never looks at the camera, but even if he had I would not be able to focus on him because the rat-faced man stands on his pneumatic legs and levels his gun at Aífe and then the back of my wife's head explodes.

"You're welcome, maic," the father says.

12.
WALLEUS

First thing I do when I return to the Gallery from a late lunch is set up Cobb with his drawing then make a beeline for Stilian. If that bastard ain't in yet, I'm going to stick my foot so far up his ass he'll be eating around my soles. Lucky for him, and my shoes, he's hunched over in his booth, organizing orders.

"How's your brain injury doing?"

He looks up, bewildered. Maybe he's scared that this is the cool thing I say before hitting him in the face with a shovel.

"Isn't that why I never found out that Henraek didn't deliver all his order? You were laid up with some cute little nurse chicky giving you a sponge bath and wiping drool off your chin?" He tries to speak but I cut him off. "Because if you don't have a dented brain, I will sure as hell give you one if that ever happens again."

I lean down and put my face in front of his. "When

something doesn't come in, I'm the first one you tell, understand?"

He says yes, though it's so quiet I can barely hear it.

"Good." I stand up and clap his shoulder. "Now where are the order sheets?"

"There's nothing here for you," he says, facing me but still not making eye contact.

"Is Lady Morrigan bringing them over herself now?" I laugh at the thought of her doing her own work.

"You're not–"

"Walleus," Lady Morrigan calls out behind me. "Why are you here?"

I'm tempted to ask her the same. For someone who doesn't enjoy being here, she sure as hell shows up a lot.

"I work here?" I say, walking to her.

"Why aren't you out gathering?"

"Because I pay other people to do that while I figure out which parts are credible. Which, as I said before, really ain't much." I glance over and Cobb's not in his booth. He's drawn an oblong shape with stick arms and reflection lines off the head that I figure is supposed to be me, though I look close to five hundred pounds, which makes me a little self-conscious. Definitely have to clear that before it syncs with the database. "I still think you're getting some bunk intel, but I'll look into it if you want."

She says yes, and look harder, then walks past me. I follow, because I don't suppose I have a choice. I still don't see Cobb. "I've been waiting for you so I can distribute the order sheets."

"You needn't worry about those. Someone else will be handling the trade for now."

"Excuse me?" I hurry to get in front of her and stand in her path, forcing her to face me. "Is Greig taking it?"

"No," she says, as if it's the most obvious thing. "Stilian will."

"Did the Promhael approve this?"

She sneers. "I don't need approval from those panty wastes. I am the Tathadann."

"Of course, that's not what I meant," I say. "But why are you taking me off?"

"I'm re-evaluating my priorities." She tries to step around me and, for once, my gigantic stomach helps me with a woman. "Now is not the time for slip-ups and half-completed jobs."

"What am I doing now?"

She looks right through me. "Whatever I tell you to do."

Pushing a suited customer out of the way, she moves around me and back to Stilian. She hands him twelve sheets of paper, Angus's on top, Henraek's on bottom, then walks past me without acknowledgment.

I stand dumbfounded, feeling that weight in my chest return, and watch her stroll out the front. I start toward the door, ready to sniff out Greig's reedy neck and squish it between my fingers, when someone yells my name from the back.

"Mister Walleus, get back here now!"

I bristle at the command until the man yells something about your son.

I hustle to the back, each slap of the shoe sending tremors through my shins. My breath comes hard before I even reach the door, then disappears as I enter the back room.

One soldier lays sprawled across the ground, his fingers and feet twitching. A large puddle surrounds him, steam or smoke coming from his mouth. Two other soldiers hold their batons extended and ready, poised around yet another rebel who has been lashed to the crossed wood and beaten unconscious.

I take a breath and taste burnt hair. Cobb is not here.

"What about my son?"

"Sir," one of the soldiers says. He looks to his partner, waiting for him to speak.

I point at the beaten man. "He's almost dead, you idiots. Put away your weapons. What about Cobb?"

"Sir," the soldier says again, this time flicking his head as if to say, look around the corner. I step to the side. Crouched behind the wooden rack is Cobb, holding a constant-charge prod in his hand.

"What are you doing?" I put my hands up, palms out by habit, then immediately lower them when I realize how it would look to Cobb. I motion for the two soldiers to sheath their batons. "Come on now, Cobb. Put it down."

He tries to click but it cuts itself short. I approach

him normally, even crouching a little like we're playing hide-and-seek. But I can't pry my eyes from the two prongs at the tip of that prod. Each shock is one hundred thousand volts and they don't need a recharge time like the old ones did. As fast as you can jab, you can electrocute.

"Hey, bud," I say to Cobb. "I like the drawing you did. But doesn't Dad look a little fat there?"

He clicks and tips his head to the side. The soldiers keep their hands near the handles of their batons. Light on their feet, ready to strike.

"Yeah, I can see that," I say. "You want to go draw a different one? Maybe Dad with some big muscles instead?"

Clicks.

"No, sweetheart, you're not in trouble. We all know you were playing, don't we?" I give a severe look to the men, who nod compulsively. "But you know you can't go running around Daddy's work. You could get hurt and neither of us would want that, right?"

A pensive click.

I take the prod with one hand and scoop him up with the other.

"Let's get some more paper and we'll do one together."

As I pass the men, they fall in line beside me.

The one who called me speaks first. "Sir, he–"

"He's a child, soldier." I fight to keep my voice below a yell, for Cobb's sake. "If I ever see an incident like that again, I will personally tie you to a board and drown you. If I ever hear word of this again, I will tie you to a board and drown you. If I ever see you using a board, I will tie you to it and drown you. Understand?"

The soldier gives a tentative nod. The murmur up front grows, someone yelling out.

I say, "Good," then stick the prod against his neck. His eyes and mouth shoot open, body convulsing until I pull it away. He collapses on the floor.

I point the prod at his partner before dropping it. "Collect your friend."

Cobb and I exit the back room. There's something brewing near the door, the customers ringing around someone. Probably some lagon forgot how to walk again. They know they can't cop in here. I grab another piece of paper for Cobb and sit him in the back booth to keep him away from whatever derelict is causing a scene, then take a few swigs from my flask. I stop at Stilian's booth.

"I need you to access the memory network and find the records of death or hospitalization for anyone who's been through the continent," I tell him. "Maybe incarceration too, but I doubt it."

"That's millions of memories."

"Look under east, struggle, revenge, hills, killing, cyanide, drowning, tags like that to narrow it down." He picks up a pencil and I snatch it from his hand. "Do not write this down. Memorize it. No records until you find something. That means nothing that will throw up an alert, so no Nimah, no mercenary, nothing."

"What am I looking for?"

I exhale hard. "You need to find me Daghda Morrigan."

Stilian looks bewildered.

"You hear me? Find him. And not one word of this gets to Mebeth or Morrigan, hear?"

"Boss," he says, glancing around the Gallery as if his soul will be sucked into the void on hearing the man's name. "He's not real. He's a campfire story."

"He's real, I can assure you, and your pain will be very real if you don't find him." He starts to protest, but I know what he's going to say before he says it. "I don't care if she's got you on a new assignment. Get three or four men to help and I'll cover here. But do not under any circumstance tell them what you're looking for. Give them generals," I say. "And I need this last week. I'm trusting you with this, Stilian."

He swallows his nervousness and nods. I push past a knot of customers, feeling a tingle in my knuckles at the thought of sinking them into whatever amadan has fallen out in my Gallery.

When I break through the crowd, I see Henraek arguing with a customer. Of course. Why should I expect anything else today? The man puts his finger in Henraek's face and he grabs it, twists it around until the man is contorted and kneeling on the ground. He begs Henraek to let him go.

"Henraek," I yell.

He looks over to me, almost like he's surprised I'm here.

"What the hell are you doing?" I say.

He releases the man and approaches me, cocking back his fist and swinging without breaking stride. I'm too shocked to block him and white dots explode across the Gallery. I stumble back, then plant my foot and raise my fists. Muscle memory never goes away.

He stands with his hands beside his waist, though, chest heaving and face deteriorating.

"Why'd he shoot Aífe?"

It's starting.

13.
HENRAEK

He sits there with that dopey look, the same one a cheating husband clings to while the betrayed wife screams in his face. I haven't the slightest idea how it happened, sweetheart. I must've tripped dick-first and she caught me between her legs. I continue to pace because it is harder to break someone's face if you can't stand and plant your feet.

"You lying piece of shit."

"What the hell did I do?" He stares at me, rubbing his jaw.

"What happened to Donael? Did the Tathadann take him? Is he alive?"

"What are you talking about?"

"Aífe. I saw her in a memory. That bastard shot her." My voice cracks as I say it, my eyes hot with tears. "So if she wasn't killed in a riot–"

"Henraek," he says.

"Did they take him?"

"Henraek, come on."

"Maybe he didn't–"

"You don't want to do this."

I charge at him, thumbs searching for his throat. "Don't you tell me what I–" and the room flips before my eyes. I blink and realize I'm staring at the bottom edge of the booths, with Walleus's knee pinning me to the floor. I smell cold dust and hot metal.

"I don't know what is wrong with you," he says. "I understand that you're upset–"

"Upset?" I scream. He grabs my arm and my shoulder flames. I gasp and my breath makes a damp circle on the marble.

"–but you need to calm yourself and not make more of a scene."

"This is the exact time to make a scene." Even with his weight pressing on me, my chest still heaves with stuttered gasps and swollen cries. "This is what scenes are for."

"Not here, they're not," he says. His voice is close to my ear, so I swing my head back, hoping to crush his nose. He tightens his grip, presses my shoulder so far I expect to hear a snap. "You need to knock it off before I really hurt you."

I take a shallow breath, tell him I'm sorry, but a bug tried to crawl in my mouth. This produces a laugh and his hand loosens slightly. I could break his grip, spin around, and catch him in the crotch with my knee then smash his fat face against the table's edge. But I still wouldn't know why Aífe was murdered or what happened to Donael. I center myself like I taught my men to do before an attack, to project a calm surface even if it is raging beneath, in order to fight wisely.

"You weigh too much for this," I tell him, maintaining as level a tone as possible. "Can you get off me?"

"Are you going to calm down?"

I exhale through my nose, feel dust and grit scatter, then nod. He releases me. I push myself off the floor, working blood back through my extremities. When I finally stand, he's staring straight at me. No, not at me. Over my shoulder.

"Is everything all right, gentlemen?" Doctor Mebeth says.

"Fine, sir." Walleus brushes dust from his knees.

My heart pounds so hard at the sight of him I expect it to crack my ribs. I can feel his neck in my fingers. This demon who destroyed my life.

Walleus looks at me. "I was telling Henraek how bad I could beat him at football, is all," he says.

"You play?" Mebeth says to me. He even sounds interested. I imagine kicking his severed head up and down the pitch, catching it on my chest the way Concho Louth did.

"He used to. In the park. Years ago," Walleus says, his brow furrowed while giving me a nudging look. "Though you'd never be able to tell by how hard he's breathing now."

"Do be sure you two don't slide tackle the patrons, yes?" He gives an airy wave, then leaves us. We watch him proceed into the back.

"You want to end up in a stochae?" Walleus said. "Ignoring Mebeth is a good way to do it."

"He was there," I say, my arms aching to pummel Mebeth. "When Aífe got shot. He walked inside the café. Then that rat-faced bastard who got his legs torn off in Amergin blew open her head."

"Whose memory was it? One of Riab's people? You know his dad could put down a bottle on his lunch break, so he might not be the most reliable source. Was he drinking again?" He gives me a condescending-parent look. "Were you?"

"No, I wasn't drinking. Who, isn't important. I know what I saw."

"It's important if the memory is tainted," he says. "And if someone had shot her, I'm pretty sure I would've been one of the first people they'd tell. Rub it in that the rebels were losing and 'Aren't you glad you're with us now?'"

"Can you even tell when you're lying?" I say.

"Goddammit, I'm not lying to you. Really? To hell with you if that's what you think."

I give a gruff snort, my way of conceding the point without actually having to do it.

"But it doesn't matter, Henraek. Knowing why something happened doesn't make it not happen. It doesn't change anything."

"It does for me. They told me both of them died in the riot. But Aífe didn't. She was murdered. Which means Donael–" I cough, choke, as all the possibilities flash through my head, reliving the sensations of the weeks after I'd heard, of my body trying to cleave itself in half. I shake away the feelings. "Someone lied to me, Walleus."

"Yeah, well, welcome to the Tathadann." He squints hard, as if he hadn't meant to say that aloud, then pulls a flask from his jacket and offers it to me. I'm tempted, but it's still afternoon and this day is shaping up to be a long one. "Why was she in the same place as Mebeth?" I nod behind him. "She went to meet him."

His eyebrows rise. "And I thought her marrying you was a risky decision."

"He was our doctor before he went Tathadann. She went to see him a couple times. Like a counselor." I loosen my collar, trying not to vomit at the thought of Mebeth knowing intimate details of my personal life. "But I don't know why she'd seek him out."

He stifles a laugh. "Maybe because he was her doctor."

"But he'd gone Tathadann by that point in the memory."

"People do all kinds of stupid, horrible things for all kinds of stupid, horrible reasons when they're stressed. Like not going home for days without telling your wife."

"Are you insinuating I did that?"

In lieu of answering, he sighs again. "Maybe she was trying to score. Maybe she was blackmailing someone. Not to speak ill of the dead, but Aífe had kind of a vindictive streak in her. Didn't mind doing what needed to be done to get what she wanted." Another belt, shorter this time. He screws on the top, sighs, gestures absently with his hands.

"Aífe wouldn't blackmail anyone," I say.

He exhales hard enough to make the papers flutter. He fidgets with his flask, then another sigh. Sighing was his tell, back during the Struggle. He'd make himself seem put upon to deflect attention. What are you hiding, Walleus?

"Like I said." Cobb clicks at him and he nods, says give me a minute, then turns back to me. "Where was this again?"

"That café near Clodhna. Why? Did you hear something?"

"I'm trying to help, Henraek," he says. "Did you see anything else? Who else was there?"

"Mebeth and the rat-face. I didn't see anyone else." I try to keep the edge out of my voice.

"Right, Toman," he says. "You know they gave him a little market to say sorry about your legs? Figured an Amergin mob wouldn't go into Macha, especially not so close to Clodhna."

Near Clodhna. Fifteen minutes from the Gallery. Maybe there is someone looking out for us.

"What's the address?"

I stomp down the street, my fingertips aching to wrap around Toman's neck and squeeze – not enough to kill him, but enough to sate my desire to make him hurt – then drain him of everything he has. I have a mind to do the same to Mebeth, even if it would be signing my own death warrant in a way that even six-years-ago-Walleus couldn't save me from.

I glance up at the numbers on the buildings, passing regal apartments with gold banisters and marble steps and regularly bleached exterior walls, all-glass clothing boutiques with mannequins whose clothes are worth more than I am, home electronics stores that project life-sized holograms out over the street so that it looks like the city is under constant attack by dinosaurs and robots in order to lure customers in.

I come to the address. I double check the numbers on either side and across the street. This is in fact the correct one. And I'm standing in front of the only burnt-out carcass of a building in this entire neighborhood.

14.
WALLEUS

It's the small moments that matter. The everyday sounds given new significance. The slide of the shades as they close. Corn kernels exploding and tumbling down into the bowl. The soft patter as Donael pours on his special recipe, which tastes a lot like sugar with some butter but I think he grabbed the garlic-salt shaker instead of regular salt. Cobb still spills half of it on the couch and flicks kernels onto the carpet, so at least someone's enjoying it. I pretend to be enthralled with the movie so I won't hurt Donael's feelings by not eating it.

With Greig and Morrigan crawling up my ass and Henraek yesterday, chasing things he doesn't need to find, I make the executive decision to take the morning off.

Which makes it perfectly OK to eat popcorn for breakfast while watching a movie.

I tell Donael to pick something out while I make a

call, then raise Stilian.

"Please tell me you've found something," I say to him, walking into the kitchen for some privacy.

"Boss, it's millions of memories to go through. Not to mention parsing the pre-Morrigan memories from the Promhael-altered ones." He lowers his voice. "And I can't really tell them what I'm looking for other than the general categories. It's going to take a while."

"Then categorize faster. Call me when you find something. Soon."

I drop the phone on the counter, pause, then pick it up again and dial.

"Is Toman dead yet?" I say when Belousz answers.

"It takes time, boss." He sounds out of breath. "I don't have boxes of bomb parts sitting around my kitchen."

There's murmuring in the background.

"Who are you with?"

"No one you know." He clears his throat. "We fought together. He's helping me cobble together a clusterbomb, so it looks like an accident. It's surprisingly hard to make something look crappy on purpose."

I sigh and press my fingers against my eyes. "Hurry it up, OK?"

When I return to my boys, I find the movie is paused.

"I told you that you could watch," I say.

"You took a long time," Donael shrugs. "I didn't

want you to miss anything." I pull them both close and hit play.

The couple in the movie spread out a blanket in a field and unpack a wicker basket of food, him feigning romance so he can get into her pants, unaware of the werewolf who will ambush them in less than two minutes as they begin to reveal their true selves to one another. Donael asks why they're eating on the dirt. When I tell him they're having a picnic, he returns a dumbfounded look.

"Communing with nature, Donael. Getting out of the normal routine and doing something different. Expanding your horizons."

"Do they eat the animals?" he says.

Cobb clicks. I return Donael's look, thinking the animal's about to eat them.

"I don't get it," he says.

I pause the movie. "You don't know what a picnic is?"

He shakes his head. Cobb mimics.

"We're going to fix that today."

At lunchtime, I take them out back with a blanket, some sandwiches and apples. It ain't the Great Outdoors, but I don't feel like driving all the way out to the mountains to eat. Plus, I've got a comfortable lounge chair on the patio; I've eaten meals on the dirt enough for my lifetime.

"Play bird sounds," I tell the house, aiming to recreate the experience as much as I can.

Cawing seagulls come through the exterior speakers. "Songbirds, you amadan, not seagulls."

It switches and they sound more like tropical birds than the ones I'm used to – all those chattering bastards that used to wake up me and Henraek when we were growing up out in the country – but neither of the kids knows better.

They only get halfway through their food before Cobb takes Donael's remote-controlled plane and flies it out of the yard, disappearing beyond the fence. Donael chases after the plane and Cobb chases after Donael.

I crack open a beer because, why not? It's only one, and maybe it'll relax my brain and help me come up with a solution to my most pressing problem: Greig. It'd be easiest if I could just kill him myself. But the old woman has taken a shine to him and would be pissed if he were dead. Better than killing him would be destroying him. The problem with that is, how?

Henraek is the other burr in my ass. Asking about Aífe isn't going to do anything but break his heart. But once Belousz stops farting around and disappears Toman, it'll both cut the number of amadans in Eitan down by one and save my friend a whole lot of heartache. One little lie is a small price to pay for not learning that the dead should be viewed through nostalgia, not fact.

Cobb creeps back into the yard. He looks in the bushes, under the patio table. Like he's stalking something.

"What are you–"

He clicks quietly and puts a hand in front of his mouth.

Sorry, I mouth to him.

He checks behind and inside the water fountain in the middle of the yard, and I have no idea what the hell he's looking for.

Above him, leaves rustle.

I clear my throat and nod to the tree, but before Cobb can look up, that monkey boy Donael unleashes a war-whoop and jumps off a branch to attack Cobb. But he misjudges the leap, one foot landing on a lawn sprinkler and flying out in front of him. His head cracks against the water fountain's base.

I push myself out of the chair and lumber over to him, pulling him into me. He blinks out the stars and presses his hands against his eyes, willing away the tears. Cobb circles us, clicking like a maniac.

"It's not your fault," I say to Cobb. "You're fine."

I rub my hand over Donael's head, checking that there's no swelling or bleeding. For all the times I got hit on the head during the Struggle, most landed on my own flat spot, like it was dispersing the pressure. It got me to wondering if someone was messing with me.

Donael shakes my hand off him. "I'm OK."

"Follow my finger," I say to him, moving my pointer finger in patterns. His eyes seem to work fine, so I stand him up and brush the grass off his back. "Next time you try to kill Cobb, do it somewhere soft, hear?"

He doesn't answer, instead taking off back beyond the fence again, Cobb chasing with stuttering legs.

Can't say Donael's resilience or hard dome surprises me. After all, he is my son.

One night during the Struggle, Aífe knocked on the door, looking for Henraek. He hadn't been home for three days. I didn't want her standing in the hallway all night while I raised the various meeting areas to track him down, so I invited her in. I figured it would give me a little time to sober up so I could enjoy getting drunk again.

When I came back into the room from making calls, she was sifting through the pictures of Liella strewn over my sofa. I gathered them up like I'd been caught with pornography.

"Does it make you feel better?" Aífe said.

I took a long belt from the rapidly emptying bottle then let out an even longer sigh. "They found Henraek. He'll be home soon."

She took the photos back from my hands, running her fingers over Liella's cheek, her whole demeanor much calmer than her normal hurricane self. That was part of what worried me. "Does it help knowing she's gone forever? Because you never have to lie there and stare at the ceiling and wonder."

I handed her the bottle with some half-assed platitude of it'll be different soon, then went to get another for myself. In the years after, it always amazed me that Henraek never noticed the physical similarities. Donael and I even have the same distinctive flat spot on the back of our heads. Maybe Henraek was too busy with the Struggle. Which would be ironic: the thing that brought Donael into the world also being the thing that kept him hidden.

When I returned from getting more booze, she'd traded tears for liquor and drained all my whiskey.

"I just want him back," she said between sobs. "I want our lives to be normal again."

"We never had normal lives. Not since before the Wars. That's what we're trying to fix."

"Henraek and I were fine. We had each other. That was all we needed. And now?" She motioned around my apartment. "When he leaves, I never know if I'll see him again. When he comes home, I never know how long he's there. When he holds me, I never know if he's thinking about me or fantasizing about bombing something." She sniffed hard. "I just want to know."

I gave her a hug, closed my eyes, and swam in the familiar smell of sweat and jasmine. Her hands clawed against my back, then she looked up at me and her breath rolled over my face, some kind of desperate need to be acknowledged, to not be alone, passing between us. And, for the ten minutes that stretched out to whatever plane my dead wife's soul occupied, Aífe was Liella. I always thought she imagined me as Henraek.

Donael's scream cuts through the air. My skin prickles. I sprint toward his voice. Only twenty feet and I'm already panting. Sweat drips into my eyes.

He tears around the fence and stops in the yard, turning to face whatever's chasing him.

"Get over here," I yell. "What's wrong?"

He points into the neighbor's yard. "He's trying to put it on me."

"What?" I slow my steps as I near him, trying to suck in air through my mouth and nose at the same time. "What on you?"

He points again, and I watch Cobb pivoting through the bright green grass holding the body of a foerge, an ash-colored bird of prey you usually only see in the mountains. Must have gotten lost to end up here.

"He's chasing you with a dead bird?"

Donael nods vehemently.

"Drop the carcass. Picnic's over," I say. "We're watching a movie."

I shepherd them back into the house, holding Cobb in my arms so he won't rub whatever germs live in dead birds all over himself, then wash his hands at the kitchen sink.

Donael has already reclaimed his position on the couch, picking up the bowl of popcorn he didn't finish for breakfast. I turn on the TV and tell it to find something funny. Cobb climbs up next to Donael, head lolled on his brother's shoulder and snoring before the movie can even upload.

I tell it to play, then sit beside them. Archrivals armed with dead birds one minute, then best friends with shoulder pillows the next. Such is the relationship between people, one could say.

And then it occurs to me. Cobb had a dead foerge. I need a dead Forgall.

15.
HENRAEK

"An Amergin mob wouldn't go near Clodhna," my aching asshole – they might as well have taken a crap on the front step.

I spent hours canvassing the streets of Macha looking for Toman's new store, not finding it until long past dark, at which point it was closed. The buildings' bright façades glimmered in the night, a stark contrast to the darkness that envelops Findchoem and Amergin. When I arrived home, the lights were off, Emeríann breathing heavy with the hint of a snore. I couldn't sleep because of the adrenaline, so I fidgeted and exhaled and stewed, replaying the memory of Aífe's death until it was flash-burned into the back of my skull.

I dressed and left for Macha before Emeríann had even woken, then spent ten minutes wandering around Toman's store. Observing, surveilling— taunting, maybe. I lifted a piece of bread when he was flirting with one of the mothers perusing the aisles, then paid for a drink to see if he'd notice. Even when staring right into my eyes, he showed no hint of recognition. The encapsulation of everything the Tathadann hated, the face that stared out from countless wanted posters and bulletins and bounty sheets, the man whose wife he murdered. Yet nothing fired in the reptilian part of Toman's brain, the part that binds us together by blood. The events that ruined my life did not even register with him.

So now, in the late afternoon, I've been watching the store all day, biding my time so I can have Toman alone. I sit on a wobbly stool in a deliberately broken-down cantina across the street – to give the people of Macha the thrill of slumming it without any of the danger – sipping at my bourbon and picking at the pilfered bread.

Even with a pair of halting pneumatic legs ferrying him around, Toman still handles fruit the way an archeologist might a fossilized wing. He has emphatic conversations with customers, uses firm yet reserved gesticulations probably meant to convey some type of authority in the arena of produce. The floor is almost immaculate, black and white checkerboard tiles contrasting with the ornate wooden moulding along the ceiling. The antique scale is completely functional – though also completely superfluous because of the mass scanner sitting at the checkout – and probably light to the customer's advantage, all of it creating a wash of nostalgia for simpler times, which no doubt helps customers spend more money. He has transitioned nicely from the man who set Amergin on fire and shot my wife in the face to that nice grocer on the corner. Macha is not the type of neighborhood where children stand on garbage piles and shout that they are Queen of the Struggle.

Jars of water line the top shelf behind the cantina's bar. Various glyphs indicate the depth from which it came, indicative of the quality and mineral content. Both are far better than what's at Johnstone's, which is to be expected in this neighborhood even though this seems to be a laborers' bar. It's telling that even workers here drink the good stuff.

A few stools down, two men whisper, clock me with sidelong glances then confer again before moving one stool closer. One man has a prosthetic copper jaw and the other is missing his hand. A bottle of water sits between them. I consider ordering a glass of Whistling Pigs.

Sixteen years ago at the Parkhead, Walleus and I ordered two glasses of fancy bourbon for a last taste of something nice before devoting ourselves to the Struggle. Walleus chose the one with the pigs in top hats because he liked the label. We toasted to the future, remembering that it was only with each other that we were able to get this far – to not starve or be disappeared by the resource companies in Westhell County, or get robbed or find ourselves on the wrong end of a knife once we'd escaped to Eitan City – and that we were only as good as the other.

Aífe could be stubborn as a dead mule – a willful woman, she used to call herself – but she always had a good heart. She was the anchor that kept me from spinning off into some insane orbit, and blackmail would be too underhanded for her. Dominance, not coercion, was her style, a game we both loved to play, trying to outlast the other. Which Walleus knows. Which is why I don't buy that she was trying to blackmail anyone.

He knows more than he's letting on, but I don't know what that is. He's protecting someone. My money is on whoever is keeping his position in the Tathadann safe.

The men shift one stool closer.

I'd never admit it to Walleus, but part of the reason I smacked him so hard when he told us he was leaving our obviously failing revolution was that, owing to our promise, he was lowering me to his level and marring the reputation I'd worked hard to build. Another part was because he had the foresight to make the move and I didn't. Mostly, though, it was because my best friend was abandoning me.

The men assume the stools beside me. I toss back my drink, ready to break the glass and swing when the one next to me with the jaw says, "You're him, aren't you?"

I keep the glass ready. "Nah. Wrong guy."

"Yeah," he says, the jaw hitching slightly when he speaks, making his words bounce off his tongue. "I know exactly who you are." He extends his hand.

"Mister, you need to drink with us. Be an honor."

I set my glass down and shake. "That's very kind of you."

They wave to the bartender for another glass, pour me water from their bottle.

"I seen all those things you done a couple years ago. Goddamn, I told my wife then, if there's anyone we need right now, it's more men like you."

Shrugging it away, I say, "I was doing what any man would've done if called on." I take a long drink of the water and my hair stands on end, long dormant taste buds perking up, synapses lighting up in parts of my brain I haven't used for years. "I was only as good as the men around me."

"Including the rats?" One-hand says.

I take another long drink, unwilling to let him ruin this sensory experience. Even if Walleus was a rat, this man didn't fight next to him for years and hadn't earned the right to insult him. "If you're referring to Protectorate Blaí, we all have our own path."

"That son of a bitch," the Jaw says. I notice patches of oxidation where his chin should be, almost like a goatee. "Rat bastard traitor."

"He's human like the rest of us."

"Yeah," says One-hand, "but he don't let you blow up that electricity barn–"

"No, it was one of them transportation buildings," the Jaw says. "You always tell it wrong."

"Anyway, you don't blow it up, none of those other people get killed in all them other firefights."

"Excuse me?" I set down the water glass.

The Jaw says, "That football match, those apartment buildings, that kids' center–"

"That was a community gathering point," I say.

They both shrug. "Not what we heard," the Jaw says. "But that ain't the point. Without your brains–"

"Sorry," I say, looking around him to One-hand. "What exactly are you trying to insinuate?"

He sips at his water. "Heard that man turned Tathadann before y'all went in. Told all the men inside to high-tail and if they don't make it, don't give no fuss. Lay down arms and go quiet, they weren't being killed."

"Who told you that?"

The two look at each other. "Everyone," they both say. The Jaw adds, "Heard someone say he was the one said it."

"It was a power substation – not a barn or a transportation building – that supplied electricity to half of the governmental communications centers that, once downed, allowed us to make the strategic strikes your friend enjoyed so much while limiting the impact on non-Tathadann-affiliated civilians, achieved through meticulous planning and the valor of some good men."

They both lean away from me. One-hand puts up his one hand. "It's cool, paírtí. Ain't no big deal either way. I saw pictures and that place blew sky high, so however you did it is cool, OK?"

"You need to learn your real history and stop

listening to them." I look away so I won't punch this mouthbreather, and see Toman closing up the market. I pick up the glass of water and pour it on the floor beside him. "You talk to this 'everyone,' and you tell them I kneel before no one."

I grab a newspaper from the rack by the door before leaving, see an archival photo of Macuil Morrigan on the front page used to announce the statue dedication a week from tomorrow, then throw it on the ground.

Outside, Toman shakes hands good evening with the greasy-handed cabbie tinkering on the engine of his vintage car. I've never seen one like that in real life, only photos. I suppose people over here can afford to piss away their earnings. A plume of smoke bursts from the car. He passes by me, still with nary a flicker of recognition. The pneumatics of his legs hiss, stopping and starting intermittently. I follow, pretending to read a wrinkled Tathadann bulletin. One of the rods on his legs begins to pump too fast, increasing his pace and throwing him off balance. He hurries across the mouth of the alley, arms flailing as he swerves, trying to stay upright. I hide behind a morbidly obese woman wobbling on an ivory leg adorned with some type of filigree then duck past her to a group of teenagers with backpacks. He bangs at his leg, now at a near gallop, trying to adjust the pressure.

Then an explosion rips through the air. I drop and cover my face by instinct. Behind me, I can hear the patter of concrete and wood raining on the sidewalk. Screams fight each other to be the loudest, the most violent, this neighborhood unaccustomed to bombings. A mother shelters her children with a housecoat held over them, hurrying away from the blast. A teenage boy scoops a fallen man off the sidewalk before the alley, winging the man's arm over his shoulder as they hobble away. More people rush toward the sound, stepping over debris and coughing against the cloud of dust.

Through the chaos, I catch a glimpse of Toman hurrying away, back to his house. Where he'll be alone with a head full of memories that will explain why he shot Aífe and maybe what happened to Donael.

Six blocks down, I find him going into a building. Sandstone façade, recently bleached to an ivory shade of bone and coated with lacquer so as to look similar to Donnculan, the Tathadann neighborhood Walleus lives in, all the houses immaculate and white. I wait for a moment to put some space between us.

Despite the impenetrable fortress the building looks to be, there's no porter and the door doesn't fully close. I slip through the lobby to a brass elevator without a glance. A browning palm fern sits in a tarnished planter, a water feature wrapping around the planter but without any water running. The exterior might look spectacular, but the rest of this building is several pegs below the housing in Walleus's neighborhood, which is an appropriate metaphor for the party itself. The Tathadann has a curious way of showing Toman their appreciation for donating his body to the cause.

Still, the people here likely have consistent hot water and don't have to time their blackouts.

My forearms tingle with anticipation.

Inside the elevator, there's a black smudge on the seven button. I push the button too, then notice the dirt and grime on my hands and wipe it on my pants. The man standing next to me has the hair of a pony and reminds me that he called my people yesterday to stop his toilet from running.

"I don't care about the water," he says, oblivious to the dust and debris covering me, "but if I have to pay utilities a dime more because of this, I'm taking that dime from your ass." He jabs a thick finger into my chest for emphasis. Eight years ago, I would have wrapped my arm around his neck and squeezed until his eyes bulged. Now, though, I take a deep breath then knead the back of my neck and apologize for the delay. Maybe Walleus was wrong. Maybe I have learned something after all this time.

The door opens at the seventh floor and I exit. He yells after me, "And this goddamned elevator needs to be cleaned again."

Sconces and patterned wallpaper on the walls instead of holes and soot marks. These lights don't flicker with the ebb and flow of electricity. I can walk down the center of the hallway without worry. I examine the door handles until I find one that is smudged with grease then press my ear against the door. It's muffled but I hear movement inside. At the far end of the hallway, a resident left a room service tray outside their door. I retrieve it, eat the remaining half of the sandwich then put the glass against the door. Sounds like the kitchen is inside the door to the left, a hologram TV playing quietly. Some type of talking heads program. He bangs around, running water and heating something up.

Seeing that he's living the good life, he really should have invested in a better lock. I pop the face of the thumb reader with my knife's tip and short-circuit the electronics in less than ten seconds. In the reflection of the room service plate, I find his silhouette. He's filling a pot at the sink. I adjust my grip and go.

He looks up, water still running, stunned with shock. His mouth opens to say, "What?" Then it explodes in red as the plate cracks his teeth. I pounce on him before his body hits the floor. I grab his shirt and smash his head against the tile.

"Why did you shoot her?"

"What?"

I smash it again, twice. His pupils become loose. He mutters something violent.

"Aífe Laersen. You shot her. Why?"

"I don't know who–"

I release his shirt, his head thumping again on the tile. I grab a shard of broken plate, hold the tip against his cheek.

"My wife. In the café." I press it and the skin puckers but doesn't break. "Why?"

He opens his mouth, ready to loose the words that will finally smother this fire smoldering inside my chest. Then a glob of spit lands on my face. Despite his recent community makeover, he is programmed to lie and kill that which stands opposed to the Tathadann, as Emeríann is only too happy to remind me.

I feel my cheeks burn and realize I'm smiling.

I stab the ceramic shard through his cheek and yank it, ripping from molars to lips. Ragged skin flaps as he yells, splattering the tile with red.

He thrashes and writhes, smearing a blood halo over the tile, until I stab the needle into his temple.

"I'm going to find out anyway. You could have just told me."

There are slivers of coal in my kit but I would rather eat them than have them grace his eyelids for the journey.

After I close his apartment door behind me, I walk down the hallway, thinking I should be floating, but my feet still touch the floor. It makes me wonder if maybe Walleus is right, that knowing won't really change anything. I'd never believed that I could close that door in my heart, that it would no longer ache for Aífe and Donael, but there should be a difference. And there is a bit, but maybe not enough. Maybe it will never be enough.

I step out of the elevator and hurry through the lobby without seeing anyone else. Outside, near the alley, the crowd has begun to thin. As the gawkers blocking my path turn away, I glimpse a hump of a body sprawled across the sidewalk.

Oh shit. Oh shit shit shit.

Even from this distance, without even seeing properly, I recognize Forgall. A man kneels beside him, smoothing his hair back off his forehead.

This cannot be happening. Not now. Not today.

I sprint toward them, slip on a glass bottle and shatter it. The man glances up and then scurries away before I can react, and I see one of his eyes is covered with skin. Did Morrigan have Belousz track me? Did Walleus? Or is he here for Forgall? But how would he know Forgall was here?

When I get to Forgall, his face is not pale so much as it's a complete absence of color. A jagged spear of metal sticks out of his stomach. I press my fingers to his neck, feeling the faint pulse beneath his skin. His eyes are closed like fists, his breath seeping between his lips. If the shrapnel hasn't shredded his intestines already, it will if I try to remove it. Between the blood flowing onto the concrete and leaking through his internal cavity, he's going to die and I can't get him back to our neighborhood by myself.

"What the hell are you doing over here?" I say, feeling an unexpected knot in my throat.

"You got sloppy." He coughs, his eyes drifting open, and blood flecks my hand. "They're watching you. They don't trust you either."

"Who doesn't?"

Even with a piece of metal lodged in his gut and blood leaking over the concrete by the glassful, he still manages to give me a withering look.

"How do you know?"

"I found out this morning. I came to clean up for you, take out the scouts and protect the revolution. I told Emeríann she should've kept you away." His head tips to the side. His lips continue to move, and I have to put my ear beside them to hear him. "I don't know why I ever believed you."

I smear his hair back, doing my best to comfort him. I have a sudden longing for Walleus and the flask in his pocket. Goddammit. We are going to bomb the hell out of them.

"Forgall," I say, jiggling him to keep him conscious. "Those maps you got, are you sure they're solid, they're not disinformation? Forgall, I can't take Emeríann into a set-up. I need to know if we're safe."

His head moves, but it could be a nod or my doing.

Blood shimmers on his stomach, on the ground beside him, a viscous puddle of dark rain. In his hand is the statuette of Nimah. It's too late. He's not even here anymore.

"Close your eyes, Forgall, and think about everyone you love. It makes it easier." Of all the people I've consoled while dying, I never thought it'd be Forgall, though for all our differences, we devoted our lives to the same thing. "Listen to the rhythms of your body. Go with them. Go meet your grandmother again."

His head rocks up and down slightly, the faintest nod that evaporates with his breath. His eyes stare past me, lips slightly parted, his mouth filled with dead air.

I slip the statuette into his pocket and lay my hand

on it, closing my eyes for a moment.

Then I let my face fall blank again. I leave Forgall's body behind me, heading home to find out what happened to my wife. But not before diffusing Emeríann. After all, she's going to need someone to help with this bombing now.

16.
WALLEUS

I'm not in my booth more than five minutes and Greig's already swaggering his way through the customers of the Gallery. Why can't anyone leave me the hell alone? The grin plastered on his mug makes me wish I had a pair of pliers, some bleach, and thirty uninterrupted minutes. It'll be some consolation when I get Forgall in here, let some of the men go to work on him while Lady Morrigan and Greig watch, and listen to all the nothing he says. Big man like Forgall? They can torture the hell out of him and he won't say a word. Not only will I re-establish my stature in her eyes, I'll do it while standing on Greig's forehead. One of the plebes leans down beside me, repeating in my ear that Lady Morrigan is urgently wanting me to raise her.

"I heard you the first six times. Go get me some more coffee." I shove a mug at him, sloshing some coffee on the stomach of his freshly pressed uniform.

"And find Belousz. I need to talk to him now."

He hurries away as Greig approaches, standing before my table without acknowledging me, looking around at the paintings like he's never seen them before.

Pinching the bridge of my nose, I take a deep breath then exhale. "Say your piece and go, Greig."

"Hadn't seen you for a while. I thought you'd like an update."

"I was out a couple hours. Sick kid." I sift through the stack of reports I'm supposed to review, separating the important ones from the others. "You have sixty seconds. Starting now."

"I spent some time out in the street."

"Your mother kick you out again for not ironing her underwear right?"

He doesn't take the bait. "People are saying some interesting things about Daghda."

I swallow, consciously tell my hands to continue sorting. There's no way he knows about Stilian. It's an age-old rumor he's now picking up on. "People have been saying things about him for twenty years. Course, you're not old enough to know about most of that." I risk a glance up at him. "He still coming back? Or is that next month?"

"Lady Morrigan might not take it so lightly," he says, then clears his throat. "What's Forgall Tobeigh planning to bomb?"

The abrupt shift makes me pause. "You're the field scout. You tell me."

"I thought Henraek might know."

The use of Henraek's name in the same conversation as bomb stops me, but I quickly resume shifting reports around on my table.

"Tobeigh's name has never been on Henraek's list, so I don't know what he'd know."

There's a shushing of paper on my table. Several pictures land beside my hand.

"That's the funny thing about dealing with memory," he says. "After a while they all start blending together. You can't tell what you've done from what you've seen."

I stare at him for a moment before picking up the top picture, yet I manage to maintain a blank expression. In the photo, Henraek and Emeríann are carrying something covered in a sheet that looks conspicuously like a bomb, but can't be one. Because Henraek swore to me that he wouldn't get involved in this again, and even if he is a prick – which he tends to be – he wouldn't be stupid enough to carry a bomb through the streets like that. Yet there he is, carrying something with Emeríann, and I can practically hear Greig's pants stretching with his erection. Or maybe it's actually my noose tightening.

"Help yourself out here, Walleus," he says. "What's the target? The statue? Clodhna? He can't be that dumb, can he?"

"Maybe it's a couch and they're bringing it to a friend."

"Don't play stupid. He's associating with someone

under active monitoring."

I shove the photos back at him. "What he does and who he sees in his own time is his own business. I'm sure it's a misunderstanding." I point at the image. "This is circumstantial."

"It might be…" He trails off, like honey drips from his tongue. "But this isn't."

He drops three more photos. I glance at them, expecting more horseshit conjecture, and instead see Belousz's face, pressed against the glass of a small car, Forgall in the background. In the next photo they are exiting a building in Findchoem that has a lagonael den in the basement and rents rooms by the hour. The last one shows them in a café, Belousz drinking coffee while Forgall reads a paper. The scene is so domestic, their body language so comfortable, it's horrifying. My closest ally in the Tathadann and the leader of the supposed uprising.

"This is only two days' worth. There are some from this morning, too. If I followed him for a week, I'm positive I would get even more. From your expression, I think you know these aren't fabricated." There's an assertive tone to Grieg's voice that makes it hard not to snap his neck. Where the hell is Belousz? "You authorize me to move on Tobeigh and Daele's operation or I show these to Morrigan."

"I'll investigate these myself and send word to you," I say. "You do not move until you hear from me. Do you understand?"

He stares at me, chest swollen with pride, jaw

muscles pulsing with newfound power, then snatches the photos. "You do not make the rules anymore, Walleus."

He strides away but pauses at the door and I stand and let him see my full profile, debate going after him.

I call out, "You will wait for my word, soldier," as much for the benefit of everyone else here as for him. He doesn't bother giving a response before walking out.

The plebe inches up beside me. "Sir? Your coffee?"

I smack it away, spilling the entire cup on him. He shrieks, batting at the steam rising from his uniform. "If you can't figure out that I'm busy, then you'd be better off in a stochae than in my division."

He scuttles toward the back. I call out to stop him, but can't remember his name, so I yell you a couple times. He turns to face me, his cheeks glistening, and hurries back. It's a wonder this territory is still standing.

"Didn't I tell you to get me Belousz?"

He nods behind me, hesitantly, though it could be an attempt to not pass out from the scalding coffee.

I look to the side and startle when I find Belousz next to me. In that moment – for once – I've got nothing to say. I have no idea where any of this will fall, where it places me. "Where'd you come from?"

"Hell," he says.

"Yeah, well, welcome home." I appraise the dirt and dust covering him. His eye is rimmed red. I wonder if it's from alcohol. "I need you to go to Johnstone's right now and collect Forgall. I know you know where it is," I say, a little more bite in my words than I'd intended. "Bring him to me. Now."

"He's dead, Walleus," Belousz says.

"Who, Toman?"

"Forgall," he says, and I feel some weird combination of relief and sadness for him. "I don't know what happened." He takes a breath and straightens himself. "It was in the alley after the market, and Toman's legs started going crazy. He sped past me and the charge didn't go off quick enough. It fired after he passed."

The skin around my skull tightens. "Wait, wait." I massage my temples. "So Toman is alive? And Forgall's dead?"

Belousz squints hard and clears his throat. Under all that dust and grime, his cheeks are flushed. "I saw his body in the alley."

"Why was he there in the first place?"

"Looked like he was following Henraek."

"Well, why was he following Henraek?" I say. Does Henraek know about them?

"I have no idea."

I clench my fists and press them against my mouth, bite down on my knuckle so I don't scream or tear some patron's throat out with my teeth. Part of me wonders how much he heard, how much he's gathered, and how much is from Forgall confiding in him. Of course this would happen. Of. Course. Everything was lined up and ready and now nothing is.

No. Get yourself together, Walleus. You are not the

problem. Greig is the problem. You will pull yourself together, figure out a plan. You will be cool, calm, and collected and, with or without Belousz, you will devise a way around this obstacle that squashes Henraek's incessant questioning and buries Greig in the ground. You can do this.

"Protectorate Blaí," the plebe says, and before I recognize a conscious thought I feel my knuckles smash against his teeth. He tumbles backward, crashing into a group of patrons. A woman's high heel snaps and she takes out her friend, who flails her arms as she falls and catches her male escort right in the dick. All three of them go down in a jigsaw of limbs and spilled drinks.

I press my finger into Belousz's chest, almost like I'm tapping out a rhythm, my hand shakes so bad. "Be where I can find you," I say.

"I have to go see Mom tomorrow. But you send word, I'll hear it."

"You better make damn sure. And do not, under any circumstance, go near Greig." I sigh hard. "He knows about you and Forgall."

His eye drops. I'm not sure if he's embarrassed that I know or embarrassed that he wasn't good enough to hide it from Greig.

"Love makes you do stupid things. It makes you sloppy," I say.

He nods. What else is he supposed to do?

"I don't know how I'm going to spin this. Anyone asks, deny everything," I tell him. "If that doesn't work, kill them and get rid of the body."

I walk away before I can see his response. I can't look at him again right now. I can't look at anyone. All I want is a dark room and a full bottle. But nothing I could do could stop this now it's been started.

Before leaving, I write up an intelligence order in Fomora, mark it urgent and forge Morrigan's signature, then give it to one of the plebes. I tell him I have important business to attend to and I'm not sure when I'll be back, but he is to put it in Greig's hands the second he walks through the door tomorrow morning, and make sure he understands that he has a date with a stochae if he fails. It won't occupy Greig long, but it gives me a day to figure something out.

I survey the Gallery with a few glances, not meeting anyone's gawking mugs, then hurry out, certain that this place will crush me within seconds.

17.
HENRAEK

Standing with my hand on the doorknob, I take a few breaths to prepare myself. I hear Emeríann inside, completely unaware. I feel churning in my gut, the proximity to Toman's memories pushing bile up my throat. As soon as my hand moves, it will change my world. And for a brief second I wonder if I could simply stand still in the doorway, let my body functions slow then eventually cease, for as much as I need to know why Aífe was killed, I don't want to know. Screw it. I open the door.

She's two steps inside. "Where the hell have you been? Are you pouting or something because I said you shouldn't be part of the plan?"

I flinch, then breathe. "We need to talk."

"You're goddamn right we do." She stomps back to the table and plops down in her seat, pushing her plate to the middle and crossing her arms. Her nose twitches and I find it perversely cute given the situation. "You don't come home for two days and think you can parade in demanding an audience?"

"I was home last night and left early." She starts to speak but I cut her off. "Look, Emeríann," I say, taking a deep breath, "Forgall's dead."

Her arms slip off her chest as if they were greased.

"There was a bomb this afternoon, over in Macha. Hidden in a trash container near the sidewalk. Definitely a Tathadann job. This wasn't random. There was some power behind it."

"Those bastards." She snatches her glass and indiscriminately hurls it. It shatters against a bar in the window, sending glass shards raining down over the alley between buildings. "Goddammit!"

"A bunch of shrapnel completely destroyed his gut. Looked like a pink and grey sieve." I let go a long sigh, the vials at my waist throbbing. "We need to send someone to bring his body back."

"I'll go."

"People are going to be watching. You should not be seen over there."

"You are a known quantity," she says. "But I put my hair up and wear some baggy clothes, no one will notice me."

I consider arguing but can see that it's useless. She's going. "At least get someone to go with you. Call Lachlan."

"They're going to get theirs for this. Swear to Nimah, we're going to bomb the everloving shit out of them." She bites her lip so hard I'm afraid she'll tear through the skin, her chin trembling, her eyes glassing over. "You were right, someone talked. Maybe followed him. They had to."

"No. He said there were scouts following me," I say, lowering my voice as if it might help me dodge some responsibility. "He said he was there to take them out and protect the plan. For all I know, the bomb was meant for me."

"Goddammit, and you want to go back over there? You've done enough for one day, thanks." I want to respond but don't, knowing she's more right than she knows. She shakes her head, runs her fingers through her hair and pulls it back, wrapping it around her fist. "Well, what the hell were you doing in Macha? They're hunting their own now too?"

I pick at the food on her plate, offer a noncommittal shrug. I have no reason to lie to her but prefer not to talk about my dead family when possible. But if I make something up it will look like I'm trying to hide something I did.

She cocks her head, runs her tongue across the edge of her teeth. "Why were you there, Henraek?"

"I had to follow up on something."

"Follow up on what?" she says. "And for the love of all that is holy, I don't want to hear about Aífe today."

I blink, sniff, smell the lingering dust on my clothes, because it's all I can do. I don't always tell her the truth, but I won't lie to her.

"Dammit, Henraek." She huffs and pushes her chair away from the table. "Really?"

"It's not that simple."

"Didn't you say you ignored her because you were so busy with the Struggle?"

"Not quite, but this–"

"If I remember correctly, you said, 'Drove her away?' Maybe by doing things like coming in when she was asleep and leaving before she woke?"

"That's not true. I never said that."

"No, you admitted it. When you were really drunk. You already did a pretty good job of ruining your marriage because of all that and now you want to repeat it by–"

"She was murdered, Emeríann." I meant to state it but it came out as a yell. Her mouth is still open, her hands up slightly as the reptilian part of her brain says to defend herself. "I'm sorry. I didn't mean to raise my voice."

Her hands lower but she does not speak.

"She was murdered. I saw it in a memory." She mutters something like surprise, but I keep going. "She went to talk to someone we used to know. They started arguing. She almost threw a chair at him." I pinch the bridge of my nose, not wanting to talk about this with her because it violates one of our most important and unspoken rules, but, with everything else, I cannot stop my mouth from moving. "Out of nowhere, he stood up and went inside the building. One of the men with him turned and shot her in the face. I saw pieces of her brain stick to the glass door. And Walleus knew about it. He won't say it,

NIK KORPON   179

but I know him. I know he's hiding something, or protecting someone. Maybe someone else, maybe himself."

"Of course he is. Maybe you've been there so long, you're starting to forget. Or maybe you've been watching too many memories."

"Emeríann, of all nights, tonight is not the one to fight about this."

The muscles in her jaw flex and roll, her cheeks sucking in as she inhales quietly. An eyetooth edges out and puckers her bottom lip.

She lets out a long breath and says, "I'm sorry."

I shrug because what else am I supposed to do? "I didn't mean to dump on you. It's been an incredibly shitty day."

"No, Henraek." She takes another breath then leans forward and touches my hand. "I'm sorry, but Aífe is dead. I know you miss her. I miss Riab every day too. But they're dead, and we're not."

"It's different." Aífe's murder changes everything. It obliterates everything I've known for the last six years.

"You're right, it is, because I'm trying my best to move on with life. You complain about all the people who buy the poison you harvest but you're no better than them because you still live in your own memories. You're a self-loathing junkie who's too proud and self-absorbed to realize it. You're held captive by the dead."

"But Donael might not be dead."

Her face falls, and I can't tell if it's sympathy or pity.

"Em, they told me back then that both of them died in the riot," I say. "So if she didn't, then maybe he didn't either."

She presses her fingers against her eyes, tears leaking around the edges. "Dammit, babe. He…" She stutters for a moment, looking for words or stalling or trying to temper the edge of her tongue. "He would've found you by now."

My shoulders sag, and her words speed up, as if she could re-inflate me with assurances, condolences.

"I'm sorry, I don't want to say this and I know how bad it hurts to hear it, I know how it rips into you until you feel like everything inside you is pouring out all over the floor and there's no way to stop any of it." She presses her hands to her chest and the tears flow freely now. "But he would've found you by now."

"He could be out there."

"The city isn't that big. Someone would've seen him and told you, or told him where you were and he would've come. I mean…" She's nearly screaming it in frustration while her voice breaks with tears. "Dammit, Henraek. He's dead."

The rushing in my ears vanishes, silence a tactile being around us. "He's not dead until I say he is."

"It's not easy to accept. I know it. I get it." She wipes her hands over her eyes, drags her sleeve across her nose. "But you have to. Stay with me, stay with the living. It's OK to hurt but letting it consume you is no different than a white flag."

My pride starts to puff up my chest, to fight anyone who says I have surrendered. But she's right. Donael was a smart boy, resourceful, and there aren't that many people in Eitan. Word would have gotten around, either about him to me, or me to him.

But probably dead does not mean actually dead. I'll prepare myself for the fact that he is likely dead, but I'll also chase down every lead I can. One way or another.

I stand and go into the kitchen, bring the bottle and two glasses, pour us each a tall one. I set my chair next to hers and pull her close. Her skin smells faintly of wood smoke and liquor sweated through pores. I wonder if she can smell Forgall's blood on me.

"I'm sorry," I say. "For a lot of things." I raise a toast to the lost and swallow it in one gulp. The liquor burns my throat and I tell myself that's why my eyes are watering.

She sucks in hard, squinting away the burn, then pours us another. She waits for me to look at her before toasting. "The future is unwritten, love. But a week from now, the ceremony, the bomb, it's going to give us a pretty big pen. We can use it to create something new, and all of them – Donael, Riab, Aífe – they'd be proud of what we're going to do."

She kisses my forehead and says she needs to go, then raises Lachlan while changing her clothes. I give her a hug and tell her to be careful before she leaves.

The apartment is eerily quiet, the ghosts of Riab and Aífe flitting through the still air.

I could change my clothes, give her a two-minute lead then follow her. Observe her from a short distance, far enough so I won't be made but close enough to help should they need it. Familiarize myself with the others in her group, the way they interact, the way they organize. Make sure they're all who they say they are.

I lean forward and feel the vials press against my stomach.

But for all I know, there are scores of scouts positioned around Findchoem to watch for me, and I will lead them right to Emeríann and the others. As observant as I may be, I can't watch entire blocks. Hell, I hadn't even noticed the scouts Forgall was trying to clear out. Forgall said that we were safe. He was a good man, and Emeríann is a smart and self-reliant woman. She will be fine out there.

So I tell myself.

I sit in the silence for a few moments. Then I open the gate to let Silas in, pull out the viewer and insert the vials.

Even if Emeríann doesn't understand the need to have closure, to have something resembling answers, she would understand that in order to create something new, you need to know what came before in order to build on it, make it better, stronger. It's not a white flag or being held captive. And even if it was, sometimes you need that. The heart wants what the heart wants, and sometimes it just wants to bleed.

I hit play.

For the reputation he had as an unpredictable liability, Toman lived a surprisingly quiet life. Even when viewing two hours per minute, he moves rather slowly, even with fully functional legs. Office, park, hologram shop, water repository. Sometimes he walks through the lower west quarter with Belousz and his elderly mother. It's odd but I would prefer to know as little as possible about Belousz so that I can fantasize about killing him without guilt. I hit play to find some insight and find them only discussing some woman. "Snakes don't care where they're going as long as there's grass, I told him. Didn't listen though, because he's the boss," he says, and I believe we may actually agree on something.

I go to the kitchen and grab a glass, debating the relative benefits of bourbon or homebrew. At the rate his life is developing, it might be a long night, so I opt for bourbon. My tongue tingles with the memory of pure water. I'd turn on the faucet but I don't want more disappointment.

When I sit down on the couch, I find Toman at an open-air café table, glancing over at Mebeth. On the far side is the other man, still behind that fern.

I hit play and hear Aífe's voice. Static crackles and Mebeth's voice drowns out some of Aífe's words, but she's threatening him. He says something about things working their course, that he can't rush a process like this, and perhaps he should prescribe her something. This bastard could not be more vague and utterly useless to me if he tried. Aífe begins to scream in her rapid-fire way that makes me anxious and homesick in equal turns and Toman glances over to the man across from him, who relaxes back in his chair and glances back. One eye is the dead grey of a shark. The other is covered with an eye patch, covering his still-fresh wound.

I should have killed him when I had the chance.

Aífe continues to scream for a moment about what will happen if he doesn't end it but Toman is getting bored and the sound of her voice goes in and out and I can't understand what she's saying. Mebeth stands and walks toward the café. Belousz watches him, and once he's inside looks to Toman and nods in a way that carries gravity. Then he follows Mebeth. Toman stands, levels his gun, and fires.

He walks into the café. Mebeth asks Toman and Belousz if they're hungry. They have great tapas here, he says, and he'll order something for everyone. Then he walks through a door into the kitchen, Belousz standing at the edge. Toman pours himself a drink, drains it, then follows Belousz to the front door. There are two loud cracks behind them that I believe to be gunshots. Outside, they lift Aífe's body by the arms and legs, carry her to the alley and, on the count of three, hurl her into a trash container to be ferried away.

I failed you again, Aífe. I let them live. I'm sorry for all those that I killed during the Struggle, that I'm betraying the oath I swore because of them. But

Belousz and Mebeth, both of them deserve to die. I'm going to kill Belousz myself, but I'll need assistance getting to Mebeth. And I know who can help.

18.
WALLEUS

Donael is in rare form when I get home, running around while kicking an imaginary ball. I have a thought to tell him to stop but I'm too hungry and instead stand in front of the refrigerator, gnawing on cold rib-eye and swigging steak sauce straight from the bottle. Apparently he's recovered from the trauma of a dead foerge. Now I need to overcome my dead Forgall. Behind me, the crashing noise stops and when I turn, Donael and Cobb are staring at me like they've stumbled on a talking horse in their kitchen.

"What?" I say.

They stare at the juice running down my forearms, the sauce smeared over the corner of my mouth.

"Can we have some?" Donael says.

"Do you want it warm?"

Donael says no. Cobb clicks twice. I set the container on the counter, get out the milk, and set the bottle of sauce between them.

"Bon appétit," I say, and they dig in without ceremony. Father of the year, here. But could you do this, Henraek? Give him meat from a farm, not a park? I don't think so.

After Donael has consumed a half-pound of grilled meat, I ask him what's gotten him so crazy.

"We're all going to dress up like Concho Louth for school tomorrow and run down the hallway."

"The hell you are dressing up." I glance at Cobb. "Don't repeat that."

"Why not?"

"You know why not."

He gives me a death glare that is eerily reminiscent of Henraek. I remember seeing that glare many times, usually followed by Henraek tipping back his bourbon then laying his gun on the table, the barrel pointed in my direction.

"You will not, under any circumstances, dress up like the best Hoeps player in history. Are you listening to me?"

"I'm standing right here," he says. "Yes, I hear you."

"But are you listening to what I'm saying?"

He chews on the edge of a bone, staring at the counter for a minute before saying he understands. "But everyone else is going to."

"And everyone else is going to be picking bamboo splinters out of their assholes for the next week. And don't you repeat that, either," I say to Cobb. "The Tathadann has brought some stability to Eitan. They've let us eat good food like this and they've provided a school for you, let you get an education so you can do something important with your life."

He nibbles at the last bit of meat then dredges it through the leavings of sauce in the container and gnaws on the bone again, mainly as a way to consume sauce. The whole time I can feel him waiting.

"What, Donael? Say it."

"I know about those memories you watch." He drops the bone in the container and wipes his face on a dishtowel. "I remember some of that. Dad used to talk about it before he got shot."

"I'm sorry you do. There's nothing good about it. You won't have to deal with anything like that again." I put my head under the faucet and take long gulps of water. The image of his face when hearing Aífe and Henraek were dead still breaks something inside me.

"Mom and Dad wrapped their dead friend up in our bathroom. They used the sheet from my bed and when I asked them where my sheets were, they told me we had bed bugs."

"Donael, come on," I say, nodding at Cobb. "He understands a lot more than you think."

"Good. He should. It happened, right? If we can't wear certain colors or say certain names, he should know why, right? What's he going to do when they beat him for it and he doesn't know why?"

"Enough." He flinches when I say it, and I didn't mean to be so loud. "Can we talk about something else, please?"

The phone in the living room rings.

"Why are you defending them?" he says. "You used to hate them."

"Things change. People change."

"I don't change."

I close my eyes and take a deep breath. "They give us food and a roof. That's a hell of a lot more than me and Henraek had when we were little."

"I don't understand how you can fight so hard for one thing then give it up and go with the total opposite."

"They teach you anything in history class?" He opens his mouth but I cut him off. "No, of course they don't. There are thousands of things that happened fifty years ago, thirty years, people who fought and people who led, but they only tell you what they want you to know. But you can't even know that's true because half of what they erased was filled in with constructed memory, so most people don't know if it's their own memory or something they've heard a thousand times. The truth is, Donael, the Tathadann's not that different from who came before them."

"That's not what my dad said."

I twinge but don't show it. "Henraek had more balls than reason. The role of any government is to screw the population slow enough that they never notice it. The ones before the Tathadann allowed the Resource Wars to happen and it tore apart countries. The ones before that started wars with each other to get revenge for the wars their parents started with each other. It doesn't matter what their name is. They're all screwing us regardless."

"But don't you feel like a liar?" he says.

"That's enough," I growl.

I chew on the bone to keep my mouth occupied. How am I supposed to explain revolution or murder? That when someone takes the land your family owned for generations, only to destroy it on the off-chance they'll find some small amount of resources they won't even let you use, the only appropriate response is a gun. That when those people ruin the world around you and tell you everything's the way it's supposed to be, the only thing to do is tear their world apart. I can't explain that to an eleven year-old.

"I don't understand," he says.

"I know you don't. And I hope that you never have to." The phone rings again.

He shakes his head. "I don't even know what that means."

With no real response or explanation coming from me, he goes to answer the phone. Cobb glances up at me then back down to the counter, and though he can't speak, I can feel disgust radiating from him.

"You too?" I say to him.

"Tyrell Deckard is downstairs," Donael yells.

I stop in my place.

"Where?"

"Tuhc from the gatehouse is on the phone."

I hurry into the living room and snatch the phone, telling Donael to go clean up Cobb. When he's in the kitchen, I speak into the mouthpiece. "Who is this?"

"Mister Walleus, this is Tuhc from the front gate. There's a man down here real insistent on seeing you. Says his name is Tyrell Deckard," Tuhc says. "Should I send him up?"

Donael reappears in the doorway holding Cobb's sauce-stained shirt.

"No," I say. "No, I'll be down." I hang up before Tuhc can respond.

"What should I do with this?" Donael says.

"Put it in the laundry. What else would you do with it?" I lay my hands on Donael's shoulders. "I need to take care of something. I might be a couple minutes. You guys watch a movie or something. Get Cobb ready for bed if I'm not back in thirty minutes."

"What kind of name is Tyrell Deckard?" he says.

"He's an old friend."

"Sounds like a dumb friend." He snickers to himself.

Instead of a proper response, I purse my lips and nod at him, then shut the door and double check that it's locked. I slip one of my keys between my index and middle finger in case, then feel guilty for doing it, but tighten my grip anyway.

Henraek's back is to me as I approach. Inside the gatehouse, Tuhc – after all these years I now know his name – has conspicuously lowered his head, focusing on something to avoid catching Henraek's anger and finding himself with some untreatable injury. There are no bricks or boards in Henraek's hands – and again I'm glad they clean this area so frequently – so as long as he doesn't have a gun shoved between his ass cheeks, there's nothing to indicate he's intent on murdering me, unless it's with his bare hands, which wouldn't be that surprising.

I slink up behind Henraek and grab him by the elbow. "Deckard?" I say, yanking him away from the gatehouse. "What the hell is wrong with you? Just because you don't care about your life doesn't mean you have to inflict yourself on me."

"I didn't use my name. That movie's a thousand years old anyway."

"Stop being a prick." I keep my head down, face tilted away from any cameras. "Come on. Not here."

We walk three blocks in silence, getting away from the immediate surveillance. Once into the alleyway, he spins me around by the shoulder.

"Belousz was part of it," he says.

"Part of what?" I swallow hard.

"Mebeth gave the nod and Belousz gave the order. Then him and that robot satyr tossed Aífe's body in the trash after they shot her."

"What? How do you know that?"

"Stop asking me that. How do you think?" He kicks the lone bottle across the pavement. This alley is probably cleaner than my house, and with the white walls, brighter too. "I'm not going to ask you to move on Belousz. I wouldn't do that. But you need to help me with Mebeth."

"Henraek, don't be stupid. That would be catastrophically bad. For both of us." Not to mention

Donael, as well.

"I'm calling in all favors right now, you son of a bitch. Don't you dare step away from me."

"You know goddamned well that going after Mebeth would be suicide. No, not suicide – torture. Stuff they haven't even invented yet but will sure as hell try on us." His nostrils curl slightly, and I know he understands. "Anyway, Toman was the one who shot her, right? Take it up with him."

"Oh, I did," he says, his voice riding on bloodlust. "You'll never see a smile as big as his."

"Then let it go," I say.

"How can you say that?" He slams his hand against the brick wall behind me, his face inches from mine. "If someone murdered your wife, destroyed your family, I would walk beside you through every acre of Hell to help you kill them."

"Listen to me, Henraek. If you go after Belousz, you're going to screw everything up for me, which means it's going to get even worse for you. And that's saying something."

"Why are you doing this? They deserve to die." His spittle speckles my face.

I slap him and he looks more surprised than angry. I pounce on the distraction to redirect. "Stop playing the martyr before you get us both killed. You take out Belousz and it proves that you still side with the rebels, because anything that isn't Tathadann is automatically against the Tathadann. And if you're a rebel, then I'm a rebel because I vouched for you. So what you need to do is go home or go to the bar or go to one of those abandoned houses in Amergin and break a bunch of stuff, then sleep it off and come into work like this never happened. You hear me?" I relax my hands, not realizing they'd balled into fists.

Face blank, breathing level, he puts his nose to mine, says, "After everything we have been through, you would choose them over me."

"I am choosing you, choosing us – keeping both of us alive – by telling you to go home to your girlfriend."

"I can't, because she's out retrieving Forgall's body, who got blown up by your new best friend."

"I'm sorry to hear that. I know you two were close." I let the barb sink in, mostly because I'd rather deck him instead. "But you're projecting again. Belousz would have no reason to hurt Forgall."

"Why, because they were sleeping together?"

I wince. I didn't know he knew, which makes me wonder how many other people know now.

"Yeah," he says, "you're not the only one privy to secrets. And still you protect Belousz."

"I'm not protecting him. I told you, Morrigan is on edge, and anything you do to push her before I can take care of things is going to royally screw me. Greig is on my ass, looking for anything at all to prove I'm a sympathizer and should be removed from my position. I'm doing everything I can to stay out of a stochae and you trying to murder a fellow Tathadann member is not going to help the situation." I lay my hands on his shoulders and am surprised he doesn't try to stick a knife through them. I'm even more surprised that, for a few seconds, he actually seems to soften, like he's finally hearing me. "So please, for me, leave it alone."

But as brief as the expression came, it disappears. He shoves me against the wall, steps back, and looks me up and down. Sizing me up, like I'm in the middle of an auction. "Who is this fat bastard before me? Who says all this 'leave it alone'? Because it sure as hell isn't the man I crawled through Hell with. Who are you? Did you eat Walleus?"

"I know you miss your family. Really, I get it." I step forward, hoping to move him a little but he stands tall. His breath crashes against my face yet I lean closer still. "But they're dead. You think knowing how helps? Trust me, it doesn't, because then you picture it over and over."

"Her murder means Donael could be out there."

"He's not, Henraek. And killing someone else won't make it so. Donael is dead." Even saying the words makes my voice hitch. "If he was alive, you would've found him by now. And you haven't."

"But I don't know that. You know what that not-knowing does to you?" He beats his fist against his chest, and it's as heartbreaking as it is infantile. "Loss is a vacuum and it consumes everything."

"Go to hell, Henraek. My wife died trying to abort my deformed child. You abandoned yours so we could play commando in the streets."

"I was fighting for–"

"She begged you to stay and you left." My stomach touches his, my face close enough that I can see the whites of his eyes shot through with red veins. "So I'm telling you, you won't live long enough to enjoy knowing why she died if you don't back off. Morrigan has a hard-on for you the size of my thigh. They know Emeríann and Forgall were planning something. I saw the photo of you and her carrying something that looks a hell of a lot like a bomb."

This doesn't faze him. "Do you taste blood when you talk? Biting your tongue to keep all those secrets in?"

"Secrets? You're talking to me about secrets? Does Emeríann even know about Riab?"

His eyes narrow. "That has nothing to do with anything."

"Oh, sure," I say. Times like this I wish I had a little girl instead so I could channel her smarm and tone and push him to punch me. "So she doesn't know you gave the order that led him to be a part of a premature attack on a site that knew we were coming, that you gave it because you were half-drunk the whole week and trying to burn down the world, and that he could barely field-strip his weapon, much less run point on an ambush."

"He was ready. He had heart and he had determination."

"Suck my dick with that pamphlet speech," I say. "You knew they'd get slaughtered and sent them in anyway because you were hurt and wanted everyone else to hurt too."

"You are no saint, Walleus. We needed every man in order to stay alive and you abandoned us. You left us to die."

A street-sweeper backfires, echoing through the alleyway.

"I tried to get you all to come with me," I say, pressing my finger into his chest. "But I'm not your whipping boy, and you're only angry because no one thinks you're important anymore."

And then he starts singing. "Down near the river where our brothers bled–"

"Henraek, shut up."

He steps forward, pushes me back two paces. "I knelt on the bank and my father said–"

"I said, shut the hell up," I shout at him. My voice careens off the washed walls.

He pushes me with both hands, slamming my back against the wall, yells in my face, "This is your land, all that you can touch–"

"You say one more thing and I'm going to shoot you."

"And we'll water our crops with Tathadann blood." Arms spread like some gigantic bird of prey, he dares me to do it.

"I warned you. You live, you die, I don't care what you do." I spit in the middle of his chest then shoulder past him. "But they're going to kill you, Henraek."

I slap a trashcan and knock it over in front of him. Full cuts of meat and empty containers spill over his feet. I kick the can then walk back toward my house, hungry to be surrounded by my family. Even when I'm blocks away, I can still hear his voice singing, the words jagged glass on my skin.

19.
HENRAEK

I head toward Johnstone's to wait for Emeríann and Lachlan. Although I prefer fighting on my own, I'm going to need help taking out Belousz and Mebeth. And involving Lachlan and his people on this will not only give them something to cheer about, it will also bring me into their circle.

As I round the corner I see Belousz standing beneath a lamppost across the street from Johnstone's, staring at the darkened window. My fingers instantly curl, feeling his phantom muscle separate beneath my fingertips, his bones clack against my nails. Leaning on the post, one arm wrapped round while the other swings casually, his posture isn't the poised one of surveillance, but a pensive one. His back foot kicks absently at the ground. For a flash I feel an odd compassion, some vicious empathy bloom in my chest. Then I kneel and grab a length of rebar from the dirty sidewalk, crushing the feeling before it can mature.

But as I approach him, he lets out a long resigned sigh, then shoulders himself off the post and walks away. I follow from far enough away to stay unseen but close enough that he won't easily slip me. I figure I at least owe Walleus the courtesy of killing Belousz privately, to keep any guilt by association away from the chicken-shit.

I trail him for several blocks, leaning against a wall with a Tathadann newspaper covering my face when he stops at a market and emerges with a wilted bouquet of flowers. We weave past alleyways and avenues, through crowded markets teeming with pickpockets and men selling "traditional" snake-oil, past stalls offering roasted carcasses and vendors hocking trinkets in guttural tongues, until we come to a tenement building that lists to the right like a tooth about to be ripped free from the gum. Six-inch gaps between the bricks, the internal structure visible even from across the street. I lean against the soot-covered wall of a building and wait, the rebar held beside my leg.

When Walleus and I arrived in Eitan City years ago, invigorated by escaping Westhell County before it collapsed under the weight of the resource companies, we'd don moth-eaten fatigues and carry sticks with bandanas tied around the end, ranting about government conspiracies with a half-bottle of tea in place of liquor between us. We were playacting with things far more serious than we could comprehend, as teenagers are wont to do, and thought we were being subversive or artistic, that we were peeling back gauze from the collective eye by provoking a reaction. Now, with a clutch of dead souls and a ruined family strung around my shoulders, I have to say: it's not so funny anymore.

After a few minutes the door opens. Belousz emerges.

I stand, toss my head to either side and feel the crack trickle down my spine. I pop my shoulders and wait for cars to pass before crossing, ready to avenge my dead wife.

A frail woman steps out behind him, wearing an assemblage of leftover burlap clippings and fabric swatches. She clutches a pocketbook in one hand and the wilted bouquet in the other.

Goddamn it.

She balances herself using his arm as she crosses the threshold, then slaps it away as she shuffles down the sidewalk beside him. I give them a head start so I won't need to walk conspicuously slowly. It still takes us a full five minutes to walk two blocks and this is shaping up to be a hell of a task, until they veer off to the right and enter the darkened mouth of a decommissioned factory. I follow them into the shadows.

It's not a factory but a clandestine temple. Rows of benches filled with the mannequins that Tathadann soldiers use for target practice, arranged in various penitent positions. Some lack an arm, a hand. A rat crawls through a hole in one of the devotee's skulls. Cobwebs hang in the corners, off the candelabra, so thick they look fake. Lording over the altar is a fifteen-foot statue, a thick serpent's tail coiled beneath a woman's torso and head, her outstretched fingers sharp like claws. The pungent smell of moldy sawdust and stale incense is expected; less so is the sting of fresh disinfectant.

I creep along the shadow line in the rear breezeway to the side wall, minding each step. In this building, even a single nail would cause an avalanche of echoes.

Two trails lead through the dust of the center aisle up to the front bench, one with footsteps and the other inconsistent shuffle lines. Belousz assists his mother down a row, sitting beside her. Their whispers are static. It appears that her clothing isn't actually patchwork, but a dress that likely predates Lady Morrigan's wardrobe, though hers didn't weather nearly as well as Morrigan's. I've never seen this goddess up on the altar before. She's not from anywhere around here. I wonder how many people know of this, how many still come to worship, what would happen if the Tathadann found out.

"I know what to do, Môr," Belousz says, bowing toward the goddess before sitting back on the bench. She smacks his knuckles and he bows twice more.

"I been telling you this for years and still you ain't listening."

"You never made Dad suffer through this."

"Your fær was a godless heathen."

"Being born in Eitan doesn't make him a godless heathen. You two were from totally different cultures." Though he remains respectful, the edge in his voice is audible. He gestures at the statue. "He didn't understand the attraction of Berôs. None of us did."

"Don't sass your mother. You listened to me more often, you wouldn't still be kowtowing to that swollen cunt. It'd be your operation, not his, and your mother wouldn't be forced to live in such a shithole. You know Moira down the hall, her son is building a room in his house for her."

"Her son is an unrepentant lagon, Môr. She's going to get sold at a market for parts," he says. "And I told you I was taking care of it."

"How? Waiting for him to die? Waiting for that useless cunt Fannae to kill him off?"

"Goddamn, Môr."

This gets him a slap across the mouth.

"Watch your damn mouth in front of her." She gestures up to Berôs and when the light shifts inside the church, the shadows give the statue's face the appearance of judgment. Whether her censure is for Belousz or me, I have no idea. I'd wager that both of us are pretty much paid up on our ticket to Hell. "If you had half the initiative your brother had–"

"Then I'd be dead too." Belousz practically spits at her, but reins himself in. He says something in another language, every word holding too many letters. She responds but doesn't sound convinced. "You're not the only one who's tired of the Tathadann. Fannae is a relic and their party is sputtering. It's time for a new day."

She holds her hand up, opens and closes it, mimicking a mouth.

"It's not talk, Môr. Others feel the same, and now there are enough of us allied. All the pieces are moving," he says, "and Ragjarøn is backing me on this."

Even hearing the name Ragjarøn – the fearsome governing party led by Ødven and Federijke Äsyr in one of the far northern lands – makes me queasy and cold.

"They're thousands of miles from here," she says. "Those elk-sodomizers aren't going to hop-to for some skuffôlse like you."

"No, not for me." A smile creeps into his voice. "But they will for Daghda."

His mother straightens slightly, as if invoking the name has inflated her body with pride. "Daghda'll never come back to Eitan. He barely even came back for that cooze and her girl he kept up in the hills."

"I don't know about any woman or kid, but he's tired of wandering. He wants to retake what's rightfully his. He is a Morrigan, after all."

"You a psychic now? Reading people's minds?"

"No," Belousz says. "Ødven told me."

"You went to Vårgmannskjør?" She says something in her language that sounds resignedly impressed.

"Three weeks ago," he says. "That enough initiative for you?"

She pauses, says, "Three weeks ago you told me you couldn't bring me to worship because Fannae had you running around."

Now Belousz pauses, likely arranging his words perfectly. "You can't confess what you don't know. If something went wrong, I didn't want it to come back on you."

"So now you care about your old Môr?"

He ignores her. "I know all about them from your stories growing up. I know Eitan. They have the firepower we need." He shrugs. "It made sense, so Ødven is calling on Daghda."

"Screw me sideways," she says.

Belousz shakes his head, scratching the patch of skin over his eye. "The rebels are going to attack again, and we'll make sure no one stops them. They'll finally have their chance to cut down Walleus, and there will be no reason not to go after the Promhael and the rest of the Tathadann too, probably destroy half of Eitan in the process. Then Daghda will swoop in with all of Ragjarøn behind him and put the city back together again. The people will see their savior returned, and my group takes control behind him, with or without a hypothetical daughter. Eitan becomes an ally of Vårgmannskjør, Daghda gets to sit on high, and everyone's happy. And then you can get a better apartment, OK?"

"Don't discount his girl. That's his bloodline. They

said she's a miracle. Conceived when he was past sixty. No man I've known can get it up that old."

Belousz conceals his shudder. "Môr, that would make him nearly eighty years old now." She gives little response, instead going through the motions of her devotionals, though it looks half-hearted at best. "Now can we please stop talking about this? It's been a really bad couple days."

She rummages around in her handbag, pulls out a tampon, and sets it in his palm.

"Why the hell do you still carry these?" This earns him another slap.

He starts to protest but she raps him on the knuckles to hush him, and nods to the front where a squat man appears from a door behind the altar, adorned in a torn velvet robe with a jeweled glyph hanging at his sternum. He holds his hands up in the air, calling out to all the gods in the same tongue as the mother. It reverberates through the empty cavity of the temple, splintering into hundreds of incantations. Belousz's mother begins to whisper in concert with the priest. Belousz moves his lips but I doubt he says any words.

I wonder how long they've been planning this, and how they were able to keep any word away from Walleus. He might be preoccupied with Morrigan at the moment, but he needs to know this. And I will be more than happy to inform him that Belousz is planning to have him killed, though I do feel a little bad for him, seeing as how his new best friend is a duplicitous asshole. That's the price he has to pay for rank, being too busy putting out the many fires at his feet to notice the axe swinging at his neck. And to think that this is who he's selling me out for. I suppose ambition and self-preservation can also be an affliction.

The incantations become louder, their voices harsher. They move through two movements of the service. The priest rolls his sleeves above the elbow, blue veins like a river map. He holds an exquisite knife above him, asking the gods to anoint the cold steel. Light glimmers on the handle, the jewels winking at me.

The mother whispers harshly to Belousz, who stands and slowly proceeds up the aisle to the altar. A flutter in the rafters, sprinkling ash down on us. I find myself suddenly missing Silas. Belousz kneels before the priest and offers his arm. The knife glides through his skin like a swan in water. His body shuddering, he raises his arms above his head, allowing the blood to flow down in quiet pulses.

The priest creates two matching marks on his own forearms. He places his wrists over the patch of skin on Belousz's face where there was once an eye, blood pooling drop by drop. He dips his finger in the blood, draws a slash on his forehead and each cheek, then does the same to Belousz.

He walks down the center aisle, flicking blood over the congregation, anointing them. It's only now I realize all the brown flecks on the mannequins I thought were dirt are dried blood. He finishes his procession not more than ten feet from me. I can smell the copper on him. He returns to the altar and resumes his chanting.

Belousz stays genuflecting for a minute, his body shaking, but I can't tell if he is laughing or shuddering. He stands and wipes clean his eye, flicking his hand at the ground as if the blood is a piece of tape he can't remove from his fingers, then goes back to the bench and bows without his mother having to rap his knuckles. While their heads are bowed, I creep through the shadow without a sound save my own pounding heart, hurrying between stone columns to a side door, and exit into the street.

They come out an hour later. I follow them back to her tenement and wait.

When the hot needles of circulation deprivation prick the bottom of my thighs, I finally admit the possibility that while I've been hiding amid the dirt and grime in the alley beside the burnt-out carcass of an official Tathadann vehicle, that bastard has been inside sleeping. The sky lightened hours ago. Emeríann has to be wondering where I am. Again. If she even came home. She might still be holed up in Johnstone's with Lachlan and the others, preparing Forgall's body and refining the plans. I wonder if she used anything I pointed out.

I don't believe Belousz's talk of Ragjarøn, that a low-level grunt like him could pull off a coup like this. He must be drawing on his mother's stories to bolster his position within the splinter group, and maybe get back in her good graces alongside his dead brother. But still, I need to tell Emeríann, make sure that she and Lachlan are prepared for what may come. Except I don't know if I can tell her yet. I promised that I would support her in her plan. And I have, by staying away, by not interfering, by telling her I believe in her. But telling her that all of her hard work and planning has only been made viable by the betrayal of one of the very people she is fighting against – I'm not sure how well she'll take that. Or maybe, more accurately: I'm not sure how well she'll take that from me. For now, we're all fighting for the same thing. I won't rob her of that accomplishment until I have to.

Walleus, though, Walleus is in for a hell of a shock with Belousz. If I was a more magnanimous man, I would knock out Belousz and bring him to Walleus, make him answer for his transgressions and let Walleus have the opportunity to right them. But I'm not. This bastard killed my family, and it's my right to kill him.

And I suppose Belousz's betrayal – of the Tathadann, of Forgall, of Walleus – shouldn't come as any shock. We've all betrayed ourselves time and again, and only sometimes was it in the name of survival.

A crooked woman shuffles up to me, woolen field blanket draped over the hump of her shoulders. Dirt covers her face, only streaks of skin visible. She carries the overall impression of a walking knoll.

"Greens, grasses," she says. "You trade. You have? Please, help."

Before I can shoo her away, I hear the door open. I watch the window reflection of a slightly less destroyed car on the street. Belousz steps out the door, stretching his arms over his head. My knees crack and the brilliant burning sensation of blood courses through my legs as I stand. The woman asks me again and I tell her I'll bury her headfirst if she doesn't leave me be. Belousz begins to walk.

I grab the rebar and take up behind him. I will learn why my wife was murdered. I will find out what he actually knows about the coup, though I have a feeling that Emeríann will be sorely disappointed: Belousz will not be the one to make me change my position on Daghda's returning, or his being a savior. A Morrigan is a Morrigan.

As we pass the next alley, I glance around to make sure there's no one to see my face. Then, rebar in hand, I approach him as quickly as I can while remaining quiet – the muscle memory never leaves – and wrap one arm beneath his armpit and around the back of his neck, my other arm cinching his wrist backward, up over his head. Part of me hopes he tries to fight so I can rip his shoulder free from its socket. I push him into the alleyway, slam him against the wall of his mother's building. Soot from the wall covers half of his face. His throat trembles, his one eye burning bright with hatred.

"I've been waiting for you," he says. Dried blood crusts his covered eye.

I push words through my teeth. "Why did Toman

kill my wife?"

"Because I told him to."

"Why?"

His lips curve upward slightly. "Because they told me to."

I smack the butt-end of the rebar against his mouth. Teeth shatter, sprinkle over the ground. The faint vibration spreads through my palm. He sucks in hard through his nose, trying not to give me the satisfaction of seeing him suffer. Blood drips from the corner of his lips. I hold the metal before his good eye. "Next time, I take your sight. What happened to my wife and son?"

A smile slithers across his face. "You want me to beg? Bargain with you so you won't kill me?"

"Rest assured, there's nothing you can say that will keep me from killing you."

"She was working with us." Every 's' whistles over his broken teeth. "Told us about every one of your raids, where and when."

I slam his head against the wall. His knees wobble, body lilting to the side but staying upright. His eyelid flutters.

"She knitted sweaters for the half-breeds we kept in the basement, crocheted gloves for the flipper-babies." He pauses a moment like he's waiting for me to laugh. "They don't have fingers."

"Answer me."

"You're going to kill me anyway. It's how we're wired." He licks the blood off his lips. "But once you and Emeríann Daele bomb the water plant – and I know you will, Henraek, because you're like me–"

"I am nothing like you." I hear Walleus's voice clanging in my head.

"–all it'll do is give Daghda more reason to return. And there's no way you can't bomb it because it'd still be hanging out there, some obstacle that got the better of the great warrior. It will eat at you for the rest of your life. Then he'll come back, and everything you fought for…" He blows a puff of air at me. Poof, it's all gone.

"Daghda's dead," I say, gauging his face for a reaction. "Years ago."

"But he's the great hope, right? The man who saved Eitan, only to be displaced by Morrigan? They'll eat that story up because they need it, and when the first shot is fired, they'll rise against the Tathadann." Smug satisfaction radiates off him. "You can kill me, Henraek, but that's not going to stop anything. It's all in motion already and it's bigger than me anyway."

"How many of you are there?"

He shakes his head, but that lazy smile persists. His top lip catches on a shard of tooth. "So you kill me today. In a couple days you'll be as empty as you are now." Faint voices in the window above us, like crinkling paper. "Without a purpose, without some feeling that you've been wronged, you have nothing. The only thing that keeps you moving is revenge. You don't know who you are, so the only way to know where you stop and something else starts is by what's pressing against you."

"That's a dangerous amount of insight for a man about to die."

That smile will not go away. Maybe blood is seeping into his brain. The voices above us get louder, become clear, and his expression finally withers. That burning in his eye shifts. Fear now, not anger. It's his mother, arguing with another old woman. Moira, probably.

"And you can keep your goddamned room, you old flappy bag," she says. "Your son is a lazy, no good schælis."

All I do is smile.

"Henraek, look at me," he says. "Look at me, Henraek."

"My Bellie, my bårn? He'll be a goddamned king, he will." The other woman crows at his mother's bragging but it doesn't dissuade her. "While you're selling out your parts for a couple coins a ride, he'll be watching over this city from his perch, watching that goddamned Clodhna burn."

He tries to jump forward but I slam him back against the wall. "Henraek, you stay the hell away from her. She's done nothing. She is not in this, you hear me? You stay away from her."

"Your bastard children are going to see statues and those damned holograms of my bårn. They'll read about him in their history books."

"This is how we're wired," I say, finally swinging my eyes down to his.

"Goddammit…" He reins in his voice, struggles to

keep it level, to not let his ragged breathing obstruct his words. "Henraek, listen to me."

"You sold out your best friend in the Tathadann," I say, "and I should listen to you?"

"It's easy to make decisions during peace." He bucks against my arm. "But we're about to start a war. He would understand, and he would make the same move if he were me."

"You don't know him at all, do you?"

"My Bellie's a good goddamned boy," his mother says. "He's a boy a mother can be proud of."

"Whether you know what happened to my wife or you don't, whether Daghda's alive or not," I say, cocking my head, "you were never going to tell me anyway."

He lunges at me, and I scream and strike. The rebar clanks when it hits the brick wall behind him. Belousz sucks in hard, his eye wide, mouth agape. Blood leaks from his mouth while more pours around the edges of the rebar now sticking out of his throat.

I slide the needle into his temple and harvest him.

"Before you disappear," I tell him, "you need to understand something."

His pupils dilate, irises vibrating like a terrified animal, trying to look up in the direction of his mother's voice.

"I am nothing like you." I switch the vials, slipping the other into my pouch, tipping his head to aid the flow. Where in all of this liquid the memories of my dead wife reside is a mystery and I will not let this be for nothing.

His eyes roll to the side, mouth moving, but the words are wet with blood and the only thing I can make out is Forgall.

"This has nothing to do with him," I say.

He whispers, "Don't watch us."

The liquid continues to drip even after his eyelid flutters, fades, and comes tō rest half-open. I'm suddenly aware of how bad this alley smells, not like the tang of rotting meat but more the acrid smell of chemicals, of bodies pumped full with medications. I wait until there is no liquid left, then slip the vial next to the others and drop him on the alley floor. If I knew anything about his mother I would leave her a memento of him, something small to remind her that her son loved her and is in a better place. But I don't, and he's not.

Her son has brought me some solace, though. The still-shining streetlamps cast everything with a weightless sort of tint through the morning haze. I will finally understand why Aífe died. I will find something – anything – that will help me discover what happened to Donael. It won't close the hole in my chest, but perhaps it will be a little less gaping.

As I pass through the city on the way back home, I feel the Earth tilt ever so slightly on its axis.

Noise inside our apartment. Scuttling. Banging. Scratching and cursing.

I was followed. Someone else saw Belousz and

Forgall. Morrigan found out about Emeríann and me. A hundred variations rush through my head as I lay my hand on the doorknob, but they're all the same: someone has come for us.

I slam open the door and hear Emeríann grunt in the bedroom. I hurry across the living room, already reaching for the rebar but realizing I left it in Belousz's throat. No matter. I will destroy them by hand.

I burst into the bedroom. Emeríann is poised on one foot, trying to slip on the only nice shoes she has. Her dress rises up her thigh and I can see the ripple of muscle as she balances herself.

"Again? Really?" she says.

I consider explaining it all – Belousz, the albatross that I no longer carry, Ragjarøn – but stop myself short. "It's a long story."

"Then tell me later." She exhales as her foot finally slips into the shoe. "We have to go."

"Go?" I can feel the vials radiating heat, my fingers and brain twitching to watch them, begging for understanding, an answer.

"Forgall's funeral starts in an hour." She grabs clothes from the bed and tosses them at me. "I picked something out for you. Get dressed. Now."

I strip off my dirty clothes and toss them in a corner, laying the padded vial belt on the foot of the bed. She picks up a bag, packed with extra clothes, and sets it by the door.

"I need to clean up," I call to her. "Go ahead without me."

She ducks her head into the bedroom, raises an eyebrow. "Your job right now is to get dressed."

I gesture to the fresh shirt, which I've already streaked with dirt. The vials ring in a frequency she can't sense, but it sets my skin on fire. "I'll meet you over there."

"For the love of god, just put on some pants."

"We can't go in together, Emeríann. You know what they'd do to me."

Though she doesn't bother to poke her head back in, I can hear her exasperated sigh in the kitchen.

"All I'm suggesting is that you leave now so you can put some space between us."

The noise in the kitchen stops. She appears in the doorway. "I have to meet with some people before the funeral, confirm our plans to blow that place sky-high, then steal a car and load all the supplies in it, and I can't very well do that when surrounded by Tathadann field scouts, now can I?" She doesn't wait for me to answer. "So what I need you to do is stop whinging and moaning and get dressed like a big boy so that you can go ahead of me and not arouse suspicion."

"You're doing it today? It wasn't supposed to be for another week. Is everything ready?" I thread my legs through the pants while following her into the living room. "Have they used these charges before? You know you have to calibrate them precisely or—"

Her hand presses against my mouth, silencing me. Her lips close to my ear, she says, "We've been planning for weeks. I know what I'm doing, Henraek." Her hand comes off my mouth and yanks up my zipper. "This morning, we will mourn. But tonight? Tonight we will fight."

20.
WALLEUS

A bell rings out in the darkness. I slap my hand around, trying to find it without opening my eyes. A glass spills over the floor. After a few rings, I finally locate the handset.

"Who's dead?" I say.

"Why are you still asleep?" It's Morrigan. The fact that she is the one calling, not one of her lackeys, should startle me upright but my head is killing me. And I don't really give a shit what she has to say right now.

The blinds are losing the battle against daylight. "What time is it?"

"Time to get dressed," she says. "The funeral starts in thirty minutes."

"I can't go there." I push myself up on my elbows, pinch the bridge of my nose. "They'll beat me to death with my own arms."

"Or I will if you do not go to gather where all

the rebels will be collected." She clears her throat, a phlegmy, rattling noise. "We will provide a car. Report to me afterward."

Dial tone.

I hurl the handset across the room, then tell the lights to turn on. "Slowly, amadans. I've got a headache." I'm relieved to see that it was a glass of water and not the rest of my bourbon that spilled over the floor. I check out my wardrobe. Wrinkled pants, stained shirt. One shoe on and the other missing. The argument with Henraek is a ball of static in my chest. The events from the rest of the evening I can figure out by my sleeping position and clothes. I take a long pull from the bottle for a little hair of the dog then weave my way to the bedroom for some new clothes and a healthy dousing of aftershave.

After ten minutes, I'm neat, clean, vaguely shaved, and passably sober.

I check on the boys and find they're still sleeping, the lazy buggers. Cobb's body stretches across the mattress like his unconscious is trying to take up as much space as possible. In the top bunk, Donael sleeps in a tight ball, a frightened pill bug. I smooth back his hair then let them sleep, leaving a note on the counter for Donael to bring Cobb over to Neicy's, promising her unspecified rewards for watching my child on such short notice.

Outside, there is a black Tathadann car idling at the curb. My escort lounges in the passenger seat like an overfed housecat. I slip inside the car and the air is so cold I almost throw up. That might also be a result of drinking a bottle of bourbon.

"You're late," the escort says.

"You ever seen the inside of your own asshole?"

"No," he says.

"You want to?" I cough into my fist and taste bile. "Then tell this thing to drive."

21.
HENRAEK

A rare gust of wind tosses around the trees surrounding the lake in Regent Park, the branches clawing at the thick air like skeletal hands through graveyard dirt. The grass beneath us is dry and brittle, nearly the same color as sand. Emeríann stands near the pond with the other mourners, her hair twisted and pulled into a bun at the back of her head to both look nice for Forgall and not get in her way during the bombing. She bites the handkerchief folded in her fist, probably pretending she's not crying. Standing at a distance, it's a little hard to tell, but by the shuddering of her shoulders, I think she's actually sobbing, surrendering herself to the moment while the priest delivers his eulogy. His robes are made of something that looks like animal skins, the coronet atop his head likely fashioned from bone and sinew. I wonder if they are boar's bones, if this same priest presided over Forgall's grandmother's funeral.

I remember years ago, at Walleus and Liella's wedding, a strong breeze whipped through the ceremony. It lifted the flowers from Liella's hair and knocked settings off the tables. Despite the disheveled bride and broken stemware glittering on the brick patio, Walleus had the biggest grin. You see that? he said to me. Mom's here. Back then, he was the type to believe that.

I look over at him, fifteen feet from me, his white suit traded for a black one, his face downturned and looking solemn – though he's likely hungover and trying not to vomit – and wonder if he still remembers that. If he remembers being capable of believing things like that.

The wind that touches my face, I don't think it carries anything but dust and soot and the ashes of long-burnt bodies. I've seen the soul leave when I'm draining someone of their memory. I've seen the vessel left behind, nothing but ribs holding up their skin like the gunwales of a flimsy boat. I would love to think it's possible for the dead to swirl around here among the living but I can't believe that anything I can steal, bottle, and hock as a commodity could be precious enough to ride on the winds.

There are masses of people in the park to honor Forgall today, but they are only solitary bodies. Each of them will shrivel and waste away and there's a good chance many will land on my list, be quarantined beneath my couch before I hand them off for some money I will use to buy bourbon that's not made in a bathtub.

Standing so far away from Walleus will likely raise flags among the Tathadann field scouts who dapple the crowd, so I approach him, close enough that we could be mistaken for comrades but far enough that I can't actually punch him.

"I'm only standing here for appearances," I tell him, scanning the faces behind him for anyone I might recognize as a scout. "You can still eat a bag of dicks."

"I see you're overwhelmed with grief." He nods. "But I'm glad you're handling it well."

The wooden raft on which Forgall's massive body rests bobs up and down in the lake, the edge of it hanging onshore and the breeze making the sheet that covers him flutter.

Forgall's parents stand beside the raft, dressed in country clothes that could be black from dirt and grime or by design, and the family resemblance is striking. His mother is a frail woman in body, but the tight, leathered expression on her face says she is a woman who bows to no one. His father likely once cut a terrifying profile but has since become soft and doughy. However, his hands could still crush my skull.

"I'm surprised to see you here," I say to Walleus.

"Really?" he shrugs.

"I expected to see your people here, but not you personally. Isn't this enemy territory? The den of snakes?"

"Yeah, well, it's all part of the job." He nods at the raft. "Guess we all take risks we know we shouldn't."

A few people in the crowd part, and Stilian emerges from between the bodies. Walleus's face tightens. Stilian hurries over to us with a portable memory viewer in hand and whispers something to Walleus. All I can read of his lips is five years ago when he shows Walleus something on the viewer. Walleus's face relaxes for a flash as he watches, then reforms again. I try to edge closer but Stilian notices. "Are you sure it's him?" Stilian nods. Walleus holds the viewer close to his face, squinting, then nods and sets it in a pocket inside his jacket. "Check the profiles. Make sure this is verified. Then verify that verification. This needs to be bulletproof, hear?" Walleus claps him on the shoulder before sending him on his way. His body language is noticeably looser.

Emeríann steps forward to join a few other people who were close to Forgall, lining the edge of the lake around him. The rest of the crowd gives them a respectful buffer. From ground level it's hard to judge how many people are here, but I'd wager a thousand or so. Most are supporters of our rebellion, I'd surmise, so that even if they didn't know him personally they understand what it means to take a stand against the Tathadann, and in my head they will remain close friends here to honor him. I'm sure there are a healthy number of Tathadann soldiers dressed in civilian clothes here to keep an eye on things – I've seen no less than five I recognize from the Gallery – and likely an equal number of people who only came to see a fight break out.

Forgall and I never got along, for a number of reasons that are both idiosyncratically petty and monumentally ideological. Emeríann would say I'm a cynic – mainly because I refuse to believe that Daghda is anything but an exiled conqueror, no matter what his intentions might have been or what characteristics we ascribe him in his absence – but I think I'm a realist. Whether or not he would have done good for Eitan after the Wars, whether or not Eitan would be a different city if he hadn't married Fannae Morrigan and been banished, whether or not his supposed return would be good or bad for us, it's all as relevant as debating water. We used to have it and now we don't. It's that simple. He's good, he's bad: he's not here, so what does it matter?

Still, in our hearts, Forgall and I weren't that different. Despite what Belousz thinks, we both knew what we were, both fought long and hard for what we believed. Sure, we might have laid waste along the road and perhaps sacrificed things we hadn't meant to – people we loved, lives we hoped for – but we did it in the hopes of making Eitan a better place for those things we sacrificed.

"She sent you here, didn't she?" I say to Walleus.

"Who?" He turns his head slowly, face conspicuously blank.

"That's pretty cold. Even for her."

He has no response, because there is none.

Forgall's parents proceed to the raft with a basin of gasoline in their hands, then pour it over their son.

Emeríann waits for them to finish before pouring hers. When her basin is empty, she hugs Forgall's father, gives her condolences. They stand beside Forgall's mother.

"Can you not stare quite so hard at her?" Walleus says. "There are people watching."

"I'm observing the service. I could be looking at any of them."

"If you're watching Forgall's father with that look on your face, you got other issues I don't know about."

An iridescent sheen floats over the lake, mixing with the already toxic water and creating a joyfully colored halo around his body. The priest lights a cloth wrapped around the end of a three-foot branch and hands it to Forgall's parents. They touch the flame to his body and the whoosh of gas lighting is audible. Emeríann chokes out a cry and buries her head in the father's shoulder. Under the rustling of fire, I hear someone singing quietly. Down near the river where our brothers bled. Another voice joins in.

Beyond them, poking out from the mountains that ring the city, are the silhouettes of the watchtowers used during the Wars, and it occurs to me that in Eitan, we are literally and metaphorically surrounded by death. On almost every corner, I know a story about someone dying or some attack being waged. Which makes me wonder: why do we stay here? Why remain surrounded by so many ghosts? Why not go someplace new and start over? But then I think, where would I go? This is my home. This is where

I've always lived, where my few friends are, where I know, where I also have stories of Donael playing and Aífe laughing and Emeríann singing. Despite all the death and dirt and danger, this is my home, and I won't be pushed out by anyone.

Forgall's parents wait for the initial fire to calm before the father lays his foot on the raft and pushes it into the lake, sending Forgall on his way. Murmurs spread through the crowd, electricity gathering. A few shouts. I breathe in the smell of his skin crackling and burning. The jumping flames are hypnotic.

"Be careful," Walleus finally says. He nods toward Emeríann, at the few men glancing up at her, trying to catch her attention. "OK?"

"You sure I'm the one in danger?"

He stares at me for a long moment, eyes searching my face for something hidden beneath the surface. Maybe looking for the time we shared eight, ten years ago, looking for something to hold on to.

"People are talking about Daghda," he says.

I swallow, say, "No one talks about him. You'll get stripped."

"Citizens don't talk. But every rebel does. They always have." He chews on his top lip. "They think he's returning."

"I'm not a rebel anymore."

When Forgall's parents can take no more, they turn and thank the priest, then return to their collected friends and begin thanking people for coming. His father gives Emeríann a hug, pecks her cheek. A short, squat man approaches Emeríann almost immediately. His face pings against my skull, the memory of a memory, and I know he must be Lachlan Parnell. As soon as he leaves, another replaces him. From their gestures, I know their tones are hushed, but they are still very obvious.

"We pulled a memory from the network. Daghda died five years ago." Walleus's eyes bore into mine, but I keep my smile hidden. I knew Belousz was full of shit. "Are they trying to scare Morrigan or inspire the rebels?"

"Can't it be both?" I shift back to Emeríann. The second man leaves, nodding to someone else. Then there's a shatter and some yelling fifty feet away on the other side. The crowd parts slightly to reveal a Tathadann scout, standing above his now-smashed notation device lying on the ground. He shouts and points at a man, who promptly punches the scout in the face. Two other Tathadann – one uniformed and one in plainclothes – swoop in and pull the man away. And behind us, there's another shatter, more yelling.

Walleus leans close to me. "What's going on, Henraek?" His voice quivers with anxiety.

"There are more holes in the dike than there are fingers," I say, "and no one has a raincoat anymore." When I glance back, two other men are walking away from Emeríann. "Belousz was planning a coup," I say to Walleus.

"Without telling me?"

"You were a sacrifice he was willing to make," I say.

"I took care of him, but you should still sleep with a gun under your pillow."

"Henraek," he calls out, but I'm already making my way over, weaving around and past the forming groups. I wait for one pocket of people to start moving and use them to block me from sight until I get near her, then someone grabs my arm. I clench my fist and turn to find Forgall's father looming over me. His wife stands next to him and appears to want to spit in my face, but I don't know if that's because her son died and she thinks it's my fault or the Struggle died and she thinks it's my fault. The mass of man leans down, puts his lips next to my ear.

"She's a pacifist, didn't much like it when he took up with you all, but you all gave him something to live for. He was pretty chuffed when you started showing round Johnstone's." His thick accent makes it hard to understand what he's saying, which surprises me for some reason because Forgall never had one. "Wanted to put a bullet in you, but chuffed nonetheless."

"I get that a lot," I say.

"It's a natural reaction to seeing your idol fall. I told him good men and evil men are still men, but you know how thick he could be." He gives a half-smile. Then the two of them shuffle away with their people.

Emeríann is standing alone. I slink over before someone else gets to her. "They're watching you," I say. "What are you doing?"

She smiles. "Creating a distraction."

As if on cue, shouts ring out as a fight erupts on

the north side of the park. Bodies pitch and move, onlookers spreading out, some giving way and others joining in. Uniformed Tathadann rush to the site to break it up as another fight spreads on the other side. A twist of smoke rises from the edge of the park.

"You go that way, I'm going this way," she says. "The car's over on Erse, two blocks down. Blue two-door with white paint on the rear passenger tire. I'll see you there in five."

We slip through the crowd, headed in different directions but both toward the car. Toward the trunk filled with a tangle of wires and blasting caps, of atomizers and pulse-charges. I hear my voice singing and didn't realize I'd started. I glance over my shoulder, through the throbbing, punching, teeming mass, and in a quick sliver between people, I catch a glimpse of her singing too.

22.
WALLEUS

Henraek and Emeríann split and leave the park, weaving through the crowd. I watch the wake of parting people become smaller as they near the buildings and rubble.

Belousz wouldn't sell me out, not my right-hand, not after everything we've been through, but Henraek isn't prone to lying. Distortion, sure. Delusion, definitely. But not an outright lie. Which makes me wonder exactly what he heard. One thing I'm positive of: Henraek was not lying about killing Belousz. My head tells me I should feel something about that, but right now all I can do is stand here and watch Henraek and Emeríann disappear into the haze of Macha like wraiths. Part of me isn't sure if they were ever even there, like I flashed back on one of the other hundred services we've attended. The other part of me, it looks around and says, What the hell are you doing here?

I don't know any of these people but could

figure out who Forgall's parents are based on family resemblance alone. The people beside them, I don't know and don't care about.

It's the hundreds of other people that worry me. Walking through the rebel supporters is like piecing together all the lost jigsaw pieces from the Struggle – remnants of my old platoons, men I fought with, boys we trained who are now men – and all those old pieces form the image of a broadsword balanced above my neck. The members of the Tathadann that I see here are probably gathering on me as well as civilians. Watching who is collected in groups and what their connection is to the Struggle. Noting who I talk to and for how long, our gesticulations and mood. All of it observed and documented to present to Morrigan. I wonder if they've heard the chatter about Daghda too, if Greig is keeping it as a present for Morrigan. Or if he even knows they were married at one point.

Seeing how massively I'm outnumbered, and that my only safe connection to these people has promptly walked off, I figure now is a good time to make my exit.

Somewhere in my grey matter, I picture another lump floating on the lake, smaller than my current swollen body because I never allowed myself to become fat and complacent. I see Henraek and Emeríann – together – standing up to their knees in the water, giving a good shove to make sure I get all the way into the middle, then Emeríann giving Henraek the last drag of her cigarette before flicking it in a cinematic arc that ends on my gasoline-soaked body. The flames scorch birds flying over and all these people crowding around the lake cheer, trumpeting me off to Nahoeg or wherever we end up.

Only a small portion of the people here really know Forgall, maybe a couple dozen more from Johnstone's, more by his reputation. But none of that matters. They don't care that they don't know how he cooks dinner or what his favorite song is. They know he was one of them and they're out here because they are all them, and once – once – I was them too. I could call on people I didn't know and they'd answer. I could trust a neighbor I hardly knew to care for my deformed newborn because we were them. The old woman who lords over me now would slit my throat as easily as give my job to someone else, and be as bored by either. I could disappear or show up with Henraek's head on a stake and all she would do is preen her feather headdress. For shit's sake, I had one friend missing an eye who might have been planning to have me killed, and I have one friend missing a soul. I have a broken child and a hidden child. There's no longer a them, only me.

So I weave my way through the park. Around fistfights. Past semicircles of citizens thrown on the ground with their hands lashed behind them. Sidestepping groups of younger teens huddled together who are sure as hell going to hurt someone. I keep my eyes down the whole time to avoid being marked as an enemy to be drawn and quartered, my arm protecting the memory viewer in my jacket. Twenty feet to my left, a uniform pushes two young men, both with a look of desperation and anger I recognize a little too well. They split and head different ways, but I know that maneuver too and they'll meet up in five minutes, probably with another ten people on either side of them. Planning. Watching. Waiting.

I'm almost out of the park when someone bumps into me. I put up my hands, saying my apologies, then hear a quick scoff.

I look up and see the man who replaced me when I took over my own platoon.

"Goerde," I nod.

"What are you doing here?"

"Paying my respects." I gesture toward the lake. "He was a good man."

"You knew nothing about him."

"I knew him longer than you did, Goerde. Don't forget who trained your soldiers," I say, reminding this prick that I – and everything I taught him – am the reason he's still alive.

"You don't belong here," Goerde says. "And you don't get to say goodbye."

"I'm being polite. Calm down."

"Leave now or I yell rat." He extends his arm, indicating everyone around us. Three people behind me watch us, elbowing those standing beside them to cue them in on the action. A low murmur spreads. "You want to see what'll happen?"

I bite the inside of my cheek, then nod. "Glad to see you, Goerde."

"Eat my dick, traitor."

"Will do, Goerde. Will do." I give him our old salute then head for my waiting car before he yells and gets me lynched.

The car weaves in and out of traffic, settling into a hypnotic rhythm, making the hectic city feel a little calmer. Vendors call out and hock their goods. Waiters drape checkerboard tablecloths over wrought-iron patio tables and turn on the holograms. Men scrub down the sandy walls of Tathadann-backed businesses. A florist fills her buckets with prism flowers.

A hunched over man totters down the street, leading a horse that pulls a half-full cart of vaguely fresh fruit and rotting vegetables behind it. The young boy with him circles the cart and collects money from the people who can't afford to buy produce from an actual market where they won't get a communicable disease. Every time the boy moves to the other side, one of the alley rats – real and figurative – makes a move for the fruit and he tears back around, swinging a long, sharpened stick.

Farther up, a family of four rides matching bikes on the side of the road in a display of nuclear affection that makes me want to either cry or crap my pants. The little girl's pigtail bows even match the streamers flowing from her handlebars. As we pass, I catch a glimpse of the dad's face – the treasurer of the

Tathadann – and I'm pretty sure I've seen him exiting a bar where they project male fisting videos above the liquor.

If I wasn't about to meet with the woman who might be plotting to kill me with little idea of how to get rid of the other man who might be plotting to have me killed, I'd go so far as to say it's a nice day out.

23.
HENRAEK

The streets and sidewalks of Fomora are quiet. It's not surprising, given that we left behind both city center and the funeral of a well-known rebel, but, as I step out of the car, it still strikes me as eerie.

Emeríann changes in the car. Then we load the supplies into two backpacks, slinging them over our shoulders. She takes a deep breath and looks around.

I know I should tell her that Daghda's dead. But she needs to stay focused on the task at hand. Neither of us can afford distraction right now. I'll tell her later. When the time's right.

She smiles. "You needed a minute?"

Goddamn it. I can't hold this.

"Hey, I'm sorry, but you need to know something." I force myself to keep going. "Walleus found a memory of Daghda."

Her breath catches.

"He's dead."

She wilts away from me, and immediately I feel terrible. I shouldn't have said anything.

But then her back straightens, shoulders pulled back. "It doesn't matter. We don't need him," she says. "We'll take the city ourselves, and no one will stop us."

I want to crush my lips against hers until we bleed.

"So you're ready to do this?" I hold her shoulders, as much to comfort her as to feel for any quivering. But there isn't any.

After a last look at the blueprints, creating a rough mental layout, I fold the plans into my backpack and lead us forward.

The security on this building – the nerve center of water distribution for half the city – is no better than what I saw in Toman's building, and I get through it even quicker. We wind down cinderblock hallways, the pale blue painted concrete floors chipped and worn in the center. Placards featuring escape routes hang on the wall at every intersection.

Each time we round a bend, I look into the high corners for cameras, waiting for them to pivot away from us before leading Emeríann across the hall. There are fewer guards than I expected, though it's understandable with resources shifted toward riot containment in the city center.

A few minutes in, we come to the main artery split. I bring Emeríann close to me. "Both of these lead to the main store room–"

"So you'll go left and I'll go right and we'll clear

both hallways then meet in the middle." She smiles, self-satisfied.

"Right, but—"

"Make sure I wait for the cameras to move before I do." She pats my cheek. "Sweetheart, I've got this."

I kiss her hard on the lips, equal parts proud and eager. "Guess I'll see you there, then."

We head our own ways.

When I first met Emeríann seven years ago, and when we got together four years later, there were a number of places I never imagined us ending up. Anywhere cold is one. A cul-de-sac, another. Inside the bowels of the main Tathadann water treatment plant would qualify as a pretty close third. Yet here we are, creeping down hallways with a grip of explosives strapped on our backs.

A cough echoes. I stick close to the wall, my palms drifting along the surface, cool and rough on my skin. As I come to the bend in the hallway, I sneak a glance ahead. One door sits on the left with a camera above it. Nothing on the right. And a guard strolling along the center of the floor. Looks like a woman, though not very large. Except for the gun sitting on her hip. She's fifty feet away from me, and fifty feet from the door at the end, the metal vats of the main storage area visible through the window. I need to move, and move quick.

I wait until the camera begins to turn away from me before strafing along the left side of the hall, sticking close to the wall to stay out of sight. Thirty feet to her. Twenty. The camera reaches the middle point. Ten feet. I can hear her whistling, smell her perfume. There's an acrid, alcohol-heavy scent to it. Something cheap, like a teenager would wear in an attempt to seem more grown up. The camera points at the other side, begins panning back this way.

I take three long strides and wrap my arm around her neck, cinching her chin in my elbow. A peek up, and the camera pans closer. Her heel swings up, glancing off the inside of my thigh. Two inches and she would have dropped me with the kick. Her nails try to pierce my jacket. I dig my heels into the cement and drag us backward. The door is five feet away. The camera pans, almost on us. Three seconds and we'll be made. She plants her feet and tries to throw us forward but her hesitation gives me an opening and I launch us back through the door, into a dark room. I can feel the camera passing above us.

Hand wrapped tight around my forearm, I stretch backward, feeling her throat tighten. She pounds her fists against my arm, becoming more frantic as she feels the air disappearing. The cement is cold beneath me. We could not exist in this room, it is so dark. We could both already be dead and simply not know it.

Her fists become softer and I loosen my grip, eventually taking her consciousness but not her life. She did nothing to deserve death. When she's finally docile, I roll her off me and search the wall for a light. I press my fingers against the underside of her jaw, making sure her pulse is still there. She's quite pretty, in an immature way. Her hair is braided into twin strands and curled against the back of her head. She's probably not even old enough to be here legally but wants to contribute, to be part of something larger than her, to feel a sense of purpose and pride.

I leave her be and, at the doorway, wager a glance up at the camera. As it pans past me, away from the main storage room, I hurry out to the door and look through the window. The room is filled with steel tanks, braids of tubes, some cameras and a control panel. Across the room, in a window identical to this, I see Emeríann, her face broad with a smile, her glittering eyes noticeable even from this far away.

24.
WALLEUS

Clodhna hums with activity, officers hustling between rooms, carrying folders stuffed with reports. A young man in fatigues follows behind a woman wearing the official uniform, finger held to her ear to engage the tiny comm device. She nods twice then hands the young man a map and points to a spot, shoos him toward the door. Disc-shaped droids skitter between everyone's feet, polishing the white marble floors. It's busier than usual, though I don't know if they're figuring a reaction to Forgall's death, planning their own offensive, or preparing for a possible coup. That kind of planning was already above my paygrade, and even farther away now.

This building could turn a sneeze into an avalanche of tanks, but even with all this movement the place is pretty damn quiet. A while back, Morrigan redid the offices with some kind of soundproofing material. One of the guards tried to explain it to me, something about the cells being specially engineered so that the hollow construction would attract sound waves and destroy them, but my eyes glazed over after the third five-syllable word. It kills almost all sound and is only available for Tathadann elite, is what I took away from it.

The woman sitting at the front desk scans the escort's badge. Her blonde hair is pulled up in a tight bun and held with hair pins that could double as field surgery tools. Four orchids sit on the edge of her desk, each of them as unnaturally white as the houses that fill Donnculan. With a quick glance I clock at least half a dozen security cameras in the entranceway and outside the door looking out over the lush gardens, covering every vantage point. The secretary taps her pencil against her cheek and raises her eyebrows twice at the escort, a gesture that makes him quickly check out the marble beneath his feet and clear his throat.

"This way," he tells me when his credentials clear. She does not seem the least bit discouraged by his lack of a response.

Floor-to-ceiling mirrors hang every fifteen feet in the hallway, a pair of ravens that look carved from onyx sitting on each of them. A stream of officers marches down the hallway in front of us, headed for the large conference room at the end. The escort stays two steps in front of me the entire time, his demeanor changing quickly if I fall behind. I'm surprised he'd turn his back on me, given that I promised to turn him inside out earlier this morning. In my defense, the hangover has worn off some.

We come to a door halfway down. He clears his throat, telling me I should proceed. I step inside and my feet are silent on the thick carpet. He closes the door and the commotion from the hallway hushes, the blood in my ears the only sound. An ornately carved desk sits in front of the window and it's about as big as my car. In the corner stands a full suit of antique knight's armor. An assortment of animal heads rings the upper wall of the office, half of which I've never even seen before. I'd assume they were Commander Morrigan's, as he seems like the type of guy to sneak up behind an unsuspecting animal and blow its head off, but I could easily see Lady Morrigan doing it.

For all the modern advances the Tathadann has implemented in the nice parts of Eitan City, this office itself is very traditional. No holograms, no automatons, no voice controls.

The door opens and I expect to see Morrigan but instead Greig walks in, his hair carefully combed.

"You're not the asshole I expected to see," I say.

"She calls, I answer," he says.

"You're a great lapdog, ain't you?" As he comes closer I notice blood splattered on his shoes, nod at them. "What happened?"

He lowers himself into a chair and sighs. "Don't you worry about it, Walleus." The self-assured smirk makes me want to stick my hand down his throat and pull his balls out through his mouth. "You know, I was looking around for that authorization. Couldn't find it anywhere."

"You were at the Gallery this morning?" I say. He nods. "Then aren't you supposed to be in Fomora?"

He cocks his head, and I can't tell if he's confused because the plebe never delivered the order – in which case I need to beat the hell out of him when I get back – or seeing if I'll call him out on his defiance.

"I think it's a little late for Forgall Tobeigh to save himself, but Belousz? You?" He clears his throat and rolls his shoulders.

How does he know about Forgall? Was he creeping around the edges of the Gallery, gathering? Apparently he doesn't know about Henraek and Belousz, which is a strange advantage to have. My legs are drained from a lack of sleep and excess of alcohol but there are only two chairs by her desk, and Greig occupies one, so I stand and stare out the window at the hedges shaped into surrealist animals or something. They remind me of a black and white movie Liella dragged me and Henraek and Aífe to go see. Something about memory or impermanence. I guess it's kind of ironic that I don't remember anything about it.

Ten silent minutes pass before the door opens again, Morrigan entering this time wearing a raven-feather headdress that I've never seen before, as well as some crushed velvet thing that makes her look like the madam of a vampire bordello.

She's not welcoming like a madam, though, ordering me to sit without even a greeting. Standing behind the desk, she leans toward me, and the resemblance to a vulture over carrion is intense.

"What did you gather at the funeral?" she says.

"There were some flare-ups, but we handled it–"

"What about Henraek?" she says.

"What about him?"

"Doctor Mebeth reported you two scuffled at the Gallery. And now there are reports that he is tied to the bombing plot." She stares straight through me. "These two are not related?"

"Last I'd heard, it was Emeríann Daele and Forgall Tobeigh." I resist the urge to acknowledge Greig beside me, or bash his skull with the heavy lamp sitting on her desk. "Still, I can assure you that you've received inaccurate information. Need I remind you of the ice cream incident?"

"It's early still for jokes, Walleus. If you're positive, you need to make sure he's aware of how this looks and what will happen if he continues to operate this way. Now that Greig has dispatched with that vile rebel Forgall Tobeigh–"

"Whoa, hold on." I sit upright. "Greig said he took out Tobeigh?" I look from Morrigan's blank face to Greig's smug smile.

"Is this a surprise to you?"

I've wanted to bury this bastard. And now I know how.

"Only because it was so easy for Greig to take Tobeigh out, since Greig has so little field training." I motion for her to continue.

"Given that there is the potential for another

uprising, we will disseminate a story that he was killed by one of his own because he had been secretly relaying information to the Tathadann, but we expect a reaction to his death regardless. The rebels have already threatened to disrupt Macuil's dedication ceremony and I need not tell you what will happen if they do."

I clear my throat, compose myself. Actually, I won't bury him. I'll let him hang himself. "Can I ask what proof you have of Henraek in this? Do you have any photos linking them?" Greig starts to speak but I talk over him. "Because I find it interesting that Greig could have such sensitive information about this bombing, especially given that the men who are supposedly the architects – Henraek and Tobeigh – were highly trained rebels who thrived on secrecy."

Her head tips slightly to the side. She's listening.

"So if this information is as reliable as you say it is – and I'm still on the record as saying it's useless at best and contrived at worst – then I would reckon it could only be gathered by someone close, someone who has intimate access to the architects." Finally, I look over to Greig. He clasps his hands, then repositions them, crossing and uncrossing his leg. He is so ready to tear into me.

"Intimate is one way to describe it." He reaches into his jacket and produces a grip of photos, dropping them on Morrigan's desk. "This is a complete broach in protocol and amounts to treason. Belousz and his superior," he says, looking at me, "should both be brought before a tribunal."

She snatches the photos from the desk and examines them. Her nostrils curl up, like he's handed her a carcass left out in the sun. She regards me with a sideways glance, holds them up for me to see as well. I close my eyes and press my thumb and forefinger against the lids, as if this is the hardest thing for me to accept. I feel a tear well beneath the skin and it takes me by surprise.

"It's true, ma'am, Belousz was with Forgall Tobeigh. Quite frequently, and for the last two weeks."

"I wouldn't begin to tell you how to govern, Lady Morrigan," Greig says, "but I doubt the people would balk at a decree for these two to be stripped. Especially given that this has been going on for two weeks, and so close to the anniversary."

"Two weeks, Walleus?" she says.

"Two weeks, ma'am." I steeple my fingers, clear my throat, and blink a few times. Don't break, Walleus. Don't you dare break. "In my experience – and, Greig, that includes six years under the purview of Lady Morrigan and another ten before I saw the light – it's incredibly difficult to gain the confidence of a source quickly without them suspecting you and providing whitewashed intel, rendering the entire operation useless."

Greig's face pales.

"Source?" they both say.

"Yes. Source." I blot my forehead with a handkerchief. "I took your advice to heart, ma'am, and decided that instead of relying solely on Henraek to infiltrate the rebel cells, I would recruit Belousz to go deep cover. Which he did," I gesture to the photos, "until Greig went and ruined that."

"Why wasn't I notified?" she says.

"It was a quick operation and, obviously, required a high level of secrecy and trust. Young Greig here, ambitious as he is, has shown he can't play well with others. And I sure as hell don't trust him. For all I know, he took out Tobeigh because he is the leak and he's protecting himself." I clear my throat. "I made an executive decision for the safety of my team to keep this one close to the chest. I apologize for leaving you in the dark."

The room hums with silence, all the commotion outside not more than a whisper.

She holds up the photo of Henraek and Emeríann. "What of this one? Is this another operation you've yet to tell me of?"

"I told you he could do it, we just needed some time. Judging from the size and shape, I'd wager that's a liquor cabinet, given they're headed into a bar."

Greig speaks up. "That's now two rebel sympathizers Walleus is tied to."

"No," she says, her voice so sharp I can nearly hear the air part in front of me. "You killed one of them. The other is useless without Tobeigh."

He bows his head, like he's actually deferring to her. "My apologies, Lady Morrigan. I was acting in the best interest of the Tathadann and Eitan. If everything were running above board, as I run my operations–"

"You have no operations, son," I say. "I give you tasks."

He purses his lips. "If we were all notified, this source would still be active. However, it was a well-intentioned operation and one that could have been used to obtain a large amount of intelligence on the rebels. Despite our difference in opinions, Protectorate Blaí is a good leader and I have learned a lot from him. I have become very good at my job under his supervision." He pauses, maybe for dramatics or to let me crap my pants in surprise at getting a compliment from him, in front of her no less. "Which is how, in addition to uncovering Belousz, I recently gathered information that none other than Daghda Morrigan plans on returning to Eitan City."

Morrigan's eyes ricochet to mine. I let her stew for a couple breaths. The noose is set around his neck. Now I make the floor disappear and hope like hell this memory can be verified.

"It's an amazing feat, I'll give it to him. He probably would've come back early for his nephew's funeral today too." I nod at Greig, whose apparent confusion leads me to believe he didn't know Daghda and Forgall were kin. "Except Daghda died five years ago."

Greig's face goes completely white. Morrigan's is stone blank.

I pull the viewer out of my jacket and set it in front of her, then hit play. "We found this memory on the network."

It's subtle, but her expression does change. At first it's something like spite or revulsion, but as she lowers herself into her chair, it softens into a sadness that's been battened down beneath years of anger and bitterness. The moment makes her uncomfortably human.

"I'd reckon that I could identify the reason for all this miscommunication," I say to Morrigan. "It would be a lack of focus, from having one eye on my seat and the other on my back, looking for somewhere to rest a knife."

"This is in fact the problem," she says, still looking at the screen. "You can't have your men's eyes going in two different directions. It's impossible."

"It's a figure of speech."

"It's attention to detail, and the lack of it here." She sets the viewer down and pushes it back to me, then leans back and assesses us like cattle. "Greig, you will be accompanied on all operations by a senior field scout of my choosing and submit extra logs with all observations verified by that scout. Walleus, you will clear everything – and I mean everything – with me first. There will be no dark operations. I will see to it that someone else investigates these rumors of Daghda."

"Ma'am," I say, "you saw that he's dead."

"This cannot be altered memory, or hallucination from too much Paradise? Have you seen his body?" Her expression is blank but I can see the anger roiling behind that purple-tinted skin. "Attention to detail, Walleus. I will make one of you an example. It's up to you to decide who it is."

I swallow hard, nod.

"And if no one decides, I'll kill you all and start over," she says. "Have Belousz report immediately for a debriefing. I want to know everything he learned from Tobeigh about the attack." She turns away, ending the discussion.

"Thank you for your time," Greig says, giving a slight bow before pushing his chair toward the desk.

Blood crashes against the inside of my face. I wait for him to start toward the door before I move, making sure he can't snake his way further into her graces.

She calls my name before I reach the door. "You've been a loyal asset to the Tathadann for many years," she says. "Both I and the Promhael recognize that."

"Thank you. I'm glad–"

"But that won't save you from the firing squad if you don't resolve this immediately."

I nod. "I know."

I push the door open and see four of myself in the hallway mirrors. As I walk toward the exit they disappear; I wonder if it's a trick of perspective or a suggestion.

Greig stands before one mirror, smoothing back his hair in a compulsive way, like he's willing his pulse back to normal. I stand behind him, watching the reflection of his hand go over the same spot repeatedly.

"I've got a hangover, so I'll give you this one," I say. "Next time you go over my head, I'll shoot off your kneecaps so you can't reach so high."

"Walleus, you ever think I'm not reaching higher, but you're sinking lower? Oh wait, maybe I am rising. After all, I'm the one who took out the legendary Forgall Tobeigh, right?" He smooths back the same piece of hair. "I'm going to bury you."

"I would love to see you try."

"You think you're so smart, don't you, old man? Undercover operations? Insinuating that I'm working with the rebels? We both know you're a rat. You've always been one," he says.

"And you've always been a spoiled shit who lives off his father's heroics."

"Your kind is a relic," Greig says. "You don't have the constitution for this anymore. It's only a matter of time before you expire, so you should do the honorable thing and step aside before someone really gets hurt. This is our war now."

Then he lets loose with a smile, adjusting his collar and smoothing the front of his shirt, and in his teeth I see the tombstones of all the men I fought with, men with conviction and spirit and more balls than this little snake who has found his way into my yard. His smile grows, knowing he has my goat.

I slam his face against the mirror. Spiderweb cracks spread, a smear of blood tinting the hundred shards of my reflection. He falls to a knee, cupping his nose.

For some reason, I don't kick him. Instead, I continue toward the entranceway.

"I warned you," he shouts behind me.

I leave the droids to clean up his blood.

25.
HENRAEK

Rows of two-foot metal tubes wind from the concrete floor, small control modules sitting at the bases before the tubes twist up forty feet, passing through a bank of filters then disappearing in the ceiling where they'll meet three more levels like this. A metal walkway sits atop girders, crisscrossing the space above the ten gleaming silver vats that line the central path, five to the left and five to the right. Each could hold thousands of gallons of processed water, but are likely only filled by whatever condensation drips down to the bottom. There's no longer reason to store water, because as soon as it's processed in the area beneath us, it's diverted out to the Tathadann neighborhoods that paid the most for the privilege. At the far end of the plant sits a larger bank of dials, levers, and knobs, a mix of localized controls and read-outs for the electrical capacitors one floor beneath us that store the power the plant runs on. The control panel for the entire operation sits inside an office in the northwest corner of the plant, separated from this space but connected by eight surveillance cameras that feed into a series of display monitors beside the guards' desk. It's fascinating that the Tathadann has manufactured a startling number of technological and biomedical advances, yet their water depends on systems that are more than one hundred and fifty years old.

I think to point that out to Emeríann, but she is twenty-five feet in the air, legs wrapped around a walkway pole while her outstretched arm is precariously balanced above the surveillance camera, trying to slip on a circular resampling device, something akin to a closed-circuit video recorder that endlessly loops. It's not a perfect patch because, if someone watches beyond the duration of the sample, they'll see a quick glitch when the sample restarts. But it's good enough for three minutes of uninterrupted work, which is about all we can hope for. She slips the base over the housing of the final camera then activates it, and from the way her body relaxes, I can tell she's done it without jarring the set-up and alerting the workers above to our presence. Eight cameras housed, no eyes on us.

The maps for the plant – however ill-gotten – have been essential to this job. Without them, we would not have known where to stand, which pilings to scale to remain unseen, which tubes run outside of the plant into the surrounding neighborhood and thereby will carry an electrical pulse all the way down. Without them, we would likely have already been caught and trussed up on wooden crosses, preparing to be stripped. It's only appropriate that we will use these maps against the people who made them.

Despite all that, I feel a selfish twinge that I'm not the one who secured the maps without anyone's help.

"You here to look pretty or are you going to help?"

I blink and Emeríann is already down from the walkway and hunkered beneath a set of tubes, attaching a pulse-charge.

"I was actually looking for the bar, but they don't appear to be too accommodating." I pull a set of wires from my bag and kneel beside her, instinctively reaching out to attach them but reminding myself to pull back, that she is completely competent and I should start hooking up the atomizers instead of supervising. But something about her hands – the way they twist the ends of the wire from the wrist, the way they massage the dial as she calibrates the pulse frequency for maximum conductivity – is mesmerizing, bordering on arousing. Or maybe that's a product of the context and a dysfunction on my part.

Whatever it is, I have to consciously tell myself to get moving before we're spotted. "You're amazing," I say to her.

"You're wasting time." She looks up at me, puffs the hair off her face, flashes a smile. "We have two minutes left."

I can't argue with that. I whip the bag off my

shoulder and retrieve the atomizers, start doubling them up on the predetermined walkway posts, then fasten the delay charges to the other posts. All of these are synched with the detonator, one single red button. I thought Walleus was screwing with me the first time he showed me one. I told him it looked straight out of a cartoon, but the heat from the explosion it triggered singed my eyebrows. After we press the button, the pulses will fire and short all the sensors on the way out, disabling the water flow, right as the secondary posts disintegrate, all of which will be followed by the ground level floor falling out. We will take it down from the inside, then destroy the outside for good measure.

One. Big. Boom.

Emeríann finishes with the last of the pulse-charges and crawls out from beneath the gaggle of tubes. She cracks her neck left and right, stretches her arms over her head.

"All set?"

"All set." She checks her timer. "With ten seconds to spare."

"They're all sequenced?"

"You want to check?" She plays with a smile, letting it shift from strained to coy to unsure.

I sling the bag back over my shoulders and fish the detonator out of my pocket. Something catches my eye in the periphery but flickers away before I can focus. An insect or something that has found its way in here. "Just making sure. We can't unpush the button."

"We're never unpushing this button." She sniffs hard. "Do it. We need to move."

I take in the detonator, not so much worn out as well used. I run my thumb over the button, try to remember the last time I pushed it, what we bombed and how long the report echoed inside my head. I taste grit in my teeth, smell a phantom tendril of powder and wood fire.

"You're doing it again," she says.

I look up at her, toss the detonator. "This is your job. You planned it, you get to push it."

The smile's real this time, irrepressible. "One minute?"

"Forty-five seconds to a minute. We're not working with high-grade explosives here."

"Then let's get out in thirty," she says, and it's not until she says thirty that I realize the flash is not an insect. It's a reflection. A resampling of a reflection. Because the resampling device slipped off the camera housing and is now trained on the reflection of a vat.

"Why are you still standing here?" she says, shoving me toward the door.

"Emeríann," I say, and the tube next to my head pings twice.

"What the hell?" She looks around. Then there's a zipping sound and a drizzle of blood lands on her face.

My right shoulder is white hot. A flash of electricity radiates down my arm, up my neck, lighting up every synapse along its path. I snatch at her with my other arm and pull her into cover behind the tangle of tubes, search inside the bag for my pistol.

The guards shout a warning then fire more shots.

She kneels beside me, staying behind the tube, and tells me to stop moving so she can look at my shoulder. "Flesh wound," she says, replacing the torn and bloody fabric of my jacket.

"Sure as hell doesn't feel like it." I can't aim with my left arm.

"You'll be fine." She reaches behind her and produces a pistol, leans around the tubes and fires a few times. One of the guards screams something about his knee. "You OK to move?"

"I'm fine. Where did you learn to shoot a gun?"

She glances around the tube again, fires twice more, though it seems more to keep the guards back than to hurt them. "I didn't tell you I grew up in the bogs?"

"No, you've never told me that." My hand touches metal inside the bag. I pull out my pistol.

"Oh," she says, popping off one more shot. "Well, I did. All kinds of stuff to shoot out there."

"That's lovely. We need to go. Now."

"Then stopping complaining," she says, before yanking me up to my feet. My shoulder throbs but I squeeze hard on the handle of my gun to focus. "I'll cover. Move."

When she dips around and fires, I jump out and sprint for the door, crouching low as I can, given I only have one arm to maintain balance, and duck between the bundles of tubes. Behind a vat, I spin around and level the pistol to cover her. As she comes toward me, the guard steps out and trains his sights on her. I pull the trigger half a dozen times. Two land, his chest and neck exploding in red. Lucky shot. Both of them are down.

Then I hear a ticking noise.

"Oh no."

The pulse-charges.

"Go!" I scream at Emeríann.

She sprints toward the door that opens into the hallway. More ticking. More charges sequencing. More concrete and rebar about to rain from the heavens. She hits the door so hard it knocks her off her feet, the glass window nearly shattering as it swings back and slams against the wall. The cameras pan across and I almost laugh. A heavy hiss behind us, the atomizers warming, building up the energy that will make the posts disappear.

I scoop her up and we round the corner and find the young guard standing in the middle of the hallway. She should still be out cold. Her gun is raised, her hand trembling.

"Look, kid," I say, "we've about ten seconds to get out of here before–"

A crack. My ears ring. A red splash at the base of her neck. The poor girl collapses on the ground, screaming and writhing. Emeríann is still in position, hands aimed, steady.

"What the hell, Em?" I start toward the girl, out of

instinct, but stop myself. Emeríann lowers her gun. "She wasn't going to shoot us. She's a kid."

"Her choices affect other people's lives too." She sniffs, swallows. "She's old enough to know that."

The girl's screaming has faded into whimpering grunts, fear and pain sluicing between her gritted teeth. Her fingers are pressed against her neck, coated with blood. "Please," she says, "please." The floor is smeared beneath her.

"We can't leave her here, she'll be crushed," I say. "That's a terrible way to die." I press my fingers against my eyes. I don't vocalize it, but I know we can't take her with us and she's going to die anyway. "Dammit," I yell, then pop out my clip to make sure I have enough bullets, and when I look up Emeríann has her gun trained on the girl. I say, "Em, I can," and there's another crack. The girl's head slaps against the floor. The hole in the middle of her face is shiny and red, framed with jagged edges of bone.

A loud hiss behind us, then a rumbling, the patter of concrete chunks hitting concrete floor, the keening of iron bars bending under tons of metal and tile and tubing. A cloud of dust beginning to form, particles of walkway posts and dust swirling.

No time to mourn this girl. It's happening.

I grab Emeríann's arm. We sprint.

Twenty feet.

A ferrous scream as the walkways tear free from their moorings and collide mid-air.

Ten feet.

A sizzling, electric roar as the charges ignite and disperse their energy.

Doorway.

We explode into the street, hurry across with hands covering our heads, hunks of the building falling down around us. I wager a quick look back. The façade of the plant is poked through with holes, giant swathes of brick and mortar tearing away from the sides and falling inward, a faint glow emanating from the lower levels where the metal burns so bright it evaporates. I feel the building's rumbling roar inside my chest as if it's pumping my blood.

We run until the streets become choked with people. Signs held aloft. Effigies on poles. Chanting. Shouting. Assembling. The plumes of dust and debris are visible even from a dozen blocks away.

"What the hell is going on?" I yell to her.

Emeríann falls on me, her face flushed, slick with sweat. Ecstatic. "The distraction."

She pounds on my chest, crushes her lips against mine for what seems like years, then pulls away and raises her hands over her head and screams.

Catharsis.

She starts singing. Down near the river where our brothers bled. The man next to us hears her and joins in. Another. Another. Another. Soon she climbs on top of a car, calling people to her with her arms, her voice. A siren song. I knelt on the bank and my father said. Someone nudges my arm. I turn to find Nael, one of our old bombmakers.

"You should come with us," he says. "You're going to want to watch this."

Emeríann starts another verse, the crowd singing so loud I can't hear the rest of what he says. At the chorus, the volume doubles. Hundreds, thousands of voices becoming one singular, massive entity.

I yell, "I need to stay here," but he screams something that looks like, What?

I point at the crowd and he gets the idea, slapping my injured shoulder before heading off with four other men. Any pain is quickly blurred by adrenaline. Emeríann stands on the car's roof, arms aloft, head back, throat elongated. Resplendent.

"This is our land, all that you can touch, and we'll water our crops with Tathadann blood."

26.
WALLEUS

More and more I'm finding myself in the car with no place to go and I wonder if there's something to Henraek's talk about unmoored spirits and all that.

Even though heading back to the Gallery is as undesirable as getting drunk with Goerde and all his buddies, I find myself telling the car to drive in that direction by force of habit. As soon as I realize what I'm doing, I tell it to turn left and drive in the opposite direction, as far away as possible from the Tathadann's personal influence on me. Petty, maybe, but I'm not in the frame of mind to give a shit at the moment.

Belousz is dead. Greig is likely plotting, looking for some way to exhume that seed of doubt planted in the Old Lady before it can bloom into a stochae with his name on it to be stacked alongside everyone else who has been stripped. And the old woman? She's probably drinking fetus-soul tea or whatever it is she does to keep her alive. I seriously doubt she's going to find anything more about Daghda – seeing that it took four of my men a couple days to find one small memory, and I don't expect she'll want to be publicly seen looking for him. This coup, though, this one I'm holding tight to my chest until I see how it shakes out – figure out if I'm a hero to Morrigan for my keen intelligence gathering that prevented a revolt that would fracture the party, or a leader of the new party that will stand on the ashes of the old Tathadann. Or a new resident of some country far away from here if the whole thing collapses and the rebels take over. I think of the hill-people who keep showing up.

Either way, I don't feel like going to the Gallery.

Donael and Cobb are still in school, but regardless, much as I love them, I don't really feel like hanging out with them and Donael is still too young to share his first beer, lest he develops a taste and turns out like me and Henraek. And Henraek, he's probably tying one on with Emeríann and her people, though I hope they keep it out of the scouts' range. I wouldn't be the least bit surprised to find him beat to hell tomorrow because one of them called him a traitor and he wouldn't let it pass. His pride is matched only by his stubbornness.

I was always the more rational of us, the one who could sniff out an angle and reason my way through a situation without letting emotion make everything go tits up. Sometimes that meant swallowing my pride when the situation needed it. Like when Henraek goes into his poor-me rants about the son he didn't pay much attention to in the first place and I sit and take it without comment. He called me cold and calculating; I preferred to think of myself as pragmatic. Henraek, though, that stubborn bastard would chew through his own coffin to avenge his death. I'd always thought of myself as tough – present physique notwithstanding – but that son of a bitch had some internal drive that destroyed any normal person's understanding of strength. I was honestly surprised he didn't overthrow the Tathadann by pure will alone.

So out of everyone I know, there are exactly zero people I can turn to. Forgall had a field of people there to remember him. It didn't matter if he knew them or not because they are kin to him.

And here I am, with my car and some food wrappers and an old bottle I should have thrown away weeks ago. The bar is the only place I can go where there are people who aren't trying to kill me and I don't feel like dealing with a hangover again.

After a thirty-minute looping and meandering drive, my car pulls into the driveway and I slouch my way to the house. As soon as I push the door open, the kids rush toward me.

"Oh my god, you're not dead!" Donael throws himself against me.

"No, I'm not." I hold him tight to me. Cobb hobbles off the couch, clicking like a maniac. "Why aren't you in school?" It takes a minute for what he said to sink in. "Why would I be dead?"

"I'm so glad you're home." His voice is muffled, speaking into my chest. Cobb reaches us and I bring him into the fold.

"Donael." I say his name again but he doesn't respond and I nearly have to pry him off to get an acknowledgment. "What happened?"

Donael points at the television. On the screen is a banner that reads Rebels Strike! and a live stream of the water distribution plant up in Fomora, a smoldering pile of rubble and steel beams jutting out at odd angles. Ropes of black smoke connect the heavens to the bombed out carcass. A close-up shows two lonely fire trucks with hoses, spraying chemicals to try to keep it under control. Two figures come up behind it and cut the supply hose with an axe. The TV switches to a shot of the Gallery – which actually looks worse than the water plant, if that was possible.

"They blew up your work," he says, finally disconnected from me. "Everyone got sent home early from school and there's no water." I heft Cobb up on my hip and we all go to the couch.

The newscaster with a politician's haircut and aspirations says that the rebels have claimed responsibility for the attacks, citing the recent murder of one of their members. The screen switches to a couple amadans with bandanas tied around the lower halves of their faces, yelling rebel slogans so loud and vehemently that you can't understand what any of them are saying.

"It's starting again, isn't it?" Donael says.

"No, sweetheart, it's OK." The boys huddle close to me and I pat their backs to reassure them that I'm here and not dead. "This is a couple idiots who have nothing better to do."

I try not to show my excitement at watching the Gallery burn. Damn if that ain't a beautiful sight. Wonder if Emeríann launched their plan early to honor Forgall's memory, or if this is a good old-fashioned riot. I wish I had a live feed of the old woman's face right now, could sit back with some popcorn and watch.

This is the opportunity I should have been looking for a long time ago. I've kowtowed to the Tathadann's wishes for too long. Morrigan doesn't care about me. Greig is trying to take me down. This isn't going to help.

What I need to do is talk to Henraek and Emeríann. With all I know about Tathadann operations, I could inform the rebellion and maybe, between their balls and my brains, we could actually take down this iron beast. Pick up where we left off, do something good for a change. Make the city a better place for Donael and Cobb.

With the thought of being able to take the boys to Hoeps matches and go see Donael play in his own without fear of being caught in crossfire, set up a campsite out near the hills and show them both what a real picnic is without keeping constant watch for tripwires or ignition devices, I feel the blood course through my head, my arms and hands and fingers, my whole chest opening with the lightness of possibility.

And then it rushes out through my feet, my chest collapsing and shattering and debris spreading under the weight of realization.

If the Tathadann was gone, there'd be nothing separating my and Henraek's lives and – oh, shitting hell – there would be nothing to keep Donael and Henraek apart. As soon as the great beast falls, so falls my family. Our movie nights and popcorn breakfasts, every first day of school and Donael's first girlfriend, teaching him how to clean a pistol and giving him advice on how to meet his love's parents and watching them walk into their own house. And, and, and.

Without the Tathadann, there is no Donael. They brought him into my life, and their destruction – their absence – will rip him away.

Henraek has to fail. The rebellion has to fail. For my son, for my family, it has to fail.

I have to help the Tathadann, Morrigan, Greig win. I lock my knees so I won't collapse in front of the boys and lay my hands on their shoulders. I need to feel them.

I need a drink.

The report switches back to the water plant. The newscaster speaks over a clip showing the smoldering building, saying officials have an explanation: the rebels are inciting riots on the basis that the man Forgall Tobeigh was murdered by Tathadann soldiers. However, Tobeigh, who was thought to be a major architect of the plot to bomb the water distribution infrastructure, had in actuality been leaking information to a Tathadann operative for several weeks. At least they got that in.

"Why are they doing this?" Donael says. "What does cutting off everyone's water prove?"

"Nothing," I say. "It's selfish and damaging to everyone." I wonder who I'm talking about.

A grainy photo flashes up on the screen and my stomach drops out my asshole. Greig's surveillance. Henraek and Emer carrying the bomb-that-can't-be-a-bomb across the street.

I see Donael squinting at the picture. It cuts back to the newscaster, but it's too late.

"That was my dad," Donael says. "Is that from today?"

"No, it wasn't. That must have been an old picture or something." My skull is suddenly too large for my skin. My body is on fire.

"They said it was the people who bombed the water thing."

"Then it wasn't him." Another photo flashes up on the screen, this one an establishing shot of Johnstone's, and in the left corner is a man who looks a hell of a lot like Belousz, leaning on a lamppost, staring inside the bar. "It wasn't a clear picture anyway. Look at that one. You can't tell anything from them."

"I know what he looks like," Donael says, turning to face me, his face flushed and eyes swelling. I swallow hard. "He's still alive? That's bullshit."

"Donael, watch your damn mouth. This is my house and you don't speak like that." My words come out brittle, my worst fears crashing down on me. If I tell him I'm his father, I shatter his world. If I tell him Henraek's his father, he'll hate me for the rest of his life for keeping them apart. If I lie to him, I'll hate myself but keep my son. "I saw his body, OK? It wasn't something I could ever forget. You want me to tell you about it? How the bomb tore off half his face? What all that bone looked like? All that skin hanging off and the way his eyes dripped down out of the socket? Trust me. You can't unsee that stuff. You're misremembering."

"I look at pictures of him and Mom every night before I sleep. I know what he looks like." He's almost screaming, his jaw tight. He's not Henraek's kid but goddamned if he doesn't look like him. Then in a flash he calms. No, not calms: he regroups. Recalculates. "The man said he shot them."

"No, I didn't – he didn't," I sputter, realizing I've just committed the worst mistake of my entire life. "I don't – they were talking about bombs. Who knows what he did to them? It doesn't matter how it happened. After we ran…" My mouth continues to flap but nothing comes out except a hollow click, and it takes a minute before I realize that clicking is Cobb.

The newscaster drones on about public reaction to the death and the bombing while a video clip plays and the room narrows to a pinpoint.

A lamppost divides the screen in half. Swarms of

citizens move on the street, a river of people. Some hold signs, some have torches. On the left side of the lamppost hangs the effigy of a short man with a pinstriped suit, a giant boar's head on his shoulders and a sash across his chest. They misspelled his name but I'd know Macuil Morrigan anywhere.

"Why the hell am I here?" Donael screams, tears streaming down his face.

But the swollen effigy on the right, it wears a white suit and has no hair.

He beats on my chest but I barely feel it, barely hear his voice. There's nothing but a hiss and white numbness pouring down a hole. "Why did you lie to me?"

The citizens hold the torches to the bottom of the effigies, setting them on fire. A wave of cheering washes over the street as my symbolic body burns. The newscaster comments on what a senseless display of destruction it is and how this unruly population should be dealt with swiftly and harshly.

"Where is my dad? I want to see my dad."

Donael collapses before me, his fists still pounding my legs, my feet. The clip ends, begins again. I die and I die and I die.

27.
HENRAEK

The chainsaw roaring through my skull this morning is not nearly as loud as I'd expected. All of the singing and shouting yesterday left my throat raw and my ears ringing, and my shoulder still throbs when I push myself upright, but all things considered I don't feel like the walking incarnation of slow death that I'd expected as we stumbled home from whatever bars we took over last night.

Emeríann lies with her arms flung over her face, her legs spread in a V. Silas is nestled between them, probably imagining he's a cat. I nudge him and shoo him away before he imagines his way into the oven.

The positive side of being a lightweight is that I can still somewhat move, though the floor does shift beneath my feet on my way to the bathroom. Given the architecture of this building, it might not be the alcohol.

Silas follows me into the kitchen to snack on crumbs then slips through the bars to rejoin his flock.

I turn on the faucet to get water and decontaminate my body, but there's nothing. Right. Water.

Echoing through the alleyway are rebel chants, as if we fell asleep and woke up ten years in the past. I'm leaning against the iron bars, listening, when Emeríann comes up behind me and wraps her hands around my stomach.

"I think I'm dying," she says.

"Look who's feeling sensitive now."

She breathes a small laugh and pats my chest. "Do you remember puking three times on the way home last night?"

I don't, but after feeling the acidic residue on my teeth, I can see how that would have happened. "I was shedding weight," I say. "Less to carry."

The phone rings and we both groan, Emeríann pressing her forehead into my back. When it stops, she retrieves some medicine she bought from a brigu woman who comes into Johnstone's. She asks for water and I can finally raise my eyebrow, give her that look. She closes her eyes and hangs her head a moment. We suck down the powder, follow it with a little hair of the dog. Praise be Nahoeg, it kicks in quickly and the urge to throw myself out the window to make the pain stop begins to subside.

Until the phone rings again.

I squint as I make my way over to it. "For the love of all that's holy, what?" I say.

Emeríann turns on the archaic television, letting it warm up.

"Oh good god, Henraek," a man says.

"Who is this?"

"Nael," he says. "Have you seen it?"

"Seen what?"

"What I wanted to show you yesterday," he says. "Turn on the news. See what you and Emeríann inspired."

Emeríann messes with the wires on the back of the ancient box, and when the picture finally tunes in, I see what used to be the Gallery lying in a pile of rubble. The word replay is in the top-left corner, and the newscaster says there are now twelve reported dead in Fomora as a result of the water plant bombing and authorities are evacuating certain buildings in order to demolish them in the hopes of stopping the spreading fire. I knew that would happen. I told her.

"Holy hell. You did that to the Gallery?"

"I had a little help," he says, that pride I remember from years ago edging into his voice. "But yeah, mostly me."

"Subtle as ever." The video switches to a collage of photos, one of Emeríann and me carrying furniture across the street. The newscaster says something about connections to a planned bombing. All I can do is shake my head.

"I called a couple times this morning. Wasn't sure if you two made it."

Emeríann sits in front of the television, almost touching the screen like a child, wanting to transport herself into the scene of the burning Gallery. "A little combat fatigue," I say, "but after some bland food we'll be ready."

"We found them," he says.

"Found who?"

"The guys who got Forgall."

No, you didn't. I did. Still, the best Tathadann is no Tathadann. "How do you know?"

"We took a couple guys aside during all the shenanigans and asked some questions." I can hear the euphemism in his voice. Nael and his men probably beat them to a bloody pulp. "We got a little carried away with creating a distraction for you two. One thing led to another. Then, well, you saw the rest on TV."

The screen broadcasts waves of people in the street, burning cars and effigies on the lampposts as Tathadann soldiers in riot gear line up in containment formation. One effigy looks strikingly like Walleus, which really makes me hope that he went home after the funeral. Then the video shifts to another effigy, this one dressed in fatigues and boots, and it takes a slow moment for me to realize that some of those aren't effigies, but actual bodies, hung from the posts and set ablaze. This is not the same revolution.

"Are you positive they are the ones who killed him?" Outside my window, the chanting has turned to singing. Down near the river where our brothers bled. Sirens wail in the background.

"The architect is still in the wind, but we're tracking him. Two of them were with him when it blew and the other five are garden variety Tathadann pricks."

They zoom in on the burning body, black globs of flame dripping from the man's fingers. They tarred him, then set him on fire, then hung him for all Eitan to see.

We didn't give the rebellion CPR, we jabbed a gigantic shot of adrenaline into its heart then rewired it with metal cylinders and violence. This rebellion already lacks the compassion and goodwill of the people's revolt at the dawn of the Struggle. There is no call for winning the hearts of the general citizenry, no admonitions against obtaining loyalty by force and coercion, which would mean we had sunk to their level. There is only the spilled blood of all who fought before us coming to a boil, mixing with the lessons of the past and a lack of concern for the future. There will be no one able to stop us, because this is not the old rebellion: this one can actually succeed.

"What do you need from me?" I say.

"We're waiting on your word," he says. "What should we do with them?"

Seven men who likely did nothing but wear the wrong uniform, sign their names on the wrong line. I look over at Emeríann, ragged as a raw nerve but vibrating with an energy I've never seen. There's no going back after this. I drew my lot when I told Emeríann I'd help her.

"Take them all," I say. "Put them up against the wall and shoot them."

"Roger, lieutenant." His smile is audible. "Good to

have you back."

I hang up.

"Get your boots," I say to Emeríann, pulling her in for a kiss. I can taste the damp wheat of last night's beer, the hotness of her breath. "This is it."

28.
WALLEUS

The phone startles me as I'm flipping a pancake and it lands on the ridge of the pan, half in and half out. Batter drips down the edge and burns in the gas flame. Cobb sits at the breakfast bar, idly drawing patterns in the pool of syrup on his plate. I don't know if he understood everything that happened last night, but he knows it's not good.

I don't even bother asking Donael to get me the phone. After I stonewalled him by watching the protestors burn my body over and over, he stormed off to his room, leaving a trail of holes punched in the wall and two broken glasses in his wake. At least he didn't knock over the liquor cabinet. I haven't seen him since and am trying to give him some space. Sure, he threatened to run away, but he's eleven. Where's he going to go?

I swallow twice before answering, smiling like an amadan with his first boner so they can hear it in my voice.

"She wants to see you," a woman says. I can't tell who's on the other end but I'm not sure it matters anyway. One is the same as all the rest.

"I'm caught up at the moment," I say, still smiling, "but I'll be over shortly."

"There will be a car to take you in twenty minutes."

"You don't need to do all that again. I can drive myself." And have my own method of escape.

"Have you been outside?" she says, then leaves me with dead air.

I drop the phone and, like it was a cue, the smoke alarm goes off. Cobb clicks like a broken bicycle wheel and runs in circles around the kitchen. I hurry to the range and throw a cover on the pan then wave a towel at the smoke to get it away from the alarm.

Cobb sits in the middle of the floor with his palms pressed so hard against his ears I can see the veins stand up on his forehead. I kneel down and scoop him up in my arms, repeating it's OK, it's OK, though he can't hear me through his hands.

I carry him into the bedroom and set him on the bed while I dress. With my back toward him I unclasp my father's necklace that my mother gave me when Henraek and I left Westhell County, pull off the gold rings Liella bought me for our first anniversary and the founding of the Struggle, then take all the money out of my pockets and tuck everything beneath my socks in the top dresser drawer. I rifle my closet for the cleanest white suit I can find. On the far right, shoved behind all my other suits in increasing order of status, is the first suit I wore. It was so white I was almost glowing. I pull it out, shake off the dust. Feel the current of all the talk I had when coming over pulse through the fabric, the way Morrigan and the Promhael hung on my words, the words I need to find to maneuver around her again.

I have to readjust tack. Turning things around on Greig won't work twice. Admitting that the memory could have been manufactured is admitting I've been duped – on top of this bombing that pretty much signs my name on a stochae since I vouched for Henraek. But I'm not going to beg her for anything. So maybe the trick is to not admit anything, to not kowtow. Come out with my balls swinging. Greig wants Daghda to be alive to show what a great scout he is and secure his place? Sure, Daghda's alive then, and he's coming to help facilitate a coup within the Tathadann. I don't particularly want to play that card yet, but my hand's getting forced. Greig sure as hell won't keep him away. Neither will the old woman. But Walleus will, like he's done for the last six years. And that shriveled bag is sure as hell going to know that.

There's a faint ripping sound. I bend my arm and examine the split seam up the forearm. This suit, lovely as it is, was made for me several years ago, when I had a different body. I peel it off like a used condom, throw it on the floor, and grab the closest suit that fits.

When I'm decent enough to meet the Old Woman, I bring Cobb to Donael's door. It's unlocked, probably from him going to the bathroom and forgetting to lock it. I knock once then open it without waiting for his response. Cobb scuttles over to his bed and climbs up next to Donael, who startles at our entrance, then pretends to look at a football magazine.

"I have to go out," I say. "If it takes a little while for me to get back, there's money in my top drawer."

He turns a page and it rips.

"Donael, listen to me." I lay my hand on his knee and am surprised he doesn't slap it. "If you need food or anything else and I'm not here, look in my top drawer. Underneath my socks. Right side. Cobb won't be able to get anything by himself. He needs you with him."

He continues to stare at the magazine.

"I'm sorry, but I have to go."

Still no response.

I suck in my lips. "I know you're upset. You're angry. You're heartbroken. I get that. But you need to understand something." I kneel beside his bed. He won't meet my eyes but doesn't turn away. "I love you. And no matter who it hurt, or how bad it hurt, I would do anything for you. For both of you."

In what seems to take a month of full moons, he raises his head to look at me.

"Fuck you," he says.

I close my eyes and nod, try to absorb everything positive about the room in case I don't make it back from the meeting.

"I love you boys."

29.
HENRAEK

As we go to leave for our meet-up with Nael, I find an envelope sitting on the floor inside the door. It is pristine white with no name on it, two light fingerprints in dirt. Must have come when we were passed out because I didn't hear anything. I bend down to grab it and see the vials I took from Belousz on the ground near the couch. I remember leaving them in the bedroom, but the viewer is on its crate, so I assume I tried to watch these and passed out first. Only an inordinate amount of luck kept our drunken asses from crushing these. Or maybe it was the hand of Providence. If anyone knows who to murder in order to take down the Tathadann, it would be this asshole.

I cup the vials in my hand, not sure of how to turn.

"Who are they?" she says.

I taste metal, sawdust.

"It has to do with Aífe." She doesn't need to ask it.

She already knows.

"The guy who made sure it was done." I go to set them down on the table but Emeríann grabs my arm.

"You're home," she says, "so I'm here. I want to watch it with you."

"I can do this later."

"We need to go and you're wasting time."

She takes the vial and inserts it. I turn over the envelope in my hands.

"Who's that from?" she says.

"Don't know. No markings, no postal information." The paper itself is silken, almost iridescent in quality. "I don't see many pieces of paper like this outside of Clodhna."

I slip my finger inside to tear open the top, but stop when I see Aífe's face in the memory viewer's steam. A fist forms in my throat. Emeríann takes the envelope from me.

Seeing Aífe this close is seeing her again for the first time. The gauntness of her cheeks. The wild river of veins that branches through her eyes. The dark circles beneath them. I don't remember her looking this exhausted since the months after Donael was born, but there is something else about her, a cornered-animal look, the sort of desperation I rarely saw outside of a battlefield. I listen to my breathing for as long as I can stand myself then hit play.

She stands before Mebeth, hip cocked, pointing her finger. Belousz sighs. "Not one more word from me until then."

"And how exactly do you plan to force my hand? Coercion? Blackmail?" Mebeth looks at Belousz and Toman and snorts a laugh. "You are in over your head, dear. This is not your battle. You do not belong here."

"You're right. I don't." She stalks closer to him, her voice dropping in the manner that always preceded an explosion. I find myself leaning forward and consciously straighten my spine, and though I'm curious as to her expression, I avoid looking over at Emeríann. This is old, Henraek. This is an immutable and irreversible past. Moving on with your life is not the same as erasing your history. "So end it."

"This is something bigger than you and I, Aífe. You should know this. You have lived it for years. It is in your food and your clothes. You carry its burden in your eyes, in your heart. Every bit you confess unburdens your mind, allows you to relax, to become present and stop worrying. You relieve the heaviness in your soul, in the soul of your boys, in–"

"You don't know what's inside me," she screams, slamming the chair down, and the mention of me in this context sets my skin on fire. Belousz adjusts the newspaper on the table as if he's impatient.

Mebeth remains impassive, waiting for her to finish. When she does, he says, "Then you must tell me. Dates, times, locations."

This sends her into another fit, something between crying and screaming. I have to turn down the viewer because the sound distorts.

"What is he talking about?" Emeríann says. "Dates, times?"

"Appointments, maybe? He was our doctor. She was seeing him at one point," I gesture absently, "in a psychiatric facility."

"Appointments?" The look she gives could scald the hair off a rat. "You really don't understand women at all, do you?"

"Well, what else could it be?" I turn up the volume before she can answer, a tingling, sinking feeling snaking through my body. Aífe jabs her finger at Mebeth, but seems incredibly aware that she cannot touch him. Watching her face contort like this, skin flushed with anger, makes me as nostalgic as it does disgusted. Before Emeríann implied Aífe might be no better than Walleus – might be worse than Walleus – I had never once entertained the thought. And now, watching her yell and scream and argue with him about the nineteenth of September, the place beyond Fomora, ten men or less, I cannot see anything but Emeríann's insinuations here.

But it could not be true, because she would never do that. We would argue and slam doors and once, in a dark period when the tactics the Tathadann used against us turned especially horrific and I slunk about for a depraved few months, she came after me with a kitchen knife while Donael was upstairs napping. One of my men had pitched the idea of bombing the nursery where a number of Tathadann officials sent their children and I didn't shut him down immediately,

even going so far as to ask Aífe what she thought of
the idea. The knife was meant to get me out of my
own head, and the thin cut on my neck was my fault
because I kept stepping forward into the blade, trying
to bring her down to my level.

And then she says, "Because your men would have
been slaughtered at the power plant if I hadn't told
you," and thousands of hot needles poke into my
temples, a band of razor wire tightening around my
head.

I hit pause. I do not rewind though I need to hear it
to confirm it, but I'm positive what she said. Emeríann
breathes heavily beside me. I can hear the contractions
of the muscles in her throat when she swallows.
Outside the window, thousands of miles away, crowds
sing and chant. Inside my chest, thousands of fathoms
beneath the darkness, something snaps.

Emeríann's hand trembles as she extends it. She
does not look to me for an OK, for consent, though
still she pauses a few seconds before hitting play.

A fissure develops in Aífe's wall of fury. It's a fleeting
moment, but there if you know where to look.

She sniffs hard, only once. Then her composure
returns to granite. "You end this and bring my
husband back home," she says, "and I will tell you
everything you want to know."

Emeríann doesn't bother to hit stop this time before
she stands and walks into the bedroom. The room
around me vibrates with emptiness. My dead wife
is the rat. Not Walleus. But he had to know. That's

why he'd never answer me when I asked about when he turned. How did he know? Did Mebeth tell him? Aífe?

"I just want Henraek back," Aífe says. "I need my husband. Donael needs his dad. Four months ago, you swore to me that he'd be back."

"Well, maybe you should not have trusted me," Mebeth says, offering a vague smile before standing to go inside the café. Belousz nods to Toman then follows behind. They wind through the lightly populated tables, and even having seen all that I have seen in the last fifteen years I still cannot believe that twelve people watched a woman get shot at point-blank range and did nothing. They didn't even pause to wipe their mouths.

A loud pop beyond the glass. Aífe dies again. I don't know if I want to save her.

I startle as Emeríann appears beside me. She grabs my hand, hits pause, and takes a long breath before speaking. "Riab never wanted to fight. I pushed him to do it, told him it'd make his children proud."

"I don't want to talk about this."

"He was scared of dying, said it wouldn't be right to leave me alone in the house. I told him that if he thought I couldn't take care of myself, he was as good as dead to me." She sniffs hard. "I wanted him around, not needed, and he had to understand the difference. I was young, you know? Hot blooded. Still at the age where you believed things like that mattered."

"Why are you telling me this?"

"Because she's not your fault."

"I never said that."

"Who are you talking to, Henraek?" She gives a half smile. I notice a small white scar, almost star shaped, beside her eye that I'd never seen before. "I cried for two years before I realized that. He could've said no, and we would've fought, and made up, and gone about our lives. But he didn't. You could've gone home, given up what you believed in, but you didn't. And that's it."

We sit for a minute before she squeezes my hand then hits play. She picks up the envelope from the floor and opens it with her finger.

Mebeth pops an olive in his mouth and exhales as he chews, then pushes open a heavy wooden door with silver rings for a handle, entering a small kitchen. Belousz waits in the doorway. Gleaming pots and pans hang on the walls. A cook chops a mound of vegetables on a marble counter. A Tathadann man stands behind one of the butcher's blocks scattered throughout, flanked by a cosanta, a bodyguard. There are several large hooks hanging from the ceiling in the middle of the room, three of which hold a slab of salted ham. A drain sits in the middle of the floor, a hose coiled on the right-hand wall.

And standing behind the far butcher's block is a young Walleus. That duplicitous cocksucker. I knew he was hiding something. He always knew about Aífe. He had to. His white suit is sharply tailored, probably bespoke, his bald head polished as ever. This was when they were still showing him how lush the Tathadann life was. He and Belousz exchange a look, but I can't get a read on it.

"They are finished," Mebeth says. "Take care of him then prepare a meal. Cheese, olives, something of that ilk. But nothing heavy. It's hot outside and I don't want indigestion."

Walleus looks down and holds out a hand, the cosanta doing the same, and they pull up Donael between them.

My chest seizes. Emeríann gasps, whispers oh my god over and over.

His eyes project abject terror, his face dirty, his lips tinted blue by candy.

My lungs are too heavy for my bones.

He is alive. He was alive in the kitchen of the restaurant where his mother was murdered not fifty feet from him.

I try to breathe but choke. My throat is swollen with loss.

And he is alive, but I have seen this before. As soon as Mebeth closes the door there will be two shots. Why didn't Walleus stop him?

"How do you want it?" the Tathadann man says.

Mebeth points at the hooks, then shrugs. "You decide."

Mebeth closes the door then turns and takes an orange slice from the tray. Grunting and a clipped yelp in the kitchen. Belousz nods to Toman and they head toward the door.

In the background are gunshots. Two claps that echo through my hollow chest.

Emeríann breaks down in choking tears. The taste of metal and bile fills my mouth. I kick the viewer off its perch. The image fizzles out.

Walleus knew. He knew? The entire time. Months, years. Mornings we got coffee, I mourned my son and he knew. Afternoons at the pub, pouring beer and liquor down my throat, letting it stoke the agony and anger that burned in my gut, and he knew. Days upon days upon days I walked around in a self-loathing, self-destructive fog, wanting to die but not having the courage to kill myself, absorbing the pain of the hundreds and hundreds of lives I'd destroyed, and he knew my son had been murdered.

And he did nothing to stop it.

"Henraek," she says.

Even if there was nothing he could do, he should have done something. Anything.

"Henraek," she says again, and in the lilting tone of her voice I can already hear insinuation. She was right with Aífe, but she cannot be right about Walleus. She's right but she can't be.

"Henraek," she says, louder this time, but I see a flash, a white and red blur pass before my eyes and my hands wrap around a chair and hurl it at the window, shattering against the grate, and I snatch the nearest leg and smash it repeatedly on the table, shards of wood flying at me, pricking my cheeks, my face, sweat running into my eyes, but I bludgeon the table, hearing Aífe's voice, Walleus's, seeing their faces break apart beneath the chair leg, and as the middle of the table finally gives and collapses on itself I hear Emeríann scream my name.

I spin and face her, approach her. Chest heaving, hands throbbing.

The envelope lies torn at her feet.

"That table wobbled," I say. She stares at the piece of stationery in her hands. It's blank but for the Gallery masthead. A photo sits between the tri-folds.

My skin flames. The photo is grainy, taken with a high-powered telephoto lens, no doubt, but even if I were blind I would be able to read the image by sensory perception alone.

Donael is much older than I have ever seen him, becoming a young man with thin ropes of muscles on his arms and the hint of an Adam's apple. He stands on a green lawn, holding a remote control plane in his hands as if he's trying to fix it, Cobb beside him holding the remote.

Printed on the back of the photo is Walleus's address.

30.
WALLEUS

Because the two-inch glass is strong enough to be bulletproof – which Donael would appreciate – and thick enough to mute all sound, all the rioting is actually pretty beautiful.

A man springs off the sidewalk, floating up to a blue canopy before leaping off and knocking a Tathadann soldier from his horse, which rears up and slashes at the air with its hooves.

Another man stands on the capsized fruit cart, picking off soldiers with a crossbow until his head explodes in a cloud of red.

Two other soldiers try to restrain a protestor and look like they could be performing an angular interpretive dance, until the man plunges a knife into one soldier's shoulder and the other soldier shoots the man dead.

Two mangled bikes lie on a corner as we pass. I look back, trying to see if they're the same ones from the fisting man with the family, but the formation of soldiers collapses on a group of protestors and the bikes disappear.

The burnt bodies hanging from the lampposts by frayed ropes sway back and forth like strange fruit.

With no soundtrack of gunshots or dying screams, even the most horrific scenes can become detached and manageable. But also, without that silence of the dead, I would have never been able to spend my days with Donael.

I had gotten word from Sere, Josihe's wife: rumors were swirling about Aífe meeting with members of the Tathadann. With Henraek in the wind and unable to keep an eye on things, Sere was worried that a few rebels would get a mind that Aífe was a threat, and neutralize that threat, leaving Donael on his own. Given that Aífe was able to fall in love and live with Henraek, poor impulse control was kind of a given, so I told Sere I'd watch her, see she didn't do something impulsive and get herself hurt.

I tailed her for days, selling it to my new Tathadann bosses as community surveillance and using my contacts while they were still willing to talk. Aífe kept her normal schedule at first – park, day school, market – and I began to think that Sere was being overprotective, that I could relax a little, until I caught the end of a conversation about her meeting Mebeth with some information about a planned attack. I stayed on her tight the rest of the week, only leaving post at night, hoping that, with Henraek a ghost, she wouldn't leave a young Donael alone in the house while the possibility of retaliation still hung heavy in the air.

It took me a few days to really understand the scope of what Aífe had told them. Plans for offensives. Addresses of outposts, artillery rooms, who led which cell. She told them about the power substation, which had been the rebel's crown jewel. They pulled out their men and told the skeleton crew to stand down, but not before diverting the power elsewhere. They knew it would make us cocky, ambitious, ready to take bigger risks, then promptly massacred half our men over the next few weeks with her intel.

All of that from Aífe's mouth, and all because she wanted her husband back. So when Henraek asks me about that night, about when I turned, how the hell am I supposed to respond?

That last day, I trailed her to the meeting with Mebeth. Getting into the café's kitchen took a surprisingly small amount of sleight-of-hand. In hindsight, they knew I was trailing her, so I think Mebeth called her to the café because he wanted me to witness what the Tathadann was capable of – possibly as a warning, possibly as reassurance that I'd made the right choice, possibly to wag his dick a little at how feeble the rebellion was becoming when compared to the Tathadann. Whatever the reason, that surprise was chickenfeed compared to walking into the kitchen and finding Donael sitting on the tile killing floor with his back against a butcher's block.

Some cosanta stood beside him, picking his teeth with a paring knife.

In all of my gathering, not once did it come up that they'd planned to kill Aífe – one of their main and most reliable leaks – and gut Donael in order to destroy Henraek, thereby cutting the head off the rebel snake. I never found out if that was the plan all along or if she'd outlived her usefulness, but it really didn't matter because when Mebeth came into the back with that self-satisfied grin of his saying that they were finished, it came as a pretty big goddamn shock to both Donael and me. He said to finish with the boy before walking out. For all the horrible things I've done both during the Struggle and after, at least I did them myself.

I felt bad about taking out the kitchen help after I shot the two Tathadann men, but he raised a knife around Donael and deserved to get it lodged in his face. Donael lay crumpled on the tile floor, not crying so much as trying to destroy his body with convulsions. I tried to carry him out but he kept beating on my chest and asking where his mom and dad were, figuring that was what Mebeth meant by they like I had, not they as in the rebellion. He finally fell against me. His tears soaked my trousers and left snot-marks down my thighs. There was no way I thought someone like Mebeth could take out Henraek, but I didn't know anything more than what I'd seen, so I stayed silent until Donael caught his breath. Then we left.

When Mebeth caught up with us the next day, his

men were ready to execute Donael – and probably
me – on the spot. I talked their guns back into their
holsters and Mebeth offered his ultimatum: I could
have Donael if I gave them Henraek. They wouldn't
kill Henraek, Mebeth promised, but they would break
him. He'd be Macuil Morrigan's guest of honor at the
press conference announcing the end of the Struggle.
He'd call for all the rebels to honor a ceasefire, swear
the Tathadann truly was the way.

When the liquor is low in my bottle, I imagine my
silence is a knife in Henraek's neck. If I'd been a true
friend and brother, I'd have told Henraek a week later
that Donael hadn't been crushed but was sleeping
on my couch. But by the time I found Henraek he
was already soaked with booze and rage. He attacked
Macuil Morrigan at the conference, then got locked in
a cell and dressed for a firing squad. He barely escaped
death a month later after I explained to Morrigan that
while he was a leader now, Henraek would become
a martyr if we killed him, and I agreed to take him
under my supervision.

Those early days slipped into weeks, most of which
Donael spent mourning Henraek and Aífe. Then the
weeks piled into months, and by then Donael had
acclimated to life with Cobb and me. He'd already
been through more than any kid should have. And
with Henraek, he would have been hurrying to
school between volleys of gunfire and chucked bricks
and eating squirrel or raccoon or whatever vermin
Emeríann dressed up. Not to mention what he would

have suffered before Henraek and Emeríann even got together. At my house he has sheets and clothes without holes and as much food as a growing boy needs. He has a brother to learn responsibility with and a school that will help him become more than Henraek and me.

And anyway, all that aside: he's my son.

"Mister Walleus," the escort says. "We're here."

31.
HENRAEK

I stalk around the rubble that had been our dining room table, slapping a chair leg in my palm. In any other circumstance, I would look ridiculous, but after an hour of doing it, my throbbing hand is the one thing keeping me in the room.

"One in the forehead and one in each eye before he blinks," I say. "That'll be a start."

"You need to talk to him first."

"To hell with talk!"

"Don't you yell at me, Henraek," she shouts back. "I'm the one sitting with you now, trying to keep you from making a mistake."

"Killing him will not be a mistake."

"No, but killing him without finding out why will be."

I snap a piece of table with the chair leg and kick it. On the television, the newscaster warns residents that those caught outdoors after the curfew has gone into

301

effect will be jailed, and that all travel outside the city has been prohibited except within authorized vehicles. The Tathadann cordoned off certain neighborhoods earlier this afternoon, which will make my trip to kill Walleus longer, but I will find a way regardless. They are locking down Eitan tighter than they ever did during the Struggle, but we weren't hanging bodies from lampposts last time. The years of Tathadann oppression are finally bearing their fruit, and violence will bloom across the city like a bloody rose.

"Can you imagine living the rest of your life without knowing?" Emeríann says. "You, of all people. The man who tried to burn down half the city to find out why your wife died. You're going to kill Walleus without any explanation as to why he took your son? Kept your son? Worked with you and drank with us and never said one word?" She shakes her head. "I'll move out if you do that, because you will lose your goddamned mind."

I drop the chair leg on the pile. "OK, I'll talk to him," I say. "Then I'm going to kill him. Then I'm going to hunt Mebeth and kill him too."

I change into an old delivery uniform we used during the Struggle to gain access to buildings, grab a clipboard and a cardboard box, then scribble Walleus's address and some bogus return address on the front. I glue a white wrapper in the top right corner to stand in for postage, though if they get more than a cursory look, it'll never pass. They shouldn't be close to me long enough to look, and if they are, they'll end up dead.

I strap on my kit beneath my shirt, set a towel inside the box to give it some weight, then get my pistol from beneath the couch and tuck it in my waistband.

In the bathroom I drag a straight razor across my face to shave off a few days' worth of stubble and look as different as possible. Emeríann appears in the mirror.

"I'll come," she says. "Nael can wait. You shouldn't have to do this by yourself."

I wipe off the blade against the porcelain sink. "That's the only way to do it."

"It's OK to accept help once in a while. It doesn't make you weak."

"I don't need help. I need to do this." Her face deflates slightly. I lay down the razor and face her. "I'm not shutting you out, Em. I promise. For the first time…" I pause, reconfigure the words in my head. "I am completely present now. I'm here with you. But this?" I pull out my pistol, tap the muzzle against my temple. "This is something you can't be a part of."

"Then what am I supposed to do?"

I snuff out a laugh, wipe my face with a stained towel. "Well, there's a whole lot of chaos going on out there." I lay my hand on the back of her neck, touch my forehead to hers. "I'm sure someone's going to want the woman who planned the bombing that kicked off the revolution."

After a belt of bourbon for good luck, I pick up the box then kiss Emeríann and head out.

She calls my name when I'm at the door. The window backlights her, forming something like an aura around her silhouette. "I'm sorry you have to do this."

A hundred voices ring in my ears. A thousand faces slip over one another. People I've known, fought with, fought against, seen in the bars, in the safehouses, in the streets. Of those, only four stick in my head. And soon, three.

32.
WALLEUS

In Clodhna's front courtyard's garden, the ferns are
so thick I can barely see the marble fountain through
them. Huge pink and purple flowers burst from root
balls in front of the ferns, all of it penned in by stones
and rocks. In the hour-plus it took us to get over
here, I ran through a hundred versions of my pitch,
mouthing the words to get the timing right, making
sure the scope and violence of Daghda and the coup
are bright-blooming in front of Morrigan's eyes,
because it's going to have to be near perfect to keep
my neck out of a noose.

I enter the marble vestibule. It's strikingly still, a hell
of a difference from the last time. Maybe people are out
in the field, or are scared and staying away. A different
secretary greets me this time – same hair as the other
– then escorts me through the door, down the mirror
hallway with the polishing droids and into Morrigan's
office. She extends a hand, offering me a seat.

I wait until the door closes behind her then scan Morrigan's desk for anything official – a decree for my head, authorization of deployment of force, hell, even a receipt for four bombs paid in cash. After a minute it occurs to me that if anyone was to approve those measures, it would be Promhael not Morrigan, and that would assume this city has an operating government in the best times. Getting a stamp before leveling a neighborhood ain't likely to happen when there are a bunch of crazy bastards singing songs and blowing everything up. Still, not seeing my name written down gives me a little hope.

I flop on a chair and watch the bushes for what feels like hours but is probably only twenty minutes. Rehash the Daghda situation, reinforce why she needs my expertise and connections, throw in a little woe is me about how I'd been tricked by my best friend into thinking he'd given up his rebel ways. Express my regret that I haven't been able to track down Belousz yet, but, you know, there's a goddamned riot going on. Then try to figure out how to extend that lie, maybe forge a report of death by one of the rioters. After another ten minutes, I have to get up and walk because my heart won't stop pounding against my ribs. Maybe this is it. My diet of meat and bourbon is finally coming back. The secretary is going to come into the room and find me sprawled over the carpet, piss over my pants and foam in my mouth. Or whatever happens when you have a heart attack.

The door opens. Relief floods through me like a drug. I put on my smile, not too broad to seem overconfident but big enough she knows I'm not cowering, and spin around to see a maintenance droid, emptying a garbage can that didn't have any trash in it.

By instinct, I look for a liquor cabinet to shush my blood.

I pace more, open the drawers of Morrigan's desk between glances at the door, flip through pages of books lining the end-table as if a death notice with my face on it will fall out like some forgotten love note. Then pace, and pace. Repeat: Daghda, death, Daghda, you need me.

After I've been waiting for almost two hours, the door opens. The secretary again.

"I'm sorry, Protectorate Blaí, but Lady Morrigan won't be able to meet with you today. We have a car waiting." She gives a little nod then turns and moves her pencil legs toward the door.

"Hold on a second." My voice is more vicious than I'd expected. "She brought me all the way down here, through all those people who want to kill me, to sit around for two hours with my dick in my hand and then tell me she's not coming?"

She stares at me, her lips twitching like a little mouse sniffing out food. "I'm sorry, sir, but she won't be able to meet with you today."

"When did she call?"

She blinks.

"When did she call?" I push the words through my teeth.

"I'm sorry, sir." She gives a tight smile then leaves.

It's happening. I did it. I'm greenlit.

Grab the boys. Grab their stuff. Head straight to the farm and hope to hell it's still there.

I hurry back to the entrance, toward my ride home. Out in the courtyard, there's laughing like a gaggle of geese. On the other side of the fountain are three Tathadann men – high-ranking ones, judging by their pins – with Greig standing in the middle of them. He says something and they all laugh again, one of them slapping his arm.

"Thanks again for these," he says, motioning with a folder. "I owe you one."

They pass by me without a glance.

I stand in his path. "What did you say?"

"Nothing of any concern to you." He adjusts his shirt to let the new pin on his shoulder shimmer. None of its luster does anything to hide the fact that his face is marked with cuts and stitches across gashes that will never heal right. Every time this shitbird looks in the mirror or has to shave carefully so he doesn't open a scar, he will think of me. "If it was, you think I'd tell you a thing after that scheme you tried to drown me with?"

"What did you say to Morrigan?" I ask.

"You mean after I provided documentation verified by Lady Morrigan's observer that exonerated me from any suspicion you might've inferred? Or after

I provided the reports that link Henraek – who was under your supervision – with the imminent arrival of Daghda?"

"Henraek doesn't even know Daghda."

"And I don't know how to blow up a goddamn building. But you taught me a lot. I wasn't lying when I said that." He shrugs then taps my chest with the folder, hands it to me. "I told you someone would get hurt. I warned you."

I open the folder and see a photo of Donael holding his airplane, Cobb beside him holding the remote control.

"I think you know who else has this." He gives a thin smile. "I'd say I'll see you," he says, "but I know I won't."

I grab his wrist. The photo falls from my grip and flutters to the ground. He tries to spin around, dislodge my hand and say what the hell? but I slam my knee into the back of his, knocking him to the ground. For all the planning and conniving he has done, this boy has spent no time in the field. He lets the official Tathadann words pass by his lips but he's never grappled with another man, both of you struggling to kill the other before he can kill you.

He scrabbles at the ground but can't grab hold. His head between my hands, I bash his face against a stone. A tooth pops out and hits my cheek. His pants are wet with urine.

When I spin him around, his eyes are wide with fear, mouth moving but broken teeth cutting the words. I wrap my hands around his neck until his face flushes. The cuts on his face weep blood, thin lines dripping down his cheeks. When his skin takes on a purple hue, I let go and he ferociously drinks air.

Then I choke him again, letting his skin turn purple once more before grabbing him by the jaw and dragging him through the ferns. The fronds whip against my face, the fountain gurgling beyond them.

At the edge of the fountain, I bend him backward and shove his head beneath the water, trying to trap his frantic legs with my knee. Ditches form in the ground as his feet kick at the dirt. Threads of blood spread across the water. Bubbles course from his mouth and in some weird way I swear I can hear what he's saying, like my hands have learned to translate the vibrations of vocal cords over the years.

Whatever he's trying to say, and whether I can hear it or not, I don't really give a shit.

I tighten my grip and try to touch my fingers around the back of his neck then push him farther down and after less than a minute he's no longer fighting. I hold him under for a thirty-count to be sure, though a boy like him doesn't have much fight inside him anyway.

After I pull him out and dump him on the ground beside the fountain, I cup some water and splash it on my face, sifting another handful to clean it of blood before sipping it. My suit is already bloody and wrinkled and now half of it is wet and speckled with dirt. I wipe my hands on it. I'm going to leave it behind anyway. I duck back through the ferns and hurry to meet the car.

33.
HENRAEK

The thin wail of sirens careening off buildings, around shouts of protest, through the static hissing out of Tathadann bullhorns.

We're going to bomb the Tathadann.

Stay behind the barricade or we will be forced to shoot.

With my broken hands I'll tear down Morrigan.

This is your final warning. Do not breach the line.

Then the clap of gunshots, screaming and singing and more warnings. Block after block after block. The barriers that striate the streets are as much to keep people in certain neighborhoods – like Amergin and Findchoem – as they are to keep people out of others. It takes me forty minutes to get where I would have been in ten last week, as much from all of the barricades creating labyrinthine city blocks as from keeping to the less populated streets, my face tilted down. Though many of the men I fought with understood my situation with the Tathadann, most newcomers don't. Not to mention the number of Tathadann soldiers who might or might not be looking for me with orders from Morrigan to shoot on sight. With all the chaos mainlining people with adrenaline, loyalties and alliances can become very flexible very quickly. Still, block by agonizing block, I'm coming closer to my goal.

Of killing my best friend.

The thought stops me in the middle of the sidewalk. People hustle by, some as if it's any normal day, others with canvas bags full of projectiles. A Tathadann soldier patrols the street on horseback.

I will kill him because he took my son from me. He lied to me, repeatedly, and that cannot be forgiven. But he also saved me numerous times, from attacks, from ambushes, from myself. But he stole my boy.

A man with an official-looking haircut sprints past me, wagering a quick glance back. A group of teenagers with pipes and boards follows close behind. One of them stumbles and hits the sidewalk. I jump backward to avoid a board in the foot. He pulls himself to his feet then looks up at me.

"Oh my god," he says, already looking for his friends. "It's you."

I start to say he's mistaken me for someone else, but he's already yelling for his friends, saying, "It's him, it's the traitor. Get him."

I'm gone before he can finish his sentence, head down and sprinting, dodging and weaving through the crowds on the sidewalk, box thrown aside. Because there are a lot of people out, it's hard for them to see me, but they can still see where I'm heading in the wake of the crowd.

At Minidae Avenue, I bolt left, letting my legs extend in the mostly deserted street. Their footsteps fall heavy behind me. I glance back and see they've picked up another kid. If I could stop and talk to them, I might find that I knew their parents, maybe fought with them, but I wouldn't be able to get the words out before their boards met my forehead. I knock over trashcans, trying to create a few obstacles, and as quickly as they fall back, they regroup. My lungs burn and feet throb. Maybe it's time to reconsider running in boots, or scale back my bourbon consumption.

Two blocks down, I push it hard, stretching my stride as far as it will go, driving my legs into the concrete with all the strength I have. A pho house sits on the corner. There should be an access road past it. I barrel down and put as much distance between the pack and me as I can, then throw myself into the access road at the last moment and run.

A dumpster on the right. A few shipping pallets piled against the wall on the left. A man sitting cross-legged on the concrete halfway down the road. That is not a road, but an alley, dead-ending at a brick tenement that looks like a lagonael den.

Wrong pho house.

It's too late to get out of the alley. They're too close. They'll catch me before I clear the edge.

I hurry to the end, put my back to the wall so at least they can't surround me. An acrid stench fills the alley, gasoline and exhaust and old food. The man looks up, his eyes far away.

"Hey, it's you," he says. I start to tell him he's got the wrong guy then realize it's the lagon from Johnstone's. The campfire man. And he's sitting in a puddle of his own piss.

"Oh, give me a damn break," I yell, right as the pack rounds the corner, bearing down on me.

I feel the gun against my back. If I get a first-time headshot on each kid, or at least enough to put them down, I could get out. But I would have no bullets for Walleus. I leave the pistol in my waistband and square up, scanning the alley for anything to use as a weapon.

"I'm never going to know," he says, oblivious to the pubescent psychopaths bearing down on me.

I find a chunk of brick on a pile of papers and snatch it. This is what your life has come to. Beating a bunch of kids to death with a brick in an alleyway or getting beat to death by a bunch of kids who are barely old enough to remember the Struggle.

"My boy ran – told him he had no direction – joined the fight. You might've known him." The lagon slots a cigarette between his lips. "They burned him – the stake."

The kids are thirty feet away. They slow as they approach, cockiness or sadism filling their steps. One pulls out a butterfly knife and flips it around, the metal glinting.

"Never found – peace with death," he says. "Drove away – mother looking."

"You kids really have no idea what you're doing," I say to them. From the menace in their eyes, I don't think negotiation or reason will hold any sway with them. I switch tacks. "Are you sure you know who I am?"

"My dad knew Forgall Tobeigh," says the one who holds a crooked piece of pipe. "I heard all about you."

"I wanted – understand what he felt – let me finally sleep." The lagon continues to talk as if there's not a horde of sociopaths with patchy mustaches about to get hurt really bad. "But those memories – the past is static. A barrier – you and the experience."

"So you know who I am." I stand tall, let the brick hang beside my hip, let them see the picture of composure, the calm before the storm. I catch a strong smell of gas. "Then you should know what I'm going to do to you if you come any closer."

Three of the kids exchange glances. The ones with the pipe and the butterfly knife advance, weapons extended. There's a small chinking sound.

This is it, Henraek. You're going to kill two kids who could easily be Donael's classmates.

I raise the brick, ready to defend myself, when a fist of heat strikes me, flames devouring the lagon's body. The kid with the knife jumps back but the one with the pipe unleashes a scream and falls to the ground. Tongues of fire lick his back. The lagon simply sits there. I cannot move.

The knife kid smacks his friend's back as the three timid ones bolt out of the alley, the other two following behind thirty seconds later when the boy is no longer on fire. I can see scorched flesh through the holes in his shirt as they run away.

I should be looking for a blanket for the man, or screaming for a hose. At the very least smacking the fire down with my shirt. But he sits there, legs crossed and peaceful, as if he's tapped into some long-forgotten part of our collective conscious, and I fear that doing anything to tamp the flames would disturb him.

I watch him burn, listening to the flames crackle, his skin bubble, his hair singe. I feel the tension in my body dissipate, and somewhere inside there I imagine I can hear him inhale on his cigarette.

He's found his peace. But I will never find mine until I know.

I drop the brick and exit the alleyway.

Walleus.

The man in the gatehouse is the same one who called me Tyrell and I should not have expected anything different. I pull the hat down farther on my head, mostly covering my eyes, and walk at an efficient pace, like I have more deliveries to make and no time for small talk.

"Afternoon," I say, motioning with the long shipping tube I found on my way over after I dropped the box during the chase.

"Can't believe you left the house without an umbrella," the man says.

"Oh, yeah, I know." He obviously has no idea who I am and for a brief second I wonder if he's actually an automaton. "I won't have to take a shower then, I guess."

The man gives a laugh and taps his temple. "Work smart, not hard, right?"

"Exactly," I say. "Got a delivery for Mister Blaí in Unit 138."

"You missed him."

Of all the places I don't want to stand around waiting for endless hours, this is number one. There's an obscene amount of foliage but too many cameras and it'll be hard enough getting to his house without getting flagged as it is.

"Hold on a minute. I'll ring one of the boys to pick it up." The man picks up the phone.

"It's OK," I say, a little too eagerly. "It's a surprise, looks like."

"Surprise?" He holds his finger on the hang-up button.

"For his son," I blurt. "Donael. It says hand deliver. It's fragile."

He shakes his head and sets the handpiece back on the base. "That man does spoil those kids rotten. Love to see a father take such an interest in the kids, you know? Never happens these days."

"Yeah." I can hear my teeth squeak from grinding

them so hard. "I hear that."

"Let me guess." He scratches his chin, stubbled with white hairs. "New soccer kit? No, not with that box. One them holograms of Canchie Lit?"

"It's Concho Louth." Shut your mouth, old man.

"Nah, that can't be it. Oh, I know. Telescope." He wags his finger in an assured manner. "Yeah, that's it. He'd talked about that a few months ago. Donael's been banging on about a telescope for years."

The shipping tube creases beneath my fingers. My breath claws through my chest. I want to bludgeon this man for destroying my heart.

"I can't see inside things," I tell him, "so I never know what I'm delivering."

"Ah, right, right." He pushes a button and the gate opens. "Tell Donael I want to see his surprise later."

I give him a short wave then walk toward Unit 138 to murder my best friend.

34.
WALLEUS

The car weaves through Eitan City, rerouting around the soldiers who patrol the barricades and road closures with rifles propped against their shoulders. With every turn, I yell at it to speed up. Which is hard, given that every other block is overflowing with larger and larger gatherings of protestors, their faces covered by bandanas or green and white scarves.

I tell the escort to direct it down certain streets, ones the car's system would have sidestepped because we used to plant bombs there, because avoiding them will add another thirty minutes to the trip. With every block that passes, my heart smacks harder against my chest.

As we swing around a blockade, the car makes to turn left and brakes hard.

"What are you doing?" I yell.

"Sir," the escort says, pointing out the window at the procession.

"So run them over. They'll move. Trust me."

But they won't. The line runs twenty people deep. Given the mood, they'll flip the car and set it on fire as likely as pause.

I duck down and pull a newspaper over my face. They march past us, singing songs that make my skin burn with nostalgia and anxiety because I remember that electric charge of leading four hundred people down a street. Some carry quickly painted signs, some with poles that hold effigies in nooses. In quick glances, I see only one that resembles me, which is sort of comforting. I crane my head around the front headrest to look for a break in the crowd and a man stops beside the window. Recognition and venom spread across his face. Doing my best to act naturally, I pull the paper back up to my face but he's already grabbing his friend.

"Tell it to move," I say to the escort. The man and his friend pound on the window, two others joining in. This procession will collapse on us in five seconds if we don't get out of here now.

"Mister Walleus, there's—"

A dull thump and the sound of breaking ice. The window spiderwebs around a depression in the glass. The protestor moves his hand, pointing the gun at a different spot, and pulls the trigger again.

"Drive!" I yell at the car.

The protestor gets off a third shot then starts screaming as the car takes off. There are thumps as bodies glance off the hood and front window. I look back and see the shooter holding his dangling leg in his hand. I press my finger against the window, the interior side barely cracked. Dumbass didn't even know you need special bullets and a gun with some ass behind it if you want to get through that glass.

We hum past more protestors, darting around other cars to beat a light or speeding up to encourage people to get the hell out of the way.

After twenty minutes, we pull up to the gatehouse. I roll down the window.

"I came back for my umbrella," I say to Tuhc. He returns that same grin then continues with whatever he's shuffling on the desk. We pull through and pass some homeless-looking deliveryman walking along the sidewalk.

When the car pulls up to the house, I jump out the door and hurry up the steps, yelling before the door is even fully open.

"Boys," I bellow, "pack your bags. You've got two minutes to grab whatever you want to keep then we're leaving. And I don't want to hear any arguments, Donael. Move it."

My voice echoes. Silence except for the murmur of voices from the television in the other room.

"Boys?"

When I turn the corner, I see Cobb with his back against the wall, near the edge of the panic room door. Donael stands partially in front of Cobb, protecting him. I step fully into the room and see Old Woman

Morrigan sitting on my nice, clean couch, with Doctor
Mebeth beside her. Three cosantas ·surround them,
each of them pointing a gun at me.

35.
HENRAEK

Bastard steals my kid and holds him hostage then spoils him rotten and doesn't have the balls to tell me about it. And does it all while destroying my reputation.

Forget history. He will receive no mercy.

I consciously have to tell myself to calm down so the residents won't see a man who is muttering to himself and holding a shipping tube that could easily hide a pulse-cannon while walking down their street. That might be the quickest way to end up in a disused garage with a car battery wired to my chest and a bunch of assholes shouting questions at me.

As I walk down his court, I scan the lampposts for small black boxes, the eaves of houses for blinking red lights. There are two past his house, three behind me.

When I cross his sidewalk to the front door, I hear voices inside. They are not the voices of children. I set the tube down and creep along behind the bushes that line the front of the house, keeping my head below the window line. I can't place the voices but they don't sound like a social call. At the edge of the house, I stand and slide over inch by inch, getting a gradually larger view of the living room.

Walleus stands with his back toward me. Morrigan sits on the couch with her legs crossed, wearing one of those hats that should be banned as an affront to human and beast alike. And sitting beside her is Doctor Mebeth. Three men stand behind her, pointing their guns at Walleus while he rapidly tries to explain his way out of some new mess he's gotten himself into. There is no sign of the kids, whether they are there, or hiding, or have already been shot.

The urge to save him first consumes me. It will not be Morrigan or Mebeth who kills him.

I chamber a round and test the window, hoping it's unlocked. But that would be asking too much and I've already had my allotment of luck for today. Instead I keep my finger on the trigger, stay out of sight, and watch.

36.
WALLEUS

"This is what I'm talking about, Walleus," she says, waving her hand up and down like she's having an epileptic fit. "You were supposed to meet me, and look at the state of you. You've even spilled food all over your pants."

I look down at Greig's blood splattered on my clothes and let the comment pass.

"I did go to meet you, Fannae. I went out through all those crazy sons of bitches that want to rip off my arms and beat me to death with them because you called a meet with me. I even wasted two hours in your lovely office staring at all those dead animals, waiting for you." I clear my throat, steadying my voice and reading the body language of the cosantas. Cobb clicks quietly behind them. "But you wouldn't know that because you weren't there."

"It's not important. We're beyond your lack of personal hygiene. You refuse to bring Belousz to me for questioning, which I believe is because there was in fact no operation. You have failed the Tathadann with your constant recklessness, allowing Henraek Laersen to commit acts of violence against and endanger the city of Eitan." She nods to the cosantas, who step forward. Donael twitches, head spinning as he takes in the room. "The punishment for treason is stripping."

"You're not going to do that," I say, pulling back my shoulder blades to expand my chest. "Not with Daghda coming."

Even though Greig already told her, she still stiffens at the mention. "The man you refer to is not an issue. And if I could strip you twice, I would for invoking his name."

Mebeth clears his throat. "I appreciate you resolving the problems with Aífe." I see Donael glance at me. "But your – how do we say it? Prowess? – is quickly fading. You have too much baggage, in your memories, in your life. You could not take care of that six years ago, so now we will do it for you."

I clear my throat. "You need me, Fannae."

"How, exactly?"

"There's a coup brewing inside the Tathadann. You're the top of their list, above me even. I helped you put down one uprising, and I'll help you put down this one, too." Donael stares at me. I flick my eyes, hoping he knows where the panic room sensor is.

"And what do you have that Greig does not, aside

from high cholesterol and the lingering aroma of spiced meat?"

"A pulse, to start." I put some bite in my words and her face blanches.

Her lips thin, part around her teeth. "You bastard."

"And twenty years' experience in the field on top of that. Fannae, I know formations, explosives, intelligence, counterintelligence, first aid." The words flow, my lips moving on their own, forming theories, creating simulations, building a future for my family and me that doesn't involve stochae. I construct a world for her that balances on a pinpoint, precariously positioned above the heaving masses of mothers eating their children and neighborhoods massacred for a glass of water, held up only because of the skills and speculations inside my skull. "I know the men fighting with me and the men I'm fighting. You want to keep the Tathadann whole, keep Daghda out, you'll need everything I've got."

I'm almost out of breath when I finish. The cosantas have leaned away slightly, taken aback at the breadth of the new reality I've laid out before them. My skin burns bright with possibility.

"Walleus," she says. She inhales through her nose, her eyes closed tight. Exhales. Opens. "I would rather die at his hands than live another day with you around me." She looks to the cosantas. "Take them all. Strip them. Dump them."

The hell you will.

I lunge, snatching at that wrinkled, veiny neck

of hers. Mebeth scuttles aside. When my fingers are close enough to almost feel her skin giving, I taste static electricity. The heavy swings his gun again, connecting with my mouth. My teeth tear into my cheeks and blood leaks into my throat. I hear the pneumatic hiss of the panic room door. My boy, my boy, my boy who – specks of light cover the room as the cosanta rakes his gun across my nose. He swings again but I get my hands up quick enough to grab his forearm and use my weight to flip him. I raise my fist and feel cold metal sink into my back, forcing me to a knee. It burrows down, digging deeper inside my flesh then is yanked out.

Pivoting on my knee, I throw my arms in front of my face. Morrigan has my fireplace poker reared back and ready to swing.

"You could have at least behaved like a man. Even Macuil accepted his fate with dignity." She motions for the two men to lower their weapons, the other one picking himself up.

"Leave him," Mebeth says. "I have tests that need bodies."

"No," she says. "I've been waiting for years. He is mine."

She begins to swing the poker, the claw end facing down and wet with my blood, as if she plans to open my head with it. Then it flies out of her hands as her right eye rockets from her head, followed by a large bloody chunk of her brain.

37.
HENRAEK

The three cosantas stand staring at Morrigan's prone body, a burnt-red halo blooming from her skull over Walleus's carpet. Mebeth crouches on the ground with his hands covering his head. I vault up onto the sill and tuck my face behind my arm before hurling myself through the cracked window. I land on my shoulder, reopening the gunshot wound, and roll behind the couch for cover. Two shots whistle over my head. Back against the couch, I risk a glance around the corner and see a fat pill bug in a linen suit lying on its side, grunting and clutching his leg.

"Get out of there, Walleus!" Old habits.

He rolls to his feet and launches himself at a cosanta, groaning again when they crash to the ground. I fire and clip one of them in the neck. He falls over the couch, gurgling and writhing on the floor. There's a red smear across the couch that is no doubt going to really piss Walleus off.

"You demon." I stand above Mebeth, my pistol floating inches from his nose. "You destroyed my wife. You knew everything about her and you preyed on her weakness."

"Henraek." He holds a palm out, as if it will stop a bullet. "You know there's more to it. Nothing is ever as simple as it seems."

Behind the couch, Walleus struggles with the man. They grunt, gasp as someone lands a heavy gut-punch. The man climbs to his knees, a massive feat with Walleus hanging on his back, and throws them both backward, smashing into the wall. As they fall to the ground and trade punches, chunks of plaster fall from the wall, leaving a large Walleus-shaped hole.

"I saw you in the memories. You ordered Aífe dead. Why?" I crack the butt of the pistol on the crown of his head. He crumples. "What did she do?"

"You of all people should know how damaged memories can be." He looks up at me, a rivulet of blood winding down his forehead. "Concho Louth."

"What?"

"The goal he scored. You said you played with your son in the park."

"I didn't say a thing to you about my son."

"Every rebel recounts it as a magnificent strike off his chest, a feat of athleticism. But he stumbled and it deflected off him. It was luck."

"It doesn't matter." I set the pistol against the bridge of his nose.

"Did you actually watch it happen, or did you

reenact it so many times that it became real?" He swallows, his eyes looking past the barrel up at me. "How do you know?"

"You can't rewrite someone's past to your liking." My voice cracks when I yell.

"Your friend Walleus might not agree."

Something slams into the side of me, my vision splintering as my head hits the wall. I roll aside as the cosanta brings his fist down and breaks through the plaster. Before I can get to my feet, he throws himself at me again. We tumble backward, my hand stuck beneath me, my pistol out of reach. There's a click, then the door slams. Mebeth. I should have shot him when I had the chance. The cosanta's thumb searches for my eye but I bite as hard as I can, and when he yanks his hand back, he's thrown far enough off-balance that I can right myself.

Arms poised and legs crouched, we face each other like ancient wrestlers, waiting for the other to make the first wrong move. He feints with an arm but I'm not fooled, so he dives for my knees. I come down with an elbow on his spine. The whoosh of breath leaving him is tactile.

I wrap my legs around his waist and squeeze, rest his chin in the crook of my elbows and pull. His arms slash and beat on me but in this position he has no power. The thumps become slaps as the blood rushes from his head, breath leaves his lungs, unable to return. His gasps are throaty, slowly asphyxiating, and when I reposition my legs and give one last pull

I feel the pop I've been waiting for, that holy space between his skull and his spine. His body falls limp, head lolling forward with no muscle control to keep it up. A small pool of urine forms at his waist, some of it soaking into Walleus's carpet and some wetting my thigh. Head tipped forward, chin down, he will no longer be able to breathe, and with a severed spinal column nature will soon repossess his body.

I push him off and glance around the corner, pistol leveled, my shoulder throbbing. Walleus has the man in a front bear hug, crushing him like a boa constrictor. He shifts his weight and throws the man forward, raises a fireplace poker above his head, then drives it down with a scream that comes from some dark place deep inside him that men only hear before their death.

His back rises and falls in great heaves that slowly begin to calm. Rolling off the body, he sprawls across the carpet, hands resting over his face. His thigh is a deep, wet red, ragged strips of flesh and cloth in the middle. Blood speckles him. Beside him, the man's face takes a severe dip where the fire poker has caved in his eyes. A gelatinous glob sticks to the handle.

Walleus cocks his head when he sees me, ignoring the pistol trained on him.

"I haven't seen that uniform in a while," he says, then shakes his head. "You've put on weight."

"You are not the one to talk about weight."

"This is true."

"Where is Donael?"

He pushes himself up to his feet. "Henraek."

Something washes over me. I don't know if it's closure, acceptance, or hatred. I don't know what separates them.

"I know you have him. I saw you in the kitchen with him." My finger caresses the trigger, the barrel inches from his face. "I saw Aífe and Mebeth. I know she told them everything. I know you took my son."

"Henraek."

"How did you do it?" I lower the pistol, raise it. "How did you look at me every day at work, at the bar, at coffee, and keep a straight face, knowing every night that I mourned my son he slept in your house? How does someone do that?"

"Don't play martyr, Henraek. You weren't a great father when he was around anyway."

"But I am his father. I could have changed, made myself better. He should have been with me."

"Put that gun down. You're not going to shoot me."

"Not until you answer."

He sighs like he has so many things to contend with and I am the last of his priorities. I see him crawling beside me in fields, hunched over a table full of maps in the back room of the Parkhead, holding me up at the memorial we had for Aífe, dressing me in Tathadann civvies on leaving the prison, pulling me up off the bar every year on Donael's birthday.

"I did feel bad. Those first couple weeks after Aífe died, after everything went sideways, I felt terrible. I actually cried once."

"Don't give me your sob story."

"I saw it was wrecking you but I did it because it was the right thing to do for him," he says. "I know you won't admit it, but he was better off here. He had food. He was safe. He could go to school and become more than we ever did."

"I could have provided that." I shift the gun to my left hand, set it between his eyes. My right hand hangs at my waist. "He should have been with his father."

And he gives me the knowing smile that has made everyone he's ever come in contact with want to bust out his teeth with a hammer, gives it to me bigger than I have ever seen it before.

"Henraek, he was with his father."

His words echo through the air, morphing, twisting, splintering. The room crumbles quietly around me. I blink, and I blink, and I blink. He opens his mouth to say something and I hear blood roaring through my skull.

I drop the gun and lunge at him, swinging my right hand up. The needle pricks his temple, slides in as silent as the breath between his lips. His eyes open wide, shocked, staring at me.

I remember watching those eyes light up as we neared the power substation, zigzagging a whole platoon of men through a field and razor wire. Clear liquid dribbles into the vial.

"You liar," I say to him, my breath crashing against his face. "You duplicitous, lying, conniving snake."

I remember seeing those eyes glass over as he stood

on a makeshift altar on the patio of Liella's favorite restaurant, some place that made great meatballs and was later razed as an early warning to dissenters, as Liella stood resplendent beside him in a handmade wedding gown, he in a suit with a bowtie that had taken us twenty minutes to figure out how to tie. The vial hits the halfway mark, the years he held my son – my son – the moment he abandoned the Struggle, all of the answers to my questions coming to me.

"I would have died for you a hundred times. I'd stand in front of a hundred bullets to save you." His eyelids flutter, lips quiver and seize. My hands tremble. "I would have forgiven you, you stupid son of a bitch. I would have understood but you lied to me, over and over. Were you ever honest with me? Even once?" My throat is scratchy and I didn't realize I've been yelling. A wave of tears rips through my throat. "This was not how it was supposed to go. You were going to be my inside man. You were going to work with me, like we used to, like when we had something to fight for, like when we were happy. You lied to me then you abandoned me." My voice cracks as I scream into his face that's quickly going blank.

I remember seeing his eyes flicker with anxiety and joy as he stood beside me, watching Donael wrap his tiny fingers around my thumb when I held him for the first time, his glance alternating between the newborn and Aífe. What passed between them? Was that the moment they agreed to never speak of it? No. Donael is my boy. I raised him and love him and

I know. And that's all I need to know. The vial fills, memory spilling out around the needle.

"You fucking abandoned me!"

His body crashes to the floor, cushioned by carpet that's thicker than my old mattress. His eyes glaze, his temple begins to depress. My breath is ragged, raging. My hands are moving of their own volition, vibrating and twitching. My chest convulses.

I want to punch him, pummel him, slam my fists against his face until his bones break beneath my knuckles and his nose caves and my hand notches inside his skull.

I want to pull him close, hold him against me and comfort him as he crosses over, mop his damp head with his ridiculous handkerchief. Recount stories from the field, from the bar, from the fields out in Westhell when we were young. Build the same fort for Cobb and Donael as his father built for us, but with a door that didn't fall off when you opened it.

But I can only stand over him, pistol in hand, and watch his shallow breaths, watch the depression at his temple become larger as his eyes drift away. Regardless of what he's done, he doesn't deserve to be one of them.

I close my eyes. The bullet lands in his forehead with the dull thump of a heart imploding.

My pistol falls on the floor without a noise. It might as well have never existed. My knees turn to smoke as my back slides down the wall. I can taste my breath. I can do nothing but stare at his bulbous form, the impression of his knee joints visible against the stretched and bloodied linen, the laces of one shoe nearly untied.

The world quiets and compresses into one single room as I sit sadly by his side, vial cupped in my hand.

The hiss of a pneumatic joint. I startle, touch the knife in my boot. A fissure forms in the far wall and I wonder if I am hallucinating.

"Walleus?" a small voice calls. Behind that is wild clicking, a clicking I recognize.

The wall opens completely and I now realize it is a panic room. A boy emerges, the room behind him decorated in old rebel scarves I remember wearing fifteen years ago. The boy steps forward into the room, casting cautious glances over the dead bodies around the room. The shape of his eyes presses pins into my heart. His defined jawline. The way he touches the side of his neck with his index and middle fingers. The immediate tactile charge I feel on seeing him that reaffirms Walleus was lying.

"Donael."

His head whips in my direction. Eyes probe me, wary and curious. He takes a tentative step forward and extends his hand, as if he could feel my skin from across the room. Cobb creeps out from behind him, head swiveling.

I push myself up to my knees.

"Dad?" he says.

I hold out my arms and he appraises me for another

few seconds. Then a smile spreads across his mouth like the first rays of a sunrise we haven't seen in years and years.

My boy runs to me. My boy, my boy, my boy.

He fits in my embrace like I am molded around him. He smells of sweat and dust and sweetened cereal.

I can think of nothing to say but repeat his name.

"I thought you were dead," he says, his voice slipping on the tears.

And I laugh, because it seems right. "I thought you were dead."

"I'm not," he says.

"I'm not either."

"Is Mom still…" he says, trailing off.

"No, she's…" and I squeeze him tighter in place of a full response, so tight I'm almost afraid I'll hurt him, but he doesn't seem to mind.

Cobb clicks wildly behind us. I ignore him but Donael pulls himself from my arms and turns to him. Cobb stands over Walleus's bent and broken body, his feet stomping the carpet beside his head, leaving small prints of blood behind.

"Oh shit," Donael says.

"Watch your mouth," I say out of paternal reflex, and the words make me tear up again. He hurries to Cobb, scooping him up and trying to get him away from Walleus's body without touching any of the others, but Cobb screeches and beats on Donael.

"Help me!" His tone says I should have thought of it first.

I get to my feet and wrap my arms around both of them, Cobb's scaled skin making me queasy when it brushes against my face, and I realize I have never been this close to him.

I usher them out the front door. Cobb's screeching becomes wilder. His thrashing shifts from violent to desperate. We hurry down the sidewalk, away from here, back to our home.

"What happened?" Donael says.

I suck in my lips, shake my head. I don't know what to say.

"Who were those guys?" he says.

"It doesn't matter," I say. "They don't matter."

"I told him," Donael says, stroking Cobb's back to soothe him.

"Told who?"

"Walleus." He shakes his head. "I told him everybody leaves. He didn't listen."

I hold his shoulder, stopping him on the sidewalk. "Donael, I'm here."

"I know." He smiles, then nods at Cobb. "We need to get him home. How far away do you live?"

"I'm not going anywhere, son." I wrap my arm around his shoulders and squeeze. "I'm done with fighting. I'm here for good."

"I know," he says. "I know."

I must be dead for the sky is almost blue, though that might be residual trauma. Walking along the narrow streets, winding away from the riots and boys with pipes and butterfly knives, I consciously bring myself back to the moment, to the fact that I'm walking beside my son. It's been years since we've seen each other. We should be chattering like birds on a telephone wire, yet we've barely said ten words. What is there to say? Where to start?

As we pass the few plate glass windows not covered by boards, I sneak a glance at his reflection. He's an older, more developed version of the little boy from the football match. His cheeks are thinner, eyebrow ridge more defined, like his mother's. His gait is confident but his countenance is slippery: one minute he's smiling at the woman watering a patch of dirt that was once a garden, the next he bares his teeth at the children who stare and point at Cobb, now asleep. When I ask if he wants me to carry him so he can take a break, he acts like he's relinquishing the honor, though I can tell he's exhausted. His mouth shifts into some crooked version of a smile.

The blocks creep past us. A subtle nostalgia wafts around me, cataloging random details of the city: the pho house where Aífe told me she was pregnant, the store where a two year-old Donael would activate every toy and unleash them in a torrent of plastic monsters, the brigu bar where Walleus and I first discussed the possibility of focusing all the anger and discontent that had been building into a full-fledged rebellion, the hall where I gave my early sermons about equality and freedom. For every detail I remember, I try to erase three more in order to devote myself to my son.

Between the burnt carcasses of buildings, I can see twists of smoke in the direction of the Gallery that still smolders, and my chest tightens: Emeríann and I will now have two children in the apartment. To get to that apartment, we will have to walk for two hours to avoid the riots that Emeríann and I incited, riots to take down the ruling party of which we are the prime targets. We will leave for school while it's still dark to avoid the crowds – I'll have to find a new one for him, but how do I do that? – and he'll have to adjust his diet to what we have available. My breath quickens as every new responsibility realized spawns three more, and as my head becomes a tangled mess of obligation and threatens to split open, he touches my hand.

"Do you need a break?" he says, pointing at Cobb, who sleeps on my chest. "I can carry him for a couple minutes so you can rest."

"I can make it."

He nods, and leaves his hand on mine.

We have an enormous change we'll have to adjust to, but we'll adjust to it. All of us. Together.

Eventually, we reach my building. I rest at the bottom of the steps, setting Cobb halfway on the old radiator before starting the journey up to the apartment.

We open the door and walk in to find Emeríann standing in the middle of the living room, covered in dust and blood and holding a large rifle in her hands, a pile of destroyed table behind her. She freezes like a child caught by her parents.

"Henraek," she says. "Donael." She rushes over and tries to wrap her arms around me and Cobb, Donael wide-eyed and watching the rifle. When she releases us, she kneels down in front of Donael.

"This is Emeríann," I tell him.

"Hi," he says, eyes still on the rifle as she gives him an awkward hug.

At the window, Silas pecks manically on the glass. "That's Silas," I say. "You'll meet him later."

"Like the cat?" he says. I smile and nod. "You named a pigeon after my dead cat?"

When he says it aloud, it sounds kind of creepy. I gesture around the apartment, indicating that this is now his home too and he should use whatever he likes.

"Where's the bed?" he says, taking Cobb from me. "He should really sleep. He'll process it better after he gets some rest." His tone is so unemotional that I wonder if he is incredibly mature and self-possessed for his age or has been living too long with the idea that love is transient and there is no reason to become attached.

I show him the bedroom. Emeríann follows, the rifle in her hand now replaced by extra blankets.

"Do you need anything else?" I say to him as he tucks the sheets under Cobb's legs with a tenderness that nearly breaks me.

"I'm OK." He folds one blanket beneath Cobb's stomach so it props him up, then covers his body with the other one, curving it around his shoulder and beneath his chin. "I'll be out in a minute."

Emeríann and I watch him a moment, then close the door behind us.

"You couldn't have washed all that off?" I say to her, pointing at the dust and blood on her.

"With what?" she says.

Dammit. I'd forgotten.

I hear Silas's pecking again and let him in. He immediately flaps to the counter near the bedroom, as if he can feel the new presence in the apartment. Behind the door I hear Donael singing softly to Cobb. Down near the river where our brothers bled. I didn't know he remembered that song. Emeríann flits around the room, collecting the table debris, organizing things, her maternal nesting instinct kicking in though she leaves fingerprints of dirt and blood on everything she touches.

I cup the vial from Walleus in my palm. It's heavier than it should be. Donael creeps out of the bedroom and I shove it back in my pocket. He regards Silas with a sideways glance, then stands in the kitchen, surveying the apartment. His eyes fall on the sculpture over the couch. He cocks his head, examining it for a minute, then lets out something I tell myself is an impressed sigh.

"Do you need anything?" she says to him.

"No. I don't know. I'm OK."

"Help yourself to anything," Emeríann says. She picks up the rifle and slings it over her shoulder.

"Everything here is yours."

"Where are you going?" I say to her.

"He's back." A huge smile blooms over her face.

"Who?"

She points at a stack of photos on the couch. The top one features an old man, his wrinkled – though defined – body atop a military vehicle that leads a formation of a hundred more. His face is covered by a boar mask, tusks gleaming. Sitting beside him is a woman, younger it appears, though her face is also covered with a mask. Holy shit. Belousz was right.

"Daghda's alive," she says. "He's come back. And he brought Ragjarøn with him."

I instinctively reach for the pistol in my waistband. Muscle memory.

"Who's Daghda?" Donael says.

"I'm sorry, love," she says. "I need to go."

I nod, say sure, sure.

Emeríann's eyes flick from me to Donael, back to me. Her words are slow, hesitant. "Are you coming?"

I look at my son, the boy I've mourned for six years, who is no longer a boy but quickly becoming a man, a man who will learn from his father what he should be. A man who will study my movements, catalog my actions and words, evaluate my beliefs, what I choose to pursue and what I stand against. It will be my responsibility to show him the world and our place in it.

"Go ahead," I say to her. "We'll meet you."

ACKNOWLEDGMENTS

This book would not have been possible if not for a number of people. Unfortunately, I have a terrible memory and will likely forget to list many of them. I apologize in advance.

Thank you to Marc, Penny, Phil, Mike, and Nick at Angry Robot for having faith in this book.

Thank you to Axel Taiari, Chris Irvin, Richard Thomas, and mi hermano de otra madre Gabino Iglesias for their attentive eyes.

Thank you to all the wonderful and supportive people I've met through the crime and sci-fi writing communities. I'd list everyone but that would take up a whole other book and I'd definitely forget someone. So thank you to you. And to you. And you, too. And of course you, how would I ever forget you.

Thank you to the world's best agent, Stacia Decker, for taking a chance on this book, for being a great sounding board, and for saying *no, you don't sound crazy at all* when I'm pretty sure I do.

And thank you most of all to my family: Amanda, Donovan, and Ruby. You keep me tethered and prevent me from spinning off into some crazy orbit. I couldn't do any of this without you, and I love you all dearly.

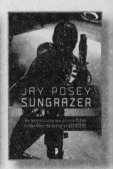

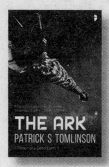
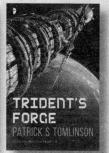

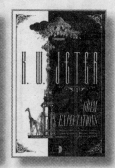

WELCOME
TO YOUR
FUTURE

BOOK ONE
NEXUS

NEXUS 1

RAMEZ
NAAM

NEXUS

INSTALL

"GOOD. SCARY GOOD."
WIRED.COM

BOOK TWO
CRUX

NEXUS 2

RAMEZ
NAAM

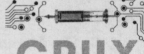

CRUX

UPGRADE

"PROVOCATIVE... A DOUBLE-EDGED
VISION OF THE POST-HUMAN."
THE WALL STREET JOURNAL

NEXUS 3

RAMEZ
NAAM

APEX

CONNECT

"A LIGHTNING BOLT OF A NOVEL WITH A SENSE OF AWE
MISSING FROM A LOT OF CURRENT FICTION."
ARS TECHNICA

BOOK THREE
APEX
WINNER OF
THE PHILIP K
DICK AWARD
2016